THE RYDLE YEAR

OR ONCE UPON A TIME IN PLYMOUTH

Angela Joyce

Published by Angela Joyce 2025
Copyright © Angela Joyce

ISBN: 9798308628521

Edited by Claire Cronshaw
www.cherryedits.co.uk

Cover design and production by Pixel Tweaks
www.pixeltweakspublications.com

The right of Angela Joyce to be identified as author of this work has been asserted by her in accordance with the Copyright, Designs and Patents Act 1988

The moral right of the author has been asserted. All rights reserved. No part of this publication may be reproduced, stored in a retrieval system, or transmitted in any form or by any means, without the prior permission in writing of the publisher, Angela Joyce, nor be otherwise circulated in any form of binding or cover other than that in which it is published and without a similar condition including this condition being imposed on the subsequent purchaser.
This is a work of fiction. Names, characters, places and incidents are the product of the author's imagination or are used fictitiously. Any resemblance to actual events, locales, or persons, living or dead, is purely coincidental.

To my mother,
who was a free spirit

CHAPTER 1

REMEMBER

Plymouth 2012

I pulled the dress out of the Co-op carrier bag. A lilac-coloured minidress with a large zip up the front. Incredible that it was still here in my mother's house. Not long till her funeral now.

I held the dress up, shook it, and sniffed it. A musty scent, slightly damp, but also with a faint perfume. Of course – patchouli. Very seventies. I sat on the bed and remembered.

Now it was all coming back – this was the dress Mum bought me in Carnaby Street, London, in 1970, with Ani! Ani Rydle. She was my best friend. She was special. We were still young then, not tainted by disillusion or depression. Everything lay in front of us. Not like now, when most of my life had been lived. I felt frightened, trapped in the moment. Alone. Should I look to the past for answers?

That year – I'll call it the Rydle Year – it was the year I met Ani, got the right jeans (Levi's), and escaped from Plymouth. I want to tell that story before I forget. And in the telling, I may understand why it ended as it did.

CHAPTER 2

AN UNUSUAL FAMILY

It was 1970 and we lived in Plymouth. My father said it was the best city in England. I didn't think so. I wanted to live in London or New York or on a farm. The Sunday Times colour supplement was to blame. Each week, the newspaper landed on our doormat and I would fetch it, extract the shiny magazine, and read it greedily. It had articles about glamorous families, but not like ones I knew. There were photos of little boys with long blond fringes like girls, and girls called Iseult or Horatia, who were allowed to run wild. I was only twelve then, just a silly shy little girl, and even worse, an only child.

Life was neat and organised: school, home, church, taking the dog out, drawing and playing Ludo with my grandmother.

I had my dreams though: I loved Levi's jeans and pop groups with names like T. Rex, The Monkees, Herman's Hermits and The Troggs. I loved Dad's pale-green Triumph Vitesse car. And all the TV programmes about spies and the Cold War and space travel – my favourites were *Lost in Space*, *Doctor Who* and *The Man from U.N.C.L.E.* We still had a black-and-white TV, but my father had promised us a colour one soon, when he saved up. And I wanted a boyfriend.

But strange things can happen. One Friday in September, I met the Rydles.

White-painted sandals. That's what I remember.

If I hadn't stayed late at high school that day, I would have missed Anita Rydle, and never got talking. A terrible thought. Was it fate or luck? I could have ended up married to an accountant and wearing M&S pleated skirts. Some of my classmates ended up like that. But I'd better keep to the story…

I hardly knew Anita, because she was in the other second-year class. She was standing alone on the steps at the front, waiting. It was a golden autumn day, with crisp brown leaves drifting across the pavements. What I noticed about her was her sandals – they were roughly painted over with tennis shoe whitener. School didn't allow white shoes – only black or brown. I was impressed that she had got away with it. I wouldn't dare. Otherwise, we were both wearing the regulation ugly uniform: brown pleated skirts, white shirts with amber ties and brown cardigans.

Ani was blonde. Everyone wanted to be blonde. I had the wrong sort of hair, dull brown and harsh. Grey eyes. I was tall and thin. The girls said I had skewy legs and fuzzy-wuzzy hair. Anita seemed confident and I wanted some of her power. It was now or never.

I swallowed and walked up to her.

"Hello…Anita?" I said.

She swung round to look at me, screwed up her face.

"Yeah? It's Ani, no one calls me Anita. Well, only my stepmother when she's angry."

"Oh. I'm Hazel. Hazel James." I started blushing. *Please don't make fun of me,* I prayed.

"Yeah, I know." She looked at me. "You're the one who's always reading, or running away from the ball in hockey. What you doing here, then? Waiting for the bus?"

"Yes."

"I'm being collected. My brother's coming. Well, he'd better…" She looked at her watch. "He's late as usual."

She looked more friendly now. She wasn't telling me to get lost, or saying I had skewy legs or stringy hair, like the others.

"Anyway, where d'you live?" she asked.

"Compton."

"Uh-huh. We live in an old house in Crownhill. It's great."

"What d'you like doing when you're not at school? I like drawing." This wasn't like me, being so daring.

"Snap! I love drawing. All our family are artists." She seemed to think for a minute and said, "Hey, d'you want to come home with me and see my drawings and stuff?"

I thought about it. Every Friday I had the same meal and watched television. It was nice and peaceful. But before I knew it, I was saying, "Yes, please."

A battered old red Cortina pulled up. It was the sort of car my father would have called 'clapped out'. A tall young man got out. He had little gold glasses and long, curly brown hair. He looked like a bigger, hairier version of Ani. Rather unsettling.

"This is my big brother, Dave," said Ani.

I didn't know what to say to him. He looked so fashionable, with a scruffy striped shirt and flared jeans, which I was sure were Levi's. You couldn't even buy Levi's in Plymouth in 1970. London was the only place, if you could get there. I'd never been.

"Hi, little sis," he said to Ani. He held out his hand to me in a jokey, formal way and said: "How do you do, Ani's friend." I shook hands, tongue-tied.

We got into his car. I sat in the back. It was messy inside, an exotic contrast to my father's immaculate Triumph. I pushed aside a heavy leather jacket to make room.

"OK, ladies," Dave said in a friendly way. "Let's get going. Gotta dash off to my flat and then pick up Bridget at five. Going to a gig later."

"His girlfriend," mouthed Ani, looking back at me. It sounded glamorous, even if I didn't know what a 'gig' was.

Dave and Ani joked and chatted in the front. I was happy keeping silent, taking it all in.

I loved roaring along in a scruffy car on a Friday evening with loud pop music blaring out. The tinny car radio was playing a song, 'Love Grows (Where My Rosemary Goes)'. Every now and then it stopped working and Dave gave it a thump. Mutley Plain shopping centre was full of traffic and people, all going home or doing weekend shopping.

We soon arrived at Ani's house. Nowhere was a long drive in Plymouth. It looked old and rambling, and was painted a curious pale-green, like icing sugar on a fairy cake. The window frames were white. The house stood in an overgrown garden, surrounded by high walls.

Ani gave Dave a big hug and said goodbye. He roared off in his Cortina. I watched him. *It must be great, being grown up and doing what you want,* I thought. I wished I had a big brother. *I could meet his friends and even get a boyfriend! Ani probably has one already.*

Ani opened the front door and we went into a hallway. I caught a whiff of herbs and wood and coffee. A small naked boy came bumping slowly downstairs on his backside to meet us. He had wild black hair.

"An-An! An-An!" he yelled, grinning.

I tried not to look down below but concentrated on his fat little face. "Hi, little Josh!" called Ani, picking him up and swinging him round. A blonde girl of four or so appeared at the top of the stairs, wearing pink silky fairy clothes.

"That's Tallulah," said Ani.

I wasn't used to children. I forced a smile and said to Joshua: "Hello. Aren't you cold with no clothes on?"

"Oh, no, Joshua *loves* being naked," laughed Ani. "Go and play on your monkey swing," she said, and he walked unsteadily across the hall and got onto a board which hung on a rope from the banisters. Ani pushed him to and fro, and he yelped with excitement. The girl, Tallulah, stood and stared down at me for a few seconds, then turned and skipped away along the landing, her fairy wings flapping. She had fat little legs in white tights.

A young woman with flowing black hair and a long, embroidered skirt came to the top of the stairs. She had bare feet. My mother never went barefoot.

"Hi, Anita, who's this?" she called.

"Hi, Mel, this is Hazel," answered Ani, and said to me: "This is Melissa, my stepmum." Ani led the way upstairs.

"How fab. Are you staying to tea, Hazel?" Mel said.

"Yes," I replied in a low voice. "Please could I ring my mother to tell her?"

"Sure," she said, pointed to the wall, and wandered off.

I saw a phone attached to the wall, which seemed strange but clever. When I rang my mother, she said *yes*, right away. She was oddly inconsistent, strict at times, but at other times surprisingly lenient.

"Come and see my room," said Ani, tugging at my cardigan sleeve. I realised that the house was topsy-turvy – with bedrooms on the ground floor and other rooms upstairs. I liked that. We both went downstairs again. Tallulah reappeared and started to follow us down, but Ani said: "Get lost, Tal, we're going to talk about something adult," and Tal stuck her lower lip out and plumped herself down on the bottom stair.

Ani's room was huge, with a view of Dartmoor out of the window. There was a double bed and even an old bath in one corner. My family had a big comfortable house but no baths in the bedrooms, just one yellow bath in the bathroom.

"All the bedrooms have got a bath 'cos Dad's a furniture designer and we like things stylish," said Ani. "Now, these are my horse drawings. What d'you think? I want to go to art college."

I harboured a hope of being an artist, too, but had no idea there were colleges to learn it.

"My stepmum went to The Slade," she said. "She paints at home now."

I didn't ask if she worked. Most Plymouth mothers I knew were housewives. Fathers were almost invisible: out at work in boring offices or away in the Navy. My parents felt sorry for mothers who 'had to work' and my father called their children 'latchkey kids'.

Ani had piles of drawing materials, paints, paper and an easel. She also had models of horses and new horse-riding clothes.

"I love horses, too," I said in a quiet voice. "But my father won't buy me one. He said we can't keep it in the garden, which is rubbish — it's big enough. And he says it's too far to go to stables every evening to feed it."

"Dad says I'll get one in a few years, when we move. He's designing a house on Dartmoor," she said.

I was filled with envy.

Ani sat on her bed and pulled off her white shoes. She threw them across the room. I hesitated, then did the same with my brown ones.

"D'you want to do a drawing? Help yourself to paper and felt pens," she said.

We both lay on our stomachs on her rug and started drawing. While we drew, Ani talked non-stop.

"I know I shouldn't have white shoes, but Mel didn't get round to buying me new ones yet. Dad says I shouldn't care what school thinks. Anyway, my family come from the Lake District. 'Rydle' comes from Rydal Water – you know? A lake up there. But it's spelt R-Y-D-L-E now. Have you been to the Lakes?"

"No. But I've got some Lakeland Pencils. They were a birthday present."

Ani went on: "My real mum and dad are divorced. Mum's got a shop in Dorset, a boutique. I call my mum 'Realmum' and Mel I just call 'Mel'," she said. "Mel tries to act like my mum, but she's not and never will be. Don't *ever* say anything about Realmum to Dad or Mel though – Dad hates her and Mel's jealous of her."

"All right," I said, feeling embarrassed.

"Anyway, I live here with Dad and Mel – and Tal and Josh, who are their kids. My dad's rich because of his work. My sister Sarah lives in a flat in London. She's at art college. And I've got half-sisters in Manchester – called Tina and Nadia."

"Oh," I said. Ani's sheer energy and outpouring of information were overwhelming me.

I could hardly keep up with it. I knew a few children with divorced parents, but it was still rare in 1970. Ani was so confident and seemed rather posh. I was jealous of her complicated family. But I also felt a bit sorry for her, not being with her own mother. Did she miss her? I didn't like to ask; it was too rude. Like asking if you were wearing a bra yet.

My family was boring compared with hers.

"I live with my parents and gran," I murmured. "In Compton," I repeated.

"Oh yeah?" said Ani, choosing a scarlet pencil.

"I haven't got any brothers or sisters, but we've got a dog called Hedley. A fox terrier. You should come and see him some time." I hoped that would impress her.

"Ooh – a dog! OK," she said.

We both had enough of drawing and sat on her bed, leaning against the wall. It had a strange red embroidered bedspread on it. My bed had a pale pink quilt. Ani plucked at her school uniform.

"Awful, isn't it?" she remarked. "But I won't have to wear uniform for ever; I'm going to *Dartmoor Manor!*"

"What's that?" I asked.

"It's a progressive boarding school in Devon. Not like the awful little schools here. Everyone at Dartmoor Manor works together and teachers have to listen to students. It's democratic! All my family go there. And you don't wear a uniform!" she finished triumphantly. "You can go barefoot in tattered jeans if you want!"

I said nothing. I had a feeling my parents wouldn't like Dartmoor Manor. And what did 'democratic' mean?

An Unusual Family

But I absolutely didn't want to go away to a boarding school. My father had been to one years ago and had suffered. His stories were full of cruelty, telling of boys being beaten with a cane there and having compulsory cold showers.

On impulse, I blurted out: "Don't you *hate* being twelve? Not being allowed to do anything or go anywhere?"

Ani said: "Gosh! Is it that bad? I mean, what do you want to do?"

"Go out alone. Meet boys. Buy nice clothes. Smoke a cigarette. All those sorts of things," I said, blushing. I was always blushing and hated myself for it.

"Wow, you do want a lot! Why not, though?" She twiddled a strand of yellow hair round her fingers. "Maybe we can do some things together?"

She gave me a big grin and I smiled back at her.

There was a thump on Ani's door. It was Tallulah. She looked in and announced in a sulky voice: "Tea's ready. But you two aren't having *ice cream*!" She ran off before anyone could catch her.

Ani looked at me with a long-suffering expression. "God… little pain. And she's only four. At least she's going to start school next year."

We went up to the kitchen. It was warm and smelt of coffee. I had never seen a kitchen like it, but recognised the style instantly, from my avid reading of colour supplements. It was the latest in kitchens – bold and bright, with dark brown walls and brown tiles with large orange flowers on them. Some jazzy music was playing quietly on a radio somewhere. The woven curtains matched the tiles and there were strange chunky orange mugs and plates on shelves. There was a mustard-yellow machine under the counter, perhaps a washing machine. The floor was covered in some kind of rush matting, which felt rough under my white summer socks but smelt nice, like dry hay. There was a big wooden table with no cloth on it. Tallulah was sitting at the table, already eating and swinging her stumpy little legs.

Joshua was crawling round on the floor, barefoot, chewing on a banana and dropping pieces everywhere. He was now dressed in loose red dungarees with a label on the back saying 'Osh Kosh'. They looked very fashionable. Melissa let him crawl about while she flapped around in flip-flops, fetching food.

"What do you two want to eat, then? French cheese and salads and rye bread?" she asked.

"Yes please," I said, sidling round the table. I wasn't sure what it all was.

"Yeah, that'll be OK," said Ani. "Come on, Hazel, you sit here."

I looked at the French cheese. It was covered in a white rind. My father hated foreign food and only ate Cheddar. Ani set out some greenish glasses on the table. She helped Mel to lay out the food and then scooped Josh up and lifted him into a bright-red wooden high chair. Ani sat next to me and smiled.

"Go on, Hazel, help yourself."

An Unusual Family

"Thanks," I mumbled. I cut a small slice of the white cheese and nibbled it experimentally. It tasted like sour milk. I took some of the dark bread and chewed it. That was better. Tallulah was staring at me, watching my every move. I blushed.

"She's gone red," she said.

"That's all right – you mind your own business, miss, and eat up," said Mel.

Despite my being embarrassed, it was fascinating observing Ani's family. I had never met anyone like them and wondered how my father, who took a scathing view of life, would react to them. I smiled to myself.

"She's in a daydream!" said someone. "Penny for your thoughts, Hazel."

I looked up, embarrassed. All of them were looking at me.

"Oh, nothing," I answered. I couldn't possibly tell them what I was thinking. "Thank you for having me round; it's very, er…nice," I managed to say.

Mel burst out laughing and patted my shoulder. "Funny girl! Have some more food, darling. Anita – get her some Coke, hurry up."

I picked out a tiny cucumber and bit into it. The sour taste made me wince.

Ani laughed. "That's a gherkin," she said. She poured me some Coca-Cola. At least I knew what that was.

Mel poured herself some coffee and started reading a newspaper. Ani helped Josh to eat, cutting cheese for him and buttering bread. He chewed things then threw them down with happy shrieks. She seemed very grown up and used to looking after little children. I was clueless about babies, but I didn't fancy having a little brother or sister. It was too late anyway, as my parents were ancient, or seemed so to me.

Mel pushed aside the paper and started talking to Tallulah as if she was an adult: "Darling, I've got a little exhibition coming up in Exeter. Would you mind staying with the Tremaynes for two nights, please? You can go to ballet with Esther and Freddy."

Tallulah considered this for a few moments, swirling her orange squash round in her glass, and then said, "No!"

"Please, darling," pleaded Mel.

Tallulah scowled.

"Perhaps I could buy you that space hopper you wanted…"

"OK, Mummy, I will then, but don't you go away again or I'll smack your bum!"

I gaped at her. I would have been slapped for saying things like that when I was her age.

Ani chipped in: "Daddy's going to take us all away on holiday soon, sweetheart. We'll have some fun together then. Just do this for Mel, this once."

"Mum's an arty fart!" chanted Tal. "Don't want any more food," she added, jumping off her chair and stomping out of the kitchen.

Mel shrugged and picked up a gherkin. She looked at it closely. "She's a pain sometimes," she murmured to no one in particular.

I tried to look adult and sympathetic. I was rather enjoying this bizarre conversation. Mel got up and fetched a wallet of tobacco and some cigarette papers from a side table. She made a fat roll-up cigarette, lit it, and looked at us. The smoke smelt unusual, rather herby.

"Could you two do me a favour and clear up?" she asked. "I need a bit of down-time. Sometimes I can't cope with being twenty-eight. I feel my life's over before it's begun." And with that, she left the kitchen with the roll-up stuck in her mouth. Ani looked at me.

"Don't worry, she's always like that. Are you OK?" she asked.

"Fine, thanks," I answered, not entirely truthfully. I could hardly cope with Ani's family. Everyone seemed to do what they wanted and say what they wanted. My mother smoked, but she would never ask guests or children to clear up, or tell them her life was awful. I stared at the mess in the kitchen. My mother always tidied up at home.

"What should we do?" I asked.

"Oh, we'll shove the food in the fridge and stick the dishes in the dishwasher. You do the food," said Ani firmly. "Hey, Josh, what are you doing?" she shouted. He had managed to slip out of the high chair and was tipping biscuits over the floor. "No, baby," she said, lifting him up and feeding him a biscuit, then releasing him. "I'll put you in the bath in a minute." She loaded the mustard-yellow machine like a little housewife. I had never seen a dishwasher before, except on television. She pressed a button and it whooshed into action.

Somehow, I piled all the food into the fridge. Mel probably wouldn't mind anyway. Things seemed easy-going here, unlike our immaculate kitchen where my mother cleaned every single thing. Ani carried Josh into the bathroom and I trailed after them. It was a real mess, with toys spread over the floor, long trailing plants in rope hangers and damp towels hanging everywhere. There were black-and-white drawings on the wall. One caught my eye, of a naked woman drying herself with a towel.

"That one's Mel," said Ani, seeing my look. "Dad did that when they first met. Now, let's run the bath for this little chap…"

I tried to imagine my mother in the nude and quickly pushed it out of my mind.

Inexplicably, I suddenly felt happy. It was lovely being here, with this big outspoken family.

"Ani – thanks for asking me here. It's fun!" I blurted out.

She grinned. "That's OK, Hazel, I like having you here. It must feel funny, with all these kids. As you're an only child."

"No, it's all right." I hadn't cared before, but at this minute, it seemed sad. I felt like a dud, having no brothers or sisters.

"Well, you're welcome to this one," she joked, lowering Josh into the bath.

He looked up at us and pointed at me.

"Lady," he said in a friendly way.

I didn't like babies; they always reminded me of ugly piglets wearing nappies, but somehow Josh was such a pretty baby he touched my heart.

I smiled down at him. He had some tiny boats floating around in the bath. They reminded me of a toy catamaran I'd had when I was little. I'd forgotten that for years. I pushed his boats along. He splashed with his little fat hands and laughed.

"Do you think Mel will have any more?" I asked.

"Nah, she takes the pill," said Ani in a matter-of-fact way. I was shocked. No one ever mentioned the pill in my house. My mother never even said the word 'contraception'.

Mel appeared at the door.

"Oh thanks, girls. You're angels!" she said. She looked happier now. "Let me take over and you go and chat."

"Actually, I ought to ring my father to collect me," I said.

"Aww! Don't go yet," said Ani.

But I was suddenly tired. It was all too much.

"I think I'd better," I said. I smiled at her. "You could come to my house next weekend – if you want."

"Oh, lovely!" she said. "Can I do that, Mel?"

"Absolutely," answered Mel vaguely, sitting on the edge of the bath and squirting some bubble bath into the water. She had balanced a cigarette on the windowsill. Ani leant over and opened the window.

"Bit smoky in here!" she said, looking at Mel. Mel shrugged.

There was still no sign of Ani's dad. He was probably working late, like other fathers.

I rang my own father, and he arrived shortly afterwards to pick me up. Tallulah thundered down the stairs to open the door.

"Evening," he said to her. "And what's your name, young lady?"

"Tallulah," she said in a gruff voice.

"Ah, after the actress Tallulah Bankhead, I assume," he said.

"Don't know," she answered and skipped away.

My father could be charming. However, he also had a dark side and was exceedingly rude to people at times. *Please don't say anything awful,* I prayed in secret.

"Correct, after the actress, well done!" said Melissa, laughing and coming downstairs. "Hello, come in! I'm Melissa, Ani's stepmother."

"Ron James," he replied, shaking hands. "I hope Hazel didn't give you any trouble," he added, ruffling my hair.

"Da-ad!" I said, ducking away, but laughing.

"She was good as gold, and so helpful," said Mel fondly. "She's welcome here any time."

I glowed inside.

"Bye, Ani, see you on Monday," I said. Ani blew a kiss at me and grinned.

We headed off down Tavistock Road in our beautiful car with red leather seats. My father had a weakness for cars.

"So how was it?" he asked.

An Unusual Family

How could I explain the Rydles? I failed to find the right words to describe them.

"Nice," I said, a ridiculous bland word, which was completely inadequate. "They're divorced and have loads of kids. They've got a dishwasher! Tallulah's really naughty!"

"Hmm!" he said. He wasn't fond of little children. "Everyone seems to be getting *divorced*," he added scathingly. "Anyway, it's the weekend – thank heavens! We'll get fish and chips tomorrow at Perilla's and give Mum a break."

"Sure thing," I said, in an American accent. Talking in accents was one of our favourite things. We got on well, except when he was in one of his black moods.

It was good to be going home on a Friday evening. I had always thought Friday was the best day of the week. No school on Saturday, and time to do what I wanted.

After getting home, I looked into the living room to say hello to my mother and grandmother. They smiled and said hello back and asked how my visit had been. My mother was doing a crossword as usual and my grandmother was knitting and half-watching *Top of the Pops*. She always got disgusted with pop groups and thought modern music was awful – "No tune to it," she often said. Most young people appalled her too.

At that moment, Jimi Hendrix came striding on, blasting out a guitar riff. She burst out: "Look at that, Fenella! All that dirty long hair – they look like girls! And those tight trousers! Absolutely disgusting!"

I smiled to myself. She always did this, every time.

My mother joined in: "Oh, isn't it revolting? Why can't they have proper music?"

"I think it's quite good," I said, but this was ignored. I left them to it and went up to my bedroom.

I felt a sick headache coming on after the strange evening with the Rydles. There was a lot to think about. Tallulah was a spoilt little child but rather fascinating. She reminded me of a small wild animal. I rather wished I was her. Josh, the baby, was quite sweet, just a little dumpling. I wasn't sure about Mel – weren't all stepmothers wicked?

I stood in my bedroom, and for the first time I took a cold critical look at the pink and white walls, the matching pink quilted curtains, and divan bed. It was like hundreds of other girls' bedrooms. The Rydles had unusual furniture and pictures in bright colours. Even Ani's room was quite original. My belongings looked babyish, including the pictures which had been bought for me. There was a picture of the nativity and a gaudy portrait of me and my toy koala, painted when I was eight. The koala looked good but I didn't like myself in it. I looked like a clown. Perhaps I could buy some new things or put up some posters of pop groups. But where to buy them?

I went and knelt by my bed and rested my face on the knitted patchwork blanket my grandmother had made me. I still liked that. It had a comforting woolly smell and I always slept with it right over my nose. I lay down on the blanket and did nothing.

An Unusual Family

As it grew dark, I half dozed and thought about families and how strange they were, and wondered what it was like not to live with one's own mother. Was Mel like a real mother to Ani? Or was she mean to her? She looked much younger than my mother. The Rydles were unlike anyone I'd ever met. I hoped I would see more of them.

I suddenly sat up straight and clicked on my lamp – it was Friday and every Friday I had an important routine: checking The List. I went to my cupboard and took out a flat box with a label on it saying, 'Scrapbook Things'. In the bottom of the box, hidden under pieces of felt, cut out pictures from magazines and dried flowers, was a piece of paper. My secret list. Not a soul knew about this. I got it out and considered it:

My Top Secret List, to make me into an Exciting Girl

Go to London and get Levi's (flared)
Get a bra
Get new hairstyle
Meet some boys
Save money
   E---------------!

The last item was so secret, I had left a gap. It was the most important thing on The List. Until Ani came along, that is. I now added a new item:

Make Ani my best friend.

CHAPTER 3

WE ARE LIBERALS

Plymouth 2012

Tobi texted me today. Short and not terribly sweet. He just asked, 'How are you? When is the funeral?' I didn't feel like answering immediately, and left my smartphone on the bed. He seemed very remote, over in Vienna. *I'll let him stew for a while,* I thought. I made a cup of tea.

I took my tea into the sun lounge and looked at the garden. Summer leaves were coming out. The house was totally silent. Life seemed on hold for a while. I liked it.

Where was Ani now? In England or overseas? Possibly even in Plymouth?

* * *

Plymouth 1970

I stretched out in bed and came to slowly. A blissful feeling came over me – it was Saturday, so no school, no hideous uniform and no getting up early. I pushed back the woolly patchwork blanket and groped for my little bedside clock. Eight thirty.

Perfect. Then I remembered – Ani was coming today. I sat up and started worrying – supposing she thought my house was boring? It was so tidy and neat and dull, compared to the Rydles' muddly, colourful place.

I hoped Ani would become my best friend. But was I interesting enough for her? I always thought I should be more interesting, but I lacked the knowledge or tools. I was an only child and most people thought that was sad, which I hated. In the stories I read, bigger brothers and sisters showed you what to do and led the way, or you could be motherly to little ones or order them about, but I had no one.

There were noises outside my room on the landing. My father was about. He always got up first, made tea for us and then shaved in the bathroom, with Radio 2 blaring out. He knocked, opened my door, and looked in.

"Morning tea, Madame?" he enquired.

"Ooh, yes please," I answered.

He came in and put a mug on my bedside table. He had a quick surreptitious look round my room, checking how untidy it was. He was ex-Navy and terribly tidy, treating our house more like a ship. My clothes from the day before were thrown onto the floor. He didn't make any comment. The door was pushed further open and a long white nose poked in.

"Hmm, what d'you think you're up to?" asked Dad. Hedley wasn't officially allowed upstairs.

"Oh, please," I pleaded.

"All right, just this once."

Hedley trotted in and jumped up on my bed. He walked unsteadily over the bumps and slid down next to me. I cuddled him and kissed his ears.

I got up, leaving Hedley curled up, went to the window and pushed the curtains apart. The weather was cool and there was a pretty peachy sunrise above the houses. Seagulls were circling in the sky, calling out. According to my grandmother, they had the voices of dead sailors, but to me they sounded like happy sailors at a party, shouting, "Yow, yow, yow!"

I fetched my drawing pad to sketch the sky, still in my pyjamas. I picked out some of my Lakeland Pencils, in oranges, pinks and reds, and began the picture. The dog jumped off my bed and I heard him going in to my grandmother next door and a voice saying, "Oh, you naughty boy, come on then."

I considered my drawing. It looked too wishy-washy and pale. I never seemed to get drawings right. Maybe I needed to try painting it instead. I sighed and gave up for now, since Ani was due at ten thirty. I dragged on some scruffy pink trousers and a blue polo-neck top. My mother didn't like me in blue; she liked dreary colours like cow-brown and sludge-green, which she said suited me. As an act of rebellion I was wearing lots of blue to irritate her. I ran downstairs to the kitchen.

My mother was sitting at the table, busy with a crossword as usual. She looked up when I appeared and smiled. She was fifty three and seemed old to me, with her wavy grey hair and sensible skirts. She was quite pretty and slim, but always on some diet or other. The current one was the PLJ diet and it involved drinking large amounts of lemon juice from little plastic lemon-shaped bottles, with hot water.

"Hello, darling – oh, blue again?" she said, looking at my scruffy clothes.

"Yeah. Mum, can I wear your nail varnish today as Ani's coming?"

"Now, you know I think it's common on young girls," she said with a frown.

I made a face and said, "That girl Celia looked OK with it, at the coffee morning last week."

My mother didn't answer; she was absorbed in her crossword again.

I sighed, then I helped myself to Frosties, purposely pouring too much gold-top milk on them so they nearly drowned and flooded over the edges of the bowl.

My mother looked up and said, "I'll make you some toast."

"No, s'awright," I mumbled, reading the Frosties packet and sulking about the nail varnish.

My grandmother Lilly came in slowly. She was about eighty and plump. Lil was a true Plymothian, born and bred, with a down-to-earth personality. My mother shuddered at her Plymouth accent, but I didn't mind. I adored her. Unfortunately, she had grown really deaf, so people had to shriek at her. She did have a hearing aid but it regularly went wrong and she generally threw it aside, muttering "Damned thing!"

"Hello, Gran!" I shouted.

"Hello, young lady. Is your new best friend coming today?"

"Yes, Ani's coming."

"No need to shout. What can I cook her for lunch?"

"Something special and foreign," I yelled. "Can you do an omelette and salad? And your apple crumble and cream? That's not foreign but everyone likes it."

"I should think so," said Lil, putting the kettle on the gas hob.

"I hope Ani's family is nice," remarked my mother.

'Nice' meant respectable and not living on a council estate.

"Of course they are," I snapped.

"I'm just nipping out for a ciggie," said Mum. The dog got up and followed her. He knew who fed him.

* * *

Just after ten thirty, the doorbell rang. My mother and I both rushed to the front door to let Ani in. She was with Melissa. Ani looked wonderful: she was wearing really flared blue trousers, a red blouse with a long pointed collar and a red bandana round her wavy primrose-coloured hair. She was like a pop star.

"Hi. Who did your hair?" I asked.

"Oh, that was her big sister, Sarah," said Mel. "She was round last night. I think it's the hippy look!"

Mum won't like that, I thought. She said nothing, but she gave a quick glance at Mel's scruffy paint-stained jeans.

"Hi, Hazel," said Ani and gave me a hug. "How do you do, Mrs James?" She strode into the house and went to pat Hedley, who was jumping about and barking. "Hello, divine dog," she said to him and rubbed his ears.

My father appeared. "Welcome on board, everyone," he said. "Come in. Can we tempt you to a coffee? Or something stronger?"

"Thanks, but I must fly," said Mel, laughing. "My two little monsters are destroying the car."

We all peered at a white Mini parked outside. Screams and yells could be heard from Josh and Tallulah, and arms waved round wildly.

"What charming little children," said Dad, a glint in his eye.

"If only. Well, see you later, Ani," said Mel. "Be good. Shall I pick you up later?"

"No, no, no – don't worry. We'll drop her back to you by five," said Dad.

"Come on, I'll show you round," I said, tugging at Ani's sleeve. The sooner we got away from the adults, the better.

She smiled at me. "Yeah, let's go."

"Your clothes are so fab," I said. "Mine are rubbish. Where do you get them?"

"London," she said casually. "We go up once or twice a year."

"Crumbs, you lucky duck!" I said and felt bitter. I'd never even been. My only option was shopping in Plymouth. And the clothes were hopeless. I decided to work on my father and see if we could go to London. "Come on, let's look round."

We went through the house, room by room. I was worried that Ani would find it boring compared with her arty place, but she was very interested, looking closely at everything, including some antique ornaments, almost like an adult. My parents were fond of antiques, and frequently dragged me round antique shops. I was flustered and made her hurry.

"This is the dining room…this is the living room but we only use it for parties…this is the TV room…that's the way to the cellars…that's Hedley's bed."

"Oh, you're so lucky having a pet. We can't have any because Mel says they'd ruin the house."

I looked at Hedley, who had once chewed up the seat of an antique chair and nearly given my mother a nervous breakdown. Mel might be right.

We gravitated towards the kitchen, where Granny Lil was busy cooking.

"Hello dear," she said. "What's your name?"

"Ani," said Ani.

"Sorry, dear? Fanny?" said Gran.

We both giggled.

"No, ANI!" I yelled. I looked at Ani and said: "She's deaf. You have to shout."

My grandmother was making Cornish pasties, for some future event. She had attached a metal hand mincer to the side of the table and was pushing chunks of meat and potatoes through it. A long sausage of ground-up food emerged and piled up in a dish. We both watched, fascinated. She had already made dough, which was sitting on a cold plate. The apple crumble was in the oven, judging by the warm fruity smell.

"Go and show Fanny your bedroom," said Granny.

"She's *not called* Fanny…oh, forget it," I muttered.

Ani said, "Yeah – I wanna see your clothes."

We went up to my pink bedroom. Ani looked around thoughtfully.

"What d'you want to see? All of them?"

"Yes, all of them," said Ani firmly.

We started emptying drawers, taking armfuls from the cupboard, throwing them on the bed, and dumping shoes onto the floor. I used to think I had nice clothes, but now I could see it was a sad little collection. We both considered it.

There were piles of white knickers and cotton vests, white ankle socks and long fawn socks, pinafore dresses, check blouses, cotton trousers, cardigans, T-shirts, a red polo-neck sweater (*Not bad*), party dresses, shorts and pyjamas. The shoes consisted of scuffed tennis shoes, brown school shoes and black patent party shoes. Finally there were my horse-riding clothes – jodhpurs, a brown velvet hat and a yellow scarf with horses on it.

"The riding clothes are good. But the others…Why haven't you got any long white socks?"

"Mum thinks they're common."

"How funny."

"I know," I said. But I felt hurt by her casual remark.

"How about a bra? Have you got…you know…tits yet? I'm totally flat."

I blushed and looked down at my chest. There were two small bumps.

"Um, yes, a bit…"

"Then you need to get a trainer bra."

"I know."

A bra was already on The List. I glanced at the cupboard, where it was hidden. Should I show it to Ani? But it seemed too soon, too risky to reveal my innermost longings.

"I need to get proper jeans – Levi's," I said. "And I want to get plimsolls, and minidresses, and white tights, and a denim jacket, and flared trousers. I need to get to London! I'm gonna ask Dad to take us. I look so awful."

Ani looked at me, her head on one side. She took my tangled hair in both hands and pushed it back gently. There was a moment of silence. I could smell her sweet toothpastey breath and see into her light, sea-blue eyes. I almost thought she might kiss me, but then she released me and spoke softly.

"You don't look awful. You're pretty and your figure's good. You just need to get a better haircut and some trendy clothes. Plymouth's a dead loss. Get to London – or Exeter even."

I felt my face burning with embarrassment. Why was I so hopeless at everything?

A voice drifted up from the kitchen… "Lunch!"

We abandoned the wreckage of the bedroom and ran downstairs. All the family were waiting in the pale-blue kitchen, sitting round a Formica table. Mum was serving the omelette.

We are Liberals

Dad was leafing through the local newspaper. Ani noticed a photo on one page.

"Oh, John Pardoe," she exclaimed. "Our family think he's great."

"Hmm, the MP, you mean?" said Dad. "Why? Are they Liberals then?"

"Yes, we are Liberals," said Ani proudly, looking him straight in the eye.

"Oh well, better than being Labour, I suppose," said Dad in a dark voice.

"What's wrong with Labour?" I asked.

"The Reds?" My mother broke in. "They want everyone to be the same – and they love Russia. You just watch and see what they'll do if they get in! That ghastly David Owen we've got, for instance! I wouldn't trust him an inch!"

There was a silence. I cut up my omelette and ate a piece, praying that Ani wouldn't cry. But she looked perfectly relaxed, eating her food.

"This is lovely, Mrs James…and Granny," she said, taking second helpings.

"What's that, what's going on?" asked Granny, who couldn't hear any of this.

"Nothing, it's all right!" Mum and I shouted in unison.

"Do you two geniuses want to go to the Barbican after lunch?" asked Dad. "We can continue the political discussion over ice creams."

"That sounds lovely," said my mother, who had simmered down again.

"I would love to," said Ani, not in the least deflated. I smiled inwardly. What a girl.

"Just give me thirty minutes to watch the horse racing on TV," said Dad. This was his Saturday ritual. He left the table.

My mother started clearing up and Ani got up to help.

"No, dear, I'll do it all."

Ani looked at my mother with surprise, but subsided.

Meanwhile, my grandmother fetched her handbag and produced two ten shilling notes for us.

"You girls buy ice creams with that," she said, and got up to help my mother.

"Ooh, thank you," said Ani, delighted. "You're lucky having a gran," she said to me in an aside.

After a while, my father reappeared and said, "Come on, then." We followed him out to the car.

He brandished the car keys. "Who wants to sit where?"

"I bags the back seat with Hedley!" shouted Ani, leaping in. I sat next to my father to keep him company, even though I really wanted to be next to Ani.

We drove off. Even Ani seemed impressed with the pale-green Triumph Vitesse, which pleased me. Hedley sat with his face out of the window and ears streaming backwards in the wind. Ani had one arm round him. It was love at first sight. I hoped she didn't prefer him to me.

We are Liberals

The Barbican was the old part of Plymouth, with ancient stone houses and cobbled streets. Fishing boats and yachts filled the harbour and crowds of tourists and locals milled around. It was the best bit of town. We came here a lot. I loved looking out to sea and sniffing the fishy air.

"Do you realise this was a Saxon fishing village once called Sudtone?" asked my father.

"Yeah, we know, we've done all that at *school*," I answered rudely.

My father looked hurt and bent to pat Hedley. Secretly, I thought that was quite interesting but I didn't want him to think he knew it all. Really, the Barbican was brilliant. I imagined characters like Francis Drake walking round these streets in his Elizabethan clothes, getting ready to sail off round the world. It made me proud to be a Plymothian, although my father said Drake and the other explorers were basically pirates. I wished I could sail off somewhere, like my father had done in the Navy.

It made me think of the poem 'Drake's Drum', which we had learnt at school. Most poems struck me as soppy but this one meant something to me, as a Plymothian girl.

Drake he's in his hammock an' a thousand miles away
(Capten, art tha sleepin' there below?)
Slung atween the round shot in Nombre Dios Bay
An' dreamin' arl the time O' Plymouth Hoe

I thought of poor Drake in his watery grave off South America, so far from Devon.

We strolled ahead of my father and Ani linked arms with me.

"Do you go to a riding stables?" Ani asked.

"Yes, Moorland Stables, usually," I said.

She sighed. "Dad hasn't always got time to take me riding. I haven't been lately."

"You could come with me; I'll ask my dad."

"Could you?" she asked, smiling. "Oh – thanks!"

"Your gran is so nice," she added. "Mine lives up north and we don't see her much."

At least something was better in my family.

We came to the ice cream shop by the fish market. My father loved ice cream; he always got excited about it like a little child.

"What do you two want then, hmm?" he asked, staring at Ani. Some of my friends were afraid of him.

"Two scoops of strawberry please," she answered at once, looking him in the eye.

"What, no cream? Come on, push the boat out!" he said.

"No thank you."

"Could I have one scoop of vanilla, one of chocolate, and clotted cream, please?" I asked.

"*Mais oui*," said my father in a silly voice. He was really greedy and bought himself a giant multi-coloured creation with clotted cream and a milk flake in it. We all walked on, licking our ice creams. He quizzed Ani about her father and his work. She prattled away about it. Something suddenly occurred to me: London. Could I work on him now?

"Dad," I said, "can I ask you something?"

"How much will it cost?" he answered, winking at Ani.

"Well, I just wondered if you'd ever thought of taking me somewhere *educational*…like London?" I said innocently.

He took a large bite from his ice cream and looked out to sea. There was a big grey Navy ship out there, which he watched for a while.

"Funny you say that. I was thinking of us all going to London before Christmas, for a pantomime, clothes shopping, et cetera…" he said.

I leapt at him and gave him a hug, which knocked the ice cream sideways and made the dog bark. "Oh, Daddy. Thank you, thank you, thank you!"

"Steady on, I'll have to think about it. Would this young prodigy like to come?" he added, looking at Ani.

"Oh, thank you, Ron, I would!" she replied, smiling sweetly.

"Well, I'll have a think and look at my long-suffering bank account and we'll discuss it again soon. All right?" he said.

"Anyway, I can pay for myself, because we're well off," said Ani.

"I see," said my father.

He thought it was vulgar to talk about money. But I was happy; I thought I would burst.

As we walked along, I had a sudden impulse to run and run. I grabbed Ani and shouted: "Race you to the Hoe swimming pool!"

We both ran ahead like mad things, screaming with laughter, and nearly crashed into the railings above the pool. Surely life couldn't get any better than this?

CHAPTER 4

PEACHES IN FLAMING BRANDY

The next weekend, my parents dragged me off to see elderly relations in Barnstaple. It was incredibly boring and not worth describing. I missed Ani terribly and wondered what she was doing. Would she still want to be my friend? Or had she asked another girl round to her house? I worried about it all weekend.

On the following Wednesday, she phoned me. I was struggling with maths homework in my bedroom, when my father called me.

"It's Ani for you."

I leapt up and thundered downstairs. Ani still wanted me.

"Hi, Haze, what are you doing next weekend?" she asked.

"Hi. Um, I don't know. Homework and taking Hedley out."

"Forget all that. Come round and have a meal with us. Dad's friend Jeffrey is coming and I know you'll like him."

"Gosh, thanks."

It was still on. Of course I would go.

"Mel is making us a treat – peaches in flaming brandy!" Ani said.

My heart sank at that. It sounded repulsive. I hated the strange perfumed smell of alcohol. But I desperately wanted to see Ani and the Rydles and be a more interesting person.

"Lovely," I said.

* * *

My father drove me round to the Rydles' on the Saturday evening. Ani let me in. Strong scents of cooking and drink drifted out of the kitchen. Ani smiled and looked excited.

"Come on up."

"Hi there!" called Melissa. She was wearing a long crimson dress, with no shoes, and her hair was spread out over her shoulders. Ani was wearing a black minidress and white tights. She had even varnished her nails and was wearing a touch of lipstick. I felt awkward in my blue cotton trousers and stretchy white polo-neck top, but they were the most fashionable clothes I had. At least my scruffy white tennis shoes looked rather artistic. I had seen people in the *Sunday Times* colour supplement wearing them.

We went into the dining room. When I saw everyone, my first instinct was to flee.

All the family were sitting round a large pine table, Josh in his highchair and Tal wobbling on a pile of cushions on an adult's chair. I saw Jim, Ani's father, for the first time. He had longish blond hair, a shade darker than Ani's, and a red beard, which I didn't like. He was wearing jeans – probably Levi's, I thought gloomily – and a purple shirt with a large collar. My father never wore jeans. He dressed in suits.

There was another man there. He had dark hair and a beard and a strange silk scarf round his neck.

"Ah, this is the famous Hazel, is it?" Jim asked, loudly. "Welcome to our little feast."

"Hello," I said, blushing, and praying he wouldn't ask me anything else in front of everyone.

"I'm Jeffrey," said the other man and smiled.

He shook hands with me.

"He's a writer," said Ani.

That seemed unbelievably glamorous and clever.

"I'm a friend of the family," he added.

"How do you do?" I said.

"What lovely manners," said Mel. "Not like our awful family."

"Boo boo bum," said Tallulah and made a face. Everyone laughed.

I sat down, blushing.

The first course was spaghetti with cheese and tomatoes. It wasn't like the spaghetti I was used to (in tins), but I rather enjoyed it. Jim poured me some white wine mixed with water. I longed for orange squash, but took a sip and pretended to be interested in him, while he expounded some theory about modern furniture. Jeffrey kept asking him questions. Ani looked at me sideways and winked.

"Boring," she whispered.

Ani's taste in food seemed unlike other twelve-year-olds'. At most girls' houses, we had bread and butter, sausages on sticks and little iced cakes. But the Rydles were far removed from such things.

On the dining-room wall, I spotted a photo of the family on holiday somewhere, and all of them were holding up glasses of wine. Ani was wearing a red sleeveless summer dress, had eye make-up on and looked about fifteen. I felt dull in comparison. My hair was a mess and I wasn't allowed wine yet. But I longed to see other countries. We had been to Ireland twice. But I knew that wasn't good enough.

Ani saw me looking at the photo. "That was the Canary Islands," she said.

"Oh – did you see many canaries?" I asked.

Jim guffawed at that. I was confused. I blushed and took a mouthful of wine.

Ani said, "Shut up, Dad."

The ordeal continued. Fortunately, Josh threw some spaghetti, which caused a diversion and took everyone's attention off me.

Mel knelt on the floor and scraped up the mess. "Bloody hell!" she muttered.

"Bloody, bloody, bloody," chanted Tallulah.

Ani said, "Can I go to London with Hazel soon? She's asked me."

"Yeah," I said in a casual voice, as if I often went. I drank some more wine.

Peaches in Flaming Brandy

"Oh sure, if you want," said Jim, shrugging. "We were there last year, weren't we Tallulah-Boo?" he went on, and added, laughing: "We had great fun sticking up two fingers at Buckingham Palace, didn't we? Harharhar! You liked the adventure playground more than that, didn't you, clever girl?"

Everyone laughed their heads off. I was taken aback; I thought everyone liked the Royal Family. But then the Rydles voted Liberal and liked art, so they were probably a bit strange. They also knew people like Jeffrey, writers. I had never ever met a writer. I thought they all lived in London.

"You'll have to excuse us, we're common," said Jim. "Nouveau riche really. Not like the old rich. I got where I am by hard work. My dad was a lowly carpenter in Carlisle. And Ma went out cleaning."

I didn't know what 'nouveau riche' was. I racked my brain and thought about our French classes. Was *nouveau* the word for 'new'? New rich? The Rydles certainly seemed rich, but why were they 'new'?

"That's enough, Jim," said Mel. "She doesn't want a sociology lecture. I'll get the peaches." She went out.

"Stop it, Dad. Hazel doesn't know what you're on about," said Ani. "And I *am* gonna come to London with you," she added, giving me a big smile.

"Sorry, love, I get carried away sometimes," said Jim, not looking sorry at all but pleased with himself. He took a swig of wine and reached over to tickle Tallulah. She screamed with delight, but that frightened Josh and he let out a yell of dismay and started howling.

"Come here, little man," said Jim, and lifted Josh on to his lap. I took another mouthful of wine. I was feeling a bit peculiar.

Jeffrey turned to me.

"What are you interested in, Hazel?" he said, as if I was an adult.

"Um, art and reading and psychology," I said in a low voice. Well, I had read *Teach Yourself Psychology* recently.

He didn't laugh out loud or tell me that was ridiculous, like most adults. He looked really interested.

"Very good," he said. "A girl with intellectual tastes, evidently."

"Hazel's very clever," said Ani.

I could have hugged her.

"Do you read widely?" asked Jeffrey, drinking some wine.

"Yes, I think so," I said.

"Use your local library," he said. "Libraries are a storehouse of knowledge."

"Jeff should know, being a writer," said Jim. "Historical novels and travel books. We met at night school, back in the fifties."

I thought that perhaps I was enjoying myself after all. I drank more wine. Ani topped it up.

At this point, Tallulah interrupted us all by screaming, "I want ice cream!"

"OK, princess," said Jim. "Go and find Mum." He took a big slurp of wine and bounced Josh up and down. Tal slid off her chair and raced out.

Mel came back in, carrying a large blue bowl. She set it down. The orange peaches were floating in a poisonous-looking sea of brown liquid. I swallowed. She lit a match and held it over the dish. Blue flames shot up and everyone went, "Ahh!"

She served out large portions to everyone except Josh and Tal, instead fetching raspberry ripple ice cream for them. I envied them from the bottom of my heart. We added blobs of double cream to our dishes. It began to melt and spread out in a greasy white layer on top of the brandy. Ani immediately began spooning it up with gusto. Jim fed Tal a mouthful but she spat it out. I managed to eat it by holding my breath and swallowing quickly, like you do with nasty medicines, while saying: "It's delicious."

Jeffrey looked at me.

"Leave it if you can't finish it," he whispered. No one else noticed; they were all arguing about furniture and art.

But I felt I must eat it all. I must learn to like Rydle food. I carried on.

At last, the dreadful meal was over. The little ones ran out and went to watch television. Jim went over to a cupboard and took out a large bottle.

"Some more brandy, my love?" he asked Mel.

She thought for a minute and batted it away with her hand. "No, I'll have to drive Hazel home soon, and I'm already a bit pissed. While I do that, you can be loading the dishwasher and getting the kids to bed."

Jim leant back in his chair, taking a big swallow of the brandy.

"What do you think I do all week, hmm? Slaving away in my design practice to keep all of you!" he exclaimed.

Jeffrey laughed but looked uncomfortable.

Ani piped up.

"Give Dad a break, Mel! Hazel could stay the night, and then you won't have to drive her home."

She looked at me. I felt unsure. The Rydles were like forbidden fruit – hugely tempting but possibly dangerous. I longed for my own familiar home, but a little voice in me said, *Go on, or you'll never get another chance.* I was setting out on a road and there was no turning back.

"OK," I said. "But I haven't got a toothbrush or pyjamas with me."

This caused much amusement.

"I'm sure we can find you a spare toothbrush, love," said Jim. "And Sarah's bedroom is free."

So it was arranged and I went to ring my parents.

"Are you having lovely fun there?" asked my mother.

"Yes," I answered, feeling slightly sick by now. "They've asked me to stay the night."

"Oh, lovely. We'll pick you up tomorrow morning then. I'll phone you first."

"Come on, let's see what's on TV," said Ani.

Peaches in Flaming Brandy

We went next door to the TV room, where Tal and Josh were lolling round on the floor, eating crisps and gaping at a film on the colour TV. It was a cowboy film. I had always fancied cowboys.

"Here," said Ani, pushing a large squashy red cushion across the floor to me. "Have a bean bag." We both sank down and sprawled with the little ones. I was glad to lie down, as I was still feeling sick. Tal held out a large bag of crisps to me. I shook my head.

"I'll get some Coca-Cola," said Ani, getting up again.

I checked my watch – nearly eleven. But no adults appeared to tell us it was bedtime. I could hear them chatting next door and laughing.

The phone rang in the hall outside. I heard Jim going to answer it, saying: "Oh, hi darling! No, of course we're up, no problem. Now, about the winter show, I think you should…"

Ani rolled over and pushed the living room door shut with her foot.

She said, through a mouthful of crisps: "My brother Dave says one day we'll all have little phones which we'll carry round with us, and we'll be able to phone people from anywhere."

"Uh?" I answered. "How can that work?"

"He watches that TV programme, *Tomorrow's World*. It was on there."

"Gosh," I said. I sipped a little Coke. If I lay quite still, I was all right.

"Will you shut up?" said Tallulah.

We ignored her. Josh was asleep on some cushions, his little hand still clutching a crisp packet.

Ani leant over and whispered to me: "We should give each other secret nicknames."

"Oh, yeah!" I said happily. This must mean she really wanted to be my best friend. I wondered if I should tell her about The List.

Ani looked at me and asked: "What's your middle name? Mine's Georgia. After Georgia O'Keeffe," she explained.

"Who?"

"The artist, silly," she laughed.

I was clueless. Anita Georgia Rydle sounded good.

"Mine's Jane – really boring," I said.

"Well, better than some," said Ani. "D'you know Caroline Morris? Her middle names are Brenda Letitia!"

We sniggered.

"My middle name is May," announced Tallulah, prodding me with her foot. We still ignored her.

Ani whispered in my ear: "I'm gonna call you Pony, 'cause you're sweet and shaggy-haired like a Dartmoor pony, but you're strong, too, and I bet you could give a good kick if you were annoyed."

I loved this – it was the perfect name for me.

"And I'm going to call you Hippy," I whispered back, "'cause you are so fashionable and American-looking." By some miracle, I felt better, less wine-fuddled.

Ani rolled around, laughing. "Oh, you funny girl."

Peaches in Flaming Brandy

From then on, those were our secret names.

It was getting very late, but still no one told us to go to bed.

I wondered about baby Josh. "Should we put him to bed?" I asked.

"Oh, it's all right, Mel will see to him," said Ani. "C'mon."

I followed Ani to her bedroom and stood while she rooted in her chest of drawers for spare pyjamas. Her shoulder bag was lying open on the bed and I couldn't help noticing a little photo sticking out. I edged over and looked. It was a pale young woman with long black hair and a sad face. She was holding a small, fat, blonde baby. Could it be Ani?

"That's Realmum with me." Ani had come up behind me.

"She's pretty," I said.

"Yep," she said, but nothing more. She pushed the photo back into the bag.

"Here are some pyjamas. I'll show you Sarah's room. It's got a bath and basin in it."

The room was large and full of paintings, records and clothes left on chairs. I washed slowly and pulled on the faded pyjamas. I climbed into the strange white bed with its geometric bedspread. The sheets felt cold and damp, but I was profoundly grateful to be alone at last.

I could hear muted sounds of the family in other parts of the house – bursts of laughter, doors shutting, a short cry from the baby. Silence descended, but I lay there for some time, thinking of the photo of the sad, dark-haired mother with baby Ani. Where was she now?

The Rydle Year

* * *

When I told my mother about the peaches and burning brandy the next day, she was appalled.

"Honestly, what a thing to give to children!"

To make things worse, I let slip about the Rydles sticking two fingers up at Buckingham Palace.

"Well! I don't like that at all. I don't know if I want you going *there* again!" she said disapprovingly. She reached for a cigarette.

"Oh, *please,* Mum. They're all right, really."

"Well, I suppose they're not Communists," she said, taking a puff of her cigarette and considering.

"No."

"Would you like sausages and baked beans tonight?" she asked me.

"Oh, yes!" I answered. Sometimes it was a relief to have ordinary food.

CHAPTER 5

A ROW – AND SARAH GIVES GOOD ADVICE

Plymouth 2012

I've arranged my mother's funeral and it's next week. My cousins helped me, thank God. A small affair in Stoke Dean church. So many of her friends are already dead. I've contacted as many as I can. All so unreal. You spend years wondering what your parents' funerals will be like, and then they come upon you. No word from Tobi or Matti. I don't want Tobi at the funeral anyway. And Matti is in Bolivia, I believe, and unreachable for now. Hope his gap year's going well. Will try to ring him at the weekend. I pray there are no family rows at the funeral. That reminds me of a row I had during the Rydle Year, with my father…

* * *

Plymouth 1970

"Hello – Pony? Is that you?"

"Yes – hello, Hippy, how are you?"

The Rydle Year

"OK, thanks. Guess what? Tallulah got into trouble at her nursery: she drew a dog doing a poo. When the teacher said, 'What's this?' she said, 'It's real-ism!' She probably heard Mel and Dad talking about art. Anyway, how are you?"

I was on the phone in our hall, curled up on the window seat, twisting the tangly green phone wire round my fingers. Ani was still my friend after three weeks.

"Oh, Tallulah's so funny! Yes, I'm all right. Dad was in one of his moods this morning – no, it's OK – he's gone out to get petrol. I was rude to him last night and said, 'Bugger off.'"

"Ooh, Pony! You look so innocent. Your parents are a bit on the strict side though, you know? Anyway, listen…I've got an idea – can you come over next Saturday afternoon, because Sarah will be twenty-one and we're gonna have a meringue and drinks? It's not her proper party; that's on her boyfriend's boat later."

"Yes please. That sounds super! I want to meet her."

"OK. What are you up to today then?"

"Oh well, Mum and Dad are going antiques shopping, really boring, but I'm staying with Granny Lil and doing homework and taking the dog out. That's it really."

"Well, having a dog is good. OK, ask your mum about next week and I'll see you in school."

"I will. Also, I want to tell you about a list I'm working on."

"A list? Ooh. Tell me on Saturday. Sounds interesting. Bye."

"Bye, Hippy." I put down the green phone receiver.

A Row – and Sarah Gives Good Advice

Ani and I were always ringing each other and running up our fathers' phone bills. It was the only way to keep in touch.

When my father got home from the garage, he was still in a bad mood. He strode around the house, finding fault with everything and everyone, even the dog. I lurked in the kitchen, trying to avoid him. But he soon found me.

"Hazel," he snapped, "I looked into your bedroom earlier and it was a mess. Will you please go up now and tidy?"

I slouched against a kitchen counter.

"Go to hell!" I muttered under my breath.

"What, what's that?"

"Sod. Off," I said, loud and clear.

There was a silence. Then all hell broke loose. He went maroon in the face and started shouting.

"How *dare* you, you insolent little…Go into the dining room *now*, I want to talk to you."

I trembled inwardly. Was I too old to be slapped now? His tempers were awful.

I slunk into the dining room. It was a chilly room, only used for big family meals or parties. I stood at one end of the dark polished table and my father stood at the other. He let rip.

"I've just about had enough of you lately, with your sulks and rudeness. I want to remind you – I slave away working to keep you, doing all hours in the office and driving miles to my clients! And all I get is damned cheek back! It's about time you showed some respect, instead of moaning about ponies and holidays. A lot of children don't have anything."

He stopped to catch his breath and then carried on.

"I reckon that wretched child Ani has put ideas into your head, with all that rubbish about Liberals and art. Believe you me, she'll end up a mess!"

I was stunned. He hadn't been this angry for ages. My beautiful friendship with Ani was being ridiculed. But I wasn't going to be beaten yet.

Trembling, I said: "I just want to have some adventures, not just bloody school and homework and going out for boring lunch with you lot and wearing little-girl dresses! I'm getting older now; I'm not a little kid any more. And Ani is *not* rubbish!" I finished, already dreading what might happen next.

"Well, you can start behaving like an adult then. Unfortunately, you're too old to be smacked, so you can go to your room for now – go on!" He left the room furiously, slamming the door so hard the china on the sideboard rattled.

I stood, numb, shocked, then burst into noisy tears.

"You git!" I whispered. I wanted to die at that moment. Ani was my special friend and I had discovered her all on my own. My father had laughed at everything I had tried to do. Life seemed totally hopeless. It would be years before I was eighteen and an adult and free.

I rushed upstairs and threw myself onto the bed. Hedley followed me and I held him and cried into his warm fur. I was so angry, I bit my hand and hoped it would bleed, but it just ended up with toothmarks.

A Row – and Sarah Gives Good Advice

After a while, I heard my parents going out, no doubt to visit antique shops. I lay there for ages. I wished Jim Rydle was my father – he probably would have laughed if I said, *Sod off*. It was so flaming unfair.

Hedley got restless, jumped off the bed, and lay on the floor. He watched me with sad eyes.

I decided to get out The List, even though it wasn't the right day for checking it. The last item said:

E--------------!

I got a Biro and filled in the word – 'Escape!' That was better.

Escape! That was my ultimate desire – to escape from all of this. My family, Plymouth, everything dull and limiting. I wasn't sure how yet, but I had faith that I would find a way, one day.

I would definitely tell Ani about The List on Saturday. It was time for action.

There was a quiet tap on the door and Granny Lil put her head round.

"Are you all right, dear? I was worried."

She came in and put a plate of sandwiches on my bedside table.

"I'm OK," I shouted so she could hear. "Dad got angry with me, that's all." I turned my face to the wall.

"Oh, don't worry about him. He's all hot air. All right, I'll leave you now. Try to eat something soon, eh?" she said kindly.

I didn't answer. She was still an adult, one of the enemy.

She tutted and went out, saying under her breath: "That child…"

Get lost, I thought, although I felt mean too. She was my friend. I reached for a cheese sandwich.

I thought it over. My father had been nasty and it hurt so much. I had a good mind to add 'Kill Dad' to my list. But murder was a bit extreme. Why did he get in these moods? I had no idea. Adults were a mystery to me. Of course they told you what to do all the time and gave you meals and loved you (sometimes). But they had other things going on, hidden things which you heard about in snatches or furtive whispers. It was complicated. I sighed.

I spent a long time holed up in my bedroom, but in the end I couldn't bear it any more and took Hedley out for a gloomy walk.

* * *

Things blew over a bit that evening. My parents came back bearing antiques and looking happy. My mother smiled at me. My father disappeared to his little office to do something connected with work.

"Come and have a drink with me," said Mum. "I bought you some Coke."

I followed her, rather sheepish as my father had no doubt told her about the row. *She* never got very angry with me. She poured me a Coke, added ice and fetched some brandy for herself. She dropped some chunks of ice into it and they made a pleasant clonking noise.

I looked at her anxiously. "Is he still angry?"

"Oh, no. He's all right now. He gets rather…upset. There are things going on at work, you see. And he broods on things which happened years ago."

"What things?"

"Oh, nothing to worry you."

"Can I still see Ani?"

"Ani? Oh, yes. I don't see why not. It's nice for you to have a good friend. Even if her family is a bit odd."

I sighed with relief. All was not lost, then.

"Just be nice to Daddy and don't be rude."

"OK." I poked my finger in my glass and dabbled the ice about.

"Shall I make some supper?" she said. "We could have fish and chips from the freezer."

"Yes, lovely." We had just acquired a freezer, my mother's pride and joy.

We all settled down to watch *Morecambe and Wise* on television. My father seemed to have calmed down and he was perfectly nice to me, saying we could look at colour televisions next week in the shops. But I couldn't completely forgive him for his mean remarks and resolved to be wary of him in future.

* * *

The following Saturday, I was back at the Rydles'. Ani came running to the front door and hugged me.

"Hello, Pony," she said, grinning. She looked marvellous as usual. This time she was wearing some baggy purple trousers and a silver top. Her hair was all loose and silky. She always managed to look better than me.

"Sarah's here for her birthday tea, and she can't wait to meet you. Mel's taken the kids out to buy a birthday cake and Dad's having a nap, so it's just us."

We both ran upstairs and a tall, thin young woman appeared – she was the most wonderful-looking woman, with long, smooth, light-brown hair, large silver earrings, a black silk shirt and tight denim jeans. She wore black socks and they had holes in them, showing white toes with bright-red nail varnish on them.

"This is Sarah, my big sister," said Ani proudly.

"Hello, Hazel, so lovely to meet you."

The voice and face were almost like Ani's, which made me feel strange. There was only one Ani, but she had lots of brothers and sisters, who were bound to be similar, like a litter of puppies or something. For an only child like me, it was an odd thought.

"Hi, I love your earrings," I answered shyly.

She laughed and said: "Thanks. Shall we have a coffee and chat in the kitchen? Cake and drinks are later."

We all went into the warm, coffee-scented kitchen. Ani made us Nescafé in chunky orange mugs.

A Row – and Sarah Gives Good Advice

"So, tell me about yourself, Hazel," said Sarah, looking at me intently. Her eyes were bright blue. Her skin was like Ani's, rosy and freckly. She flicked a strand of hair behind one shoulder and the light shimmered off her earrings.

"Well, I'm nearly thirteen," I said, (true, if you added five months), "and I live in Compton in a big house with Mum, Dad and Gran, and my dog Hedley. I'm the only child. And I love art and clothes and horse riding, and interesting places. I want to do things, and travel all over the world, but sometimes Mum and Dad are strict. They're really old you see – fifty-three!" I blushed.

Sarah didn't laugh. She looked very interested.

Ani chipped in: "They're nice but they're old-fashioned, that's the trouble. And Hazel has no brothers or sisters."

Sarah stroked her chin. "Aah, right. Yeah, Ani's lucky in that way, having us sisters, because we've all done outrageous things and got into trouble already, so we've paved the way." She took a sip of coffee and looked affectionately at Ani.

"Anyway, I'll never change anything," I said, sadly.

"Of course you will," said Sarah. "You seem like an intelligent girl and good-looking…yes, you are! You'll gradually find your own style. You just need to learn to be assertive and make your point, and realise that you can't always get your way. Try to see your parents' point of view too. They probably want the best for you and they have needs too – they might get fed up sometimes."

"This isn't Dartmoor Manor School, Sarah," interrupted Ani. "She can't go back home and be all modern, you know."

"Doesn't matter," said Sarah. "She can make small changes. You two girls are both growing up and good things are coming; just be a little patient."

I drank in her words. No one had ever talked to me like this. This must be how adults felt.

I am Hazel, and nobody can change that, I thought.

"How's art college and London?" asked Ani.

"Great. You know I'm finishing in two years. Yeah? Then I want to look for work as an illustrator – for children's books. My friend Lenny has contacts, so I hope it'll work out."

I said nothing but lapped it up. It was a world beyond my experience.

All this was interrupted by a loud crash – Mel and the children were back.

The front door was flung open and Tallulah yelled, "We've got cake, we've got cake!"

Chaos set in, with Tal and Josh screaming and racing around. Jim emerged from his nap and started chasing the children, which caused more chaos. I watched from the sidelines, enjoying it.

"Help me to unpack the party food, Hazel?" said Ani.

She put out bowls, and we poured crisps and peanuts in.

Mel arranged the giant meringue on a plate, chatting with Sarah as she did it. I suppose Sarah was only a little younger than Mel and they seemed to get on well.

A Row – and Sarah Gives Good Advice

Jim arranged champagne and orange juice on the counter with a flourish, humming a little song.

"Hazel," said Sarah, "I just wondered if you needed any more jeans or anything? I'm sorting out some old clothes which I've left here. Do you want to have a rummage?"

More jeans? I had no jeans.

"Yes please," I said.

Ani, Sarah and I went down to her old bedroom, the one I'd slept in. She had a pile of clothes strewn on the bed – jeans, smock tops, scarves and velvet jackets. Ani and I started going through them. I saw a pair of faded grey cord jeans. I was desperate for cords or denim jeans. Even better, they were Wrangler's. Sarah was a bit taller than me but they fitted. My first proper jeans.

Sarah held out a black polo-neck sweater to me. "Try this."

I pulled it on. It still had a faint aromatic scent of something.

"There. Now you look like a French existentialist," she said, sounding amused.

"A what?"

"You know, poets and intellectuals – yep, it suits you."

"Oh, Hazel, you look good," said Ani. "Sarah, can I have that long black dress, d'you think?"

I was in heaven. Ani and I looked like a pair of students now. I threw my babyish old trousers and top in a corner. Sarah went and picked up a guitar, which was leaning against a chair, and started playing.

"That's folk music," whispered Ani.

"This one's called *'Quicksilver Boy'*," she said and started strumming a song:

I saw you by the lake
Shining in the shadows
My Quicksilver Boy

Tried to run and catch you
But you melted away
My Quicksilver Boy

She stopped and looked a bit shy. "That was one I wrote, just a stupid song," she said, pushing her hair back.

"That was good!" I said, looking adoringly at Sarah.

"I'm not very good really; it's just for a laugh," she said. "I play a bit at folk clubs."

A voice shouted down to us – "Are you coming to your party, or what?"

"Better go up," said Sarah.

I would have been happy, just staying in Sarah's room. But the Rydles were waiting and they loved parties.

Jim held out his arms to Sarah and shouted: "Welcome, my darling twenty-one-year-old girl! Have a hug, sweetheart."

The Rydles were always hugging and kissing each other.

He pulled a little shiny package out of his pocket and gave it to Sarah. She unwrapped it.

A Row – and Sarah Gives Good Advice

"Oh, Daddy! I adore it," she exclaimed and held out a tiny glittering ring for us all to see. It looked like silver and had tiny jewels in it.

"Diamonds for my girl," Jim said. Sarah put on the ring and flung her arms around him. He took out another package for her – a thin one.

"What's this? Oh my God! Air tickets to Paris? Thank you, wonderful Daddy," she said.

"Thought you might like to see the art there again," Jim said.

The afternoon went by in a blur of excitement. Mel put on records and we danced. We gorged on party food and meringue, and Ani and I had a small glass of champagne each. The little children rampaged around, and no one minded.

After a while, when we were tired and full of food, Sarah sat with Ani and me and we chatted like three old friends. Sarah finally left in the early evening, to see her boyfriend.

I remembered my list. Could I get Ani alone?

I said to her in an undertone, "I'm going to the toilet. Can I tell you something?"

She nodded and followed me to the bathroom. We locked ourselves in.

"What is it, Pony?"

"Ani," I said, pushing aside a damp dirty towel and perching on the bath, "I want to tell you something."

"OK – what?"

She sat next to me.

I hesitated.

"It's a secret – don't tell anyone. The thing is – I've got a list, of all the important things I want to do."

"Uh-huh…"

So I told her all the things on my list, in a great rush – a bra, meeting boys, getting to London and finding Levi's, getting a good hairstyle, saving money and escaping. I decided not to mention getting a best friend. That sounded too desperate.

Ani burst out laughing.

"You are so wonderful and different, Pony," she said. "All the other girls at school are such dimwits, just going on about pop magazines or what they did at Guides."

"I hate the sodding Guides!" I said. "Have *you* thought about these things – you know, bras and boys and everything?"

"Well, not much – I just think they'll happen in the end. I'm not really worried."

I couldn't believe it. I was terrified of being trapped for ever at home, like a little girl.

"What about escaping, though? Have you ever thought about that?" I asked.

"Not till now, no. But you're making me think. What did you have in mind – Exeter – or Cornwall?"

"Are you joking? No, I mean, far away. London or another country. Yes, definitely another country."

Ani looked at me, seeming a little uncertain.

"Well," she said, "we can do more things together. If we want to escape, we'd better practise first. I tell you what – let's

A Row – and Sarah Gives Good Advice

get away from our parents and go hiking on Dartmoor. Out into the wilds. It's half term next week."

"How will we get to Dartmoor?" I asked.

"Uh – ever heard of buses?"

"Yes, but which one? Where?"

"Yelverton – we'll go to Yelverton. You know the village near Plymouth? I've been with Sarah. I'll pinch the bus timetable from Dad's office."

Ani always had an answer.

She unlocked the door and listened.

"They're all in the kitchen," she said. "I'll just nip up and get the timetable."

We took the dog-eared booklet into Ani's bedroom and looked up buses to Dartmoor. It was easy enough. We made a plan: we would tell our parents we were doing a nature study project there. That should stop them being suspicious.

I had an inkling of adult life that day, and what it could be like. For it was then I realised that I could quite possibly make things happen – one day, at least. Sarah had opened my eyes.

CHAPTER 6

INTO THE WILDS

"Are you sure you two can manage on the bus?" said my mother. She was fussing around in the kitchen, making me sandwiches and filling a flask with hot chocolate.

"Yes. I've said we can. You know we get buses all round Plymouth, so what's the difference?"

"There are some strange people on the moors," said my Granny Lil, looking up from her knitting.

"Exactly," said my mother. "Now, I want you to go to Yelverton and stay near people. Are you listening, darling? Don't go off on any lonely walks. You can do your nature study round there."

"Mum!" I shouted. "I'm twelve. I know what I'm doing." She made me sick sometimes.

She sighed. "Better get on with the hoovering," she said, and went to the cupboard. "Can you peel the vegetables for lunch, Mother?"

"Yes. Hazel – don't you go near any bogs, and stay away from boys," said Granny.

"Yes, all right," I shouted.

Boys were exactly what I *was* looking for.

I shoved my packed lunch and anorak into my shoulder bag – the essentials for a trip to the moors.

"Right, I'm going."

"You're not wearing those scruffy tennis shoes, are you?" said Granny Lil.

"Honestly, I can't wear party shoes, can I?" I slammed out of the house.

I walked to the bus stop near Ani's. She was late. Finally, she appeared, hurrying down the road, wearing a huge baggy jumper and stripy scarf.

"Hi, Pony, sorry I'm late," she puffed. "I lost my gym shoes and had to borrow Mel's." She lifted a foot to show me a dirty old canvas shoe with paint on it.

There was always some drama at the Rydles'.

We sat on the wall by the bus stop and swung our legs.

"My mum's driving me mad at the moment," I moaned. "She won't let me do anything."

"Same here. Mel keeps on at me and makes me help with Josh. And Dad's never there. That's the whole point of doing this trip today, though – escaping from parents," she said, unwrapping a Curly Wurly bar and tearing off half for me.

"How's Realmum?" I asked.

"Realmum? Oh – she's all right. I might see her soon," said Ani.

"Is she still in Dorset?" I asked, through toffee-covered teeth.

"What? Yeah, of course."

She never said much.

The big green Western National bus arrived and we went rumbling out of Plymouth. We compared packed lunches. Ani had some outlandish things, as usual – some disgusting-looking pink paste in a white bread roll, which she said was pâté and was made of squashed animal leftovers.

"God, how can you eat that?"

"Oh, it's really nice. It's French."

She also had some stinking cheese, called 'Brie', and a packet of shiny yellow crisps.

"Chinese snacks," she said.

She had a quick glance at my chicken sandwich, fairy cake and apple. I sighed. I could never be as interesting as her.

As the bus came into Yelverton, I got up to leave. But Ani grabbed me and pulled me down again.

"What? Why?" I said, struggling.

"We're staying on," she said. "We're going out to the real moors for a proper hike."

"What?" I shrieked. "What d'you mean?"

It was funny though, and I started laughing. Some old women in the front of the bus looked back at us disapprovingly.

"Yelverton is boring. What we want is somewhere wild, to practise escaping."

Ani was in charge, as usual.

"Where then?" I said and Ani ignored me. The bus carried on. I nudged her and pinched her, but she laughed and wouldn't say.

"Here," said Ani.

We got out in the middle of nowhere, at a bus stop by a little gravelly car park.

She said, "I think I went here with Sarah. Come on then."

All around us was wild land – green hills with rocky tops, bogs, wild ponies and stone walls. I looked longingly at the ponies. I hadn't made any progress with my father buying me one, but Ani said Jim had promised her one when she was fifteen.

"Come on, Pony, let's get going. We're going to walk, then build a shelter and eat our food there and pretend we're camping."

"All right," I said, cheering up. Ani knew what she was doing. I had never built a shelter. I'd never been camping, either. We went to hotels for our holidays.

We set off across the moors, with Ani in the lead. The air smelt sweet and fresh. There was nobody else around. All I could hear were little birds chirping somewhere in the sky and a rushing stream. Ani was already eating her squashed animal pâté sandwich. She was always hungry.

"I love this!" I shouted, waving my arms and whirling my shoulder bag round and round.

"Madwoman," said Ani and smiled. I caught up with her.

Suddenly she said, out of the blue, "Do you know about sex?"

"What? Yeah, of course," I said.

"How did you find out?"

"My mum bought me a Ladybird book, and I read about it in my gran's magazines too – ones like *Woman's Own*. But my mum and dad never say anything. They're so old-fashioned."

"Sarah told me," said Ani.

"I couldn't believe it when I found out," I went on. "You know – thinking of old aunties and uncles doing it naked. Or the vicar. Or parents. Bouncing up and down. Awful." I started giggling.

"I know – yuck!" Ani said.

"But I can't wait to do it," I said. "If I found a lovely boy, I'd kiss him for hours and roll around with him naked!"

"You're boy-mad, you are," she said, laughing. "A sex maniac."

"No I'm not, shut up!"

But I felt worried. Was I abnormal? I would have to check in some women's magazines and find out more. A few girls at school had boyfriends and wore tarty make-up, but most of them stayed in with their parents all the time. I wouldn't have minded trying on some tarty make-up, just to see.

"Don't you want to try sex, though?" I went on.

"Don't know. Not till I'm about twenty," said Ani.

I was amazed. I looked sideways at her, striding along. What did she really want?

Ani said, "Tell you what, though, we could join a youth club and just hang around with boys and mess about, and then we'd get away from our parents as well."

That sounded like an excellent idea.

Into the Wilds

"But don't you have to go to church, to join a youth club like Mutley Methodist or Peverell Baptist?" I asked.

"No, you idiot, they don't mind. Our family are all atheists and Sarah and Dave went to church clubs. You can always lie."

I had never met any atheists before. But I said, "That sounds good, Hippy, let's do that."

"Anyway, who needs stupid boys when we've got each other?" she said.

We kept on walking for a little while, over marshy ground. Our feet sank in alarmingly. It was growing cloudy and a few raindrops fell. My feet felt damp and cold in my tennis shoes.

Ani stopped and pointed to a tumbledown wall.

"There – let's build our shelter now," said Ani.

We were coming towards a little wood. I was getting tired and I didn't feel like building a silly shelter. I wanted to eat up my lunch and head back to the bus.

"Can't we eat our food first?" I asked.

"No we can't," she said.

I frowned but she took no notice.

Ani started to collect sticks and pile them up, humming a little song. I almost hated her at that minute.

"Come on, Pony, help me," she said.

I made a sour face and picked up a few sticks. This was stupid. I didn't know how to make a shelter. The Brownies and Guides did pathetic things like that, and I had refused to join, ever since I saw a Brown Owl arrive at my primary school one day for their meeting, carrying a home-made felt toadstool for their dancing. And they wore a hideous brown uniform. Brown was the worst colour ever, for clothes.

We made a crude little shelter, up against the stone wall. Just two lines of sticks, leaning against each other in a crooked A-shape. Then Ani made us crouch in it, in our anoraks. We started eating our lunches and I gulped down my hot chocolate and didn't offer her any, for revenge. She looked happy. It was raining steadily on us now.

"This is pointless," I dared to say.

"Why? Don't you want to escape from Plymouth? You'll have to practise if you do, making shelters and things. You can't just leave without making plans, you know."

Ani stuffed herself with food. After she finished, she sat and started biting her nails. She did that a lot.

"Yes – well, I don't want to live in the wilds. I want to live in a town. Or a village, anyway," I said.

Up till now, I had thought how grown up Ani was, and clever. But seeing her crouched in her shelter, scoffing her food like a schoolgirl in a comic, I thought she was childish. I wanted to do adult things, like talking about books or what we would do in the future.

I looked at my watch – it was nearly four. I jumped up.

"I'm not staying here. It's late and – and we need to go back," I said.

Ani crossed her arms. "Don't be such a little pansy!"

"Well, what do you think we should do, if you're so clever?"

Into the Wilds

"We could probably sleep here tonight," Ani said. But she chewed her thumb and looked worried.

"That's ridiculous."

I started walking away, not looking back. If she didn't follow, I would still keep going. But she did follow. It was pouring with rain and getting foggy. All around was misty moorland with a few wet ponies. We were totally alone. There was a real danger we could get lost and sink into a bog. I thought to myself: *What's the best thing to do?* It was mad to keep going across the moors; we needed to go to the road and look for the bus stop. I looked round. Then I saw something – car headlights. The road was nearby.

"Come on, this way," I ordered.

"Wait for me, Pony," Ani called. She started running after me, puffing away. I refused to look at her.

"Oh, shit, I've just stepped in a bog," she shouted. I couldn't help giggling at that.

"Oh, come on, you twit, I'll pull you out." I squelched over to her and caught her arm. Her jeans were brown and soaked.

"Thank you, Pony. Are we friends again?" she asked.

"I s'pose so," I said. It was better to be with someone, however idiotic they were, than alone on the moor.

We headed for the road, which was up on a ridge. Once we got there, we could see lights in the distance.

"A farm! I knew it would be all right," said Ani, as if it was her idea to do this. But I was beyond anger. We were at more of a survival stage. My trousers were sopping wet now too. We stumbled along the road, arm in arm.

Soon after, we saw a man coming our way with a dog, whistling a tune. He wore a battered hat, a long black coat with coloured patterns on it, and Wellington boots. His hair was blowing about and his beard was wet.

"Hello, young ladies," he said, and stopped. "What are you up to, on a rainy afternoon like this?" He had a rolling Devon accent.

"We're fine, thanks, just looking for the bus stop," I said in an unfriendly voice, hurrying on.

But Ani stopped and said, "Hi there. Can we use your phone? We need to get a lift back to Plymouth."

"Your friend doesn't trust me, does she?" he said, laughing. "Don't worry, I'm all right. My name's Wolf. I live at the farm up there. What you called?"

"Ani and Hazel, and we live in Plymouth," said Ani before I could stop her. My gran had warned me about this sort of thing.

"I live just down this lane, see? With my girlfriend. I've just been checking on the sheep. If you come back, you can phone your mums."

"No," I mouthed at Ani and jerked my head towards the main road.

"Don't be daft, he won't do anything," she whispered to me, grabbing my anorak and forcing me along with her.

"I love your coat – is it an Afghan coat?" she said to Wolf.

Into the Wilds

"Sure is," he answered. "Bought it when I was doing the overland thing."

It was too late now; we had to go with him. In any case, it was pouring and we were soaked. We had a choice – murder by a madman or death by drowning.

A gloomy old farmhouse came into sight. There was mud everywhere and old crumbling walls. Another sheepdog came rushing out, barking.

"Shut up, Blackie," shouted Wolf. The dog wagged its tail and went quiet. Ani bent down and stroked it and fussed over it.

A woman came to the door. I had never seen such a sight – her hair was in dozens of plaits and dyed crimson. She appeared to be wearing rags. However, she looked friendly.

"Hello, Wolfie. Hello girls. Oh, come on in, it's all right," she said to us. "Don't worry about Blackie or Bob, they won't hurt a fly. And Wolf won't do no harm, neither." She cackled at that.

Wolf seemed to find it very funny as well.

Ani strode in, and I trailed behind.

"I'm Annie," said the ragged woman, holding out a hand to shake.

I shook hands, feeling silly.

"Welcome to our commune."

"I'm an Ani, too," said Ani.

"Ain't that funny, two Annies," said Annie, cackling with laughter again.

I didn't think it was *that* funny,

I had heard about communes in the Sunday colour supplements. They sounded terribly shocking. Sometimes there were drugs. My mother didn't like communes. I looked at Ani but she seemed relaxed.

We were in a dark kitchen, which seemed very old. There was an ancient stove and a wood fire burning. Pieces of washing hung down from a wooden frame attached to the ceiling. It felt quite cosy, but I was on edge, wondering what might happen. Ani was asking them questions about their farm and where they were from. Wolf said he was born in Yelverton, but Annie said she came from 'foreign parts' – Cornwall. That sounded silly. Cornwall was really near.

"There's the phone, girls," said Annie, pointing to an old black telephone on a side table. "Off you go."

"Can you phone Mel and get her to ring my mum?" I said to Ani. I had an idea my parents wouldn't be very pleased if I said I was in a commune on the moors.

"Come and sit by the fire, darlings, and I'll make some herb tea to warm you up," said Annie, fetching cups and putting a kettle on the old stove. Herb tea sounded strange – I thought herbs were used for making stuffing. I sat on the old sofa, on a dog-scented hairy blanket.

Ani dialled her number.

"Hi, yes it's me. Get Mum – hurry up," she said.

It must have been Tallulah answering.

"Hi Mel…umm, Hazel and I got caught in the rain near Yelverton and missed the bus. Can you come and get us?

We're at a farm. What? Yeah, on the main road that goes to Princetown."

"Blackbrook Farm," said Annie. "There's a sign."

"Blackbrook Farm, there's a sign. On the main road out of Yelverton to Princetown. What? I know but we got lost. I can't help it!"

"God," she muttered, "Mel's so annoying."

"Is she cross?" I said.

"Sort of," said Ani, shrugging.

"Can I have the phone?" asked Annie. She took it and told Mel exactly where we were.

I relaxed a bit and patted the damp sheepdogs, who were lying down in front of me. I tasted my herbal tea. It reminded me of old lawn clippings. I pushed it away.

"How long have you lived here?" I dared to say to Annie, who was less intimidating than Wolf.

"Four years, my love, living off the land," she said. "Hardly ever go to Plymouth or anywhere. We share with our friends."

"Oh. Where are they?"

"Just in Tavistock, buying some tinned food. We want to live off the land, but we aren't there yet. There's only so many turnips and spuds you can eat." She laughed loudly at that.

I tried to imagine living out on the moors, and not going into Plymouth. I had my doubts. On the other hand, you could have a horse out here.

"We live in Plymouth and it's really boring. There's nothing to do there," I said, trying to sound clever.

"Oh, well…lots of dropouts and cool people are heading this way, down to the south west," said Annie. "There's a vibe round here."

I didn't know what she meant, and I sat and stared at the fire. Ani sat down next to me.

"It's fun here, isn't it?" she whispered.

"It's not bad," I admitted. Annie fed us with digestive biscuits while we were waiting, and the fire warmed and dried us. Wolf went off to see to the animals and Annie started cooking supper.

A little later there was a loud knock on the old wooden front door, which made us jump, and it was pushed open to reveal a group of Rydles – Mel, Tallulah and Ani's brother Dave. They all burst in, shouting hello, exclaiming about the farmhouse and saying, "Sorry for bothering you," and, "Where are those naughty girls?"

Mel didn't seem too annoyed, just interested in the farm, and Dave looked around and started chatting to Wolf.

Tal came running over to us and snapped, "You stinkies, why didn't you take me with you?"

Ani lifted Tal on to her lap and hugged her. "Sorry, Sugar Baby. We will next time. But we got all wet and muddy – you wouldn't like that, would you?"

Mel stared at us and laughed. "Look at you both. What a sight! Have you been swimming in mud or what? Hazel – I rang your parents to tell them you're all right."

"Thank you."

"I've got to see round this commune," Dave said. "Hey, Wolf, can you show me things?"

"Sure, man. Why don't you all come on a tour?"

So we all followed Wolf, with Tallulah holding Ani's hand. There was a big barn with goats and chickens and a tumbledown outhouse, which Wolf said was going to be a holiday cottage one day. Then we went back in.

"What a wonderful place," said Mel. "Sometimes I'd like to get away from city life, live more simply like this."

"It's pretty cut off in winter, with the snow," said Annie and laughed. "But we just dig in and smoke and relax."

We all trooped upstairs. There were various bedrooms with unmade beds and piles of stuff on them, rather like the Rydles' house, but somehow less appealing.

A tabby cat was sniffing around up there. "That's to keep the rats away," said Wolf, picking up the cat which struggled in his arms. I shivered.

"Can I use the bathroom?" I asked.

It was shocking: the bath had a rusty stain in it, a cracked lump of dry green soap sat in the basin, and damp towels lay everywhere. The toilet hadn't even been flushed. It made the Rydles' bathroom look palatial. I felt disgusted. This was too much; maybe communes weren't so wonderful, after all. I thought of our yellow bathroom at home, which my mother or the cleaning lady, Brenda, scrubbed till it shone. I had a sudden urge to clean this one and looked around for a cloth or scouring powder. But there was nothing.

The Rydle Year

Someone banged on the door. "What are you doing, Pony?" called Ani. "We're going home now."

"Coming," I said, and hurried downstairs with her.

Mel was chatting to Annie about the commune.

"Are we going then?" asked Ani, fending off Tallulah, who was trying to climb up her.

Mel sighed. "Yes, girls, we'd better go, back to the big city. Thank you so much for looking after them, Annie."

"No trouble," said Annie, smiling. "Come back any time."

"Come on, then. Hang on – where's Dave?"

But Dave wasn't coming back. He liked the commune so much, he wanted to stay longer. Annie and Wolf invited him to stay the night, and he said he would hitch back the next day. I wasn't too surprised – the Rydles did things like that.

We drove back to Plymouth in the twilight. Tallulah enjoyed being squashed between us, like a sardine. She was quite sweet for once. It made me wish I had a sister or brother. Ani promised to take her to the toy shop the next day, to make up for missing our hike. Mel talked to us about the commune, saying how interesting it was and how she wanted to "explore new things". Everyone was jolly except me. I had a slightly sick feeling, wondering what sort of reception I would get back home.

When we arrived in Compton, Mel rang our bell, and my parents came rushing out. My mother looked worried and my father looked angry. They were both smoking, even though Dad had officially given up. Granny Lil was there, too, lurking in the doorway. A complete audience. It was so embarrassing.

Into the Wilds

Mum gave me a hug.

"Darling – what on earth happened? We were so worried!" she exclaimed.

"Where have you been?" demanded my father.

"It's all right, Ron," said Mel. "No harm done. They had a walk and got rained on, but they found a farm."

"Hazel was really clever – she found the road and we went to a commune and we phoned Mel," said Ani.

"Hmm, well, thank you, Mel," my father said. "I'm sorry about all the trouble."

He looked at me. "I'll have a word with you in a minute."

I trembled.

"No trouble, Ron," Mel said. "Bye, sweetheart." They turned to go. Ani looked back at me and smiled in a 'hope you're all right' kind of way. At that minute, I fervently wished I was her.

I went in, full of dread. We all stood around in the hall.

"A *commune*? Do you realise what these places are like?" my father said.

How do you know? I thought. There was no point answering back, though.

But then something weird and wonderful happened: my mother winked at me. She stood behind my father and winked.

"Come on, Ron," she said. "Didn't you ever do silly things when you were a boy?"

"Well, I…" he spluttered.

"They were just being normal girls," said Granny Lil.

"And you can stay out of it!" shouted Dad.

I felt sorry for my gran. She went out, muttering, "We used to play in the streets…"

"What about a hot bath?" said my mother, smiling at me. "And don't forget, Ron, we're going to Althea's cheese and wine do this evening."

"Oh, God, I'd forgotten that blasted party," he exclaimed. "I'd better get a clean shirt on then." He didn't like Althea.

By some miracle, things calmed down for the time being. My parents left and I had a peaceful evening with my grandmother, who cooked us corned beef hash and told me stories about the old days in Plymouth. She was a naughty girl who loved playing tricks on neighbours.

When I was finally in bed, in the warmth, I thought about the day's events. The tables had turned for once, and I had become the boss, taking us back to safety. Ani had shown a childish side. It made me thoughtful.

* * *

Unfortunately the whole escapade was not forgotten, though. The next evening, my father asked me to come with him to buy petrol – the usual method of getting me alone.

He wasn't too angry, but not exactly joyful either.

"What upsets me is that you didn't stay in Yelverton. You went off into the wilds. That could have been dangerous."

Into the Wilds

Adults do dangerous things, I thought, *like getting drunk and driving into walls*. He had done that once or twice, according to my mother.

"Sorry, we just wanted to have an adventure. And we were all right in the end." I didn't say it was Ani's idea.

"Mum and I think Ani may be a bad influence on you," he said.

My parents were obsessed with bad influences.

"No she isn't! Please don't stop me seeing her!"

"Why can't you have other friends?" he asked. "You hardly see Dora or Pat now."

"Ani's not like them."

"Yes, well – we think you should stay here for a few weekends, and do some things with us, instead of going to the Rydles' all the time."

"Oh, no!"

"We need to make plans for our trip to London too," said my father.

"All right."

That was better. I refused to smile at him, however, since he was being so mean about Ani.

"And next month we're having lunch with Uncle Charles and Aunty Louise at the Duke of Cornwall Hotel."

"Oh, not them!" I burst out. My uncle and aunt were the most old-fashioned people I knew. I was plunged into the depths of despair again. And I didn't like having lunch out and wearing little girlish dresses.

"Shall we invite Ani? She can't do much harm at a lunch," said my mother later on.

"As long as she behaves herself," said my father.

That was something. If Ani was there, it would be much more fun. Two of us against the grown-ups, instead of me, the only child.

After the moors incident, things didn't go too smoothly for Ani either. Her father usually kept out of things and left any discipline (very little in reality) to Mel. But this time he suddenly homed in on the events and grounded her for two weeks. She phoned me to moan about this. So we were both kept apart.

I enjoyed sulking and being miserable for a few days until my father cracked and shouted at me. Then I cried. The dog barked and ran around like a mad thing. My mother told him to be reasonable. Things gradually went back to normal and Ani was asked to the family lunch and allowed to come.

CHAPTER 7

EXTREMELY OLD-FASHIONED

Plymouth 2012

The funeral is over. Heart-rending and somehow unreal. But it went well. Good to see some friends and family. My old schoolfriend Pat appeared, so we're in touch again. She remembers Ani and filled me in on a few details. She knows Ani went to work in London, at a luxury hotel, but that was over ten years ago, and she doesn't know where she is now. When my life calms down, perhaps I could look for her.

Mum would have liked the funeral flowers – wild ones and more formal ones – pink roses, Michaelmas daisies, gerberas, campions and milkmaids.

Hated people asking what I'm doing now. Was evasive. Said I'm "freelancing". Said Tobi too busy to come, and Matti away on his gap year. Half true. I haven't done any translating work for weeks. What am I doing here? Hiding in my mother's house and reliving the Rydle Year.

* * *

Plymouth 1970

It was mid-October and my aunt and uncle arrived for their visit (my mother's cousins really, but as children we had to call all older relatives 'aunty' or 'uncle'). My mother rushed around cooking meals for them, and my father muttered dark comments about in-laws and retreated to the garden whenever possible, despite the blustery October weather.

On the Sunday, the family proceeded to the Duke of Cornwall, a gloomy Victorian hotel in Plymouth where we often had lunch. We squeezed round a table – myself, Ani, my parents, Granny Lil, Aunty Lou and Uncle Charles. Ani and I were wearing dresses. No jeans were allowed by my parents on Sundays.

She had on a long, black, lacy dress, borrowed from her sister Sarah. ("The Lady Macbeth look," said my father in a scathing aside.) I was resplendent in a turquoise pinafore dress and check blouse and long fawn socks, which my mother thought was "smart".

Aunt Louise plumped herself down next to me. She looked me up and down.

"You've grown!"

Outwards as well as upwards, I thought, adjusting my pinafore dress round my chest.

"How's school, dear?" asked Charles, the usual tedious question from old people.

"OK, thanks," I said. "I'm in the second year now, and I like art and languages and I hate maths and sport."

"I see," he said, stroking his moustache. "Girls don't really need maths, though."

"Doesn't she have a Plymouth accent!" said Lou to my mother. She was from Godalming.

"Hazel's doing really well," said my mother, and gave me a big loyal smile. *Thank you for sticking up for me*, I thought.

Charles looked at Ani. "And what's your name, dear?" he asked.

"Ani," she said.

"She's my best friend," I said, and I thought how perfect she looked.

"And where do you live?"

"In Plymouth, with my dad and stepmum. My real mum can't look after me."

"Oh, dear," he said.

"She's on Valium," said Ani, cutting her bread roll in half and stabbing a bit of butter.

Everyone went quiet at that. I bit my lip and tried not to smile.

Other smartly dressed families were arriving, in suits and their best clothes. Well-behaved children were trooping in, the girls wearing hideous dresses, the boys with ties and school trousers. There was a specific hotel scent, which you didn't get anywhere else – a wonderful mix of roasting meat, potatoes and hot puddings, a soapy smell from the cloakroom, and a whiff of drinks and cigarette smoke from the bar.

"Oh, look – there's the vicar and his wife," said my mother, waving. "Must have just finished at church. Having a break for once, poor things."

My aunt turned to me. "What hobbies do you have, dear? Are you in the Brownies or Guides? Meryl loved that and had all the badges!"

"No, I'm not a Brownie; I'm not interested. I'd rather read psychology books and draw," I answered, thinking of Sarah and assertiveness.

"What a funny girl you are," she said with a tinkling laugh. "You'll soon settle down though. All girls do. Once you get a home and children."

Not likely, I thought. *That's the last bloody thing I'm going to do.* I hated babies. I bit off a piece of bread and looked away.

Out of nowhere, I imagined Aunty Louise and Uncle Charles having sex. It was so appalling, it made me choke on my bread roll.

"Oh, dear, are you all right?" said Louise, patting my back. I nodded furiously and dug my nails into my palms. Ani smirked at me.

She seemed to be getting on well with my uncle. I felt a nasty little twinge of something inside. Could it be jealousy?

"…And then Mum and Dad had some problems, so they got a divorce, and Mum was ill for ages, she nearly went mental, and then she met Karl, who's a lot younger, but she says he's immature, and I've got stepsisters and a brother, and…"

And on and on.

Extremely Old-fashioned

Charles looked rather amused and kept asking Ani questions. Louise started listening. My parents exchanged disapproving glances. I was enjoying all this. I loved having Ani with me, instead of being the only child outnumbered by dull old people. But I really wanted to get her alone and talk more about escaping.

"Come and help me with the drinks," said my father, winking. He knew Louise and her questions all too well. We got up and went to the hotel bar.

"I can't go in there, Dad," I said. "Bars won't let children in."

"Just wait by the door," said Dad. He leant towards me. "I think The Witch has put on *even more* weight," he said, looking back at Aunty Lou. "Especially her backside!" We both laughed at that.

"Ani's being really funny, isn't she?" I said.

"Hmm, she certainly is outspoken."

"What d'you think of Uncle Charles?" I asked.

"A good chap, as long as you don't get him started on cars he's had. Then he's unbearable!"

My father went to the bar to order, then we returned, carrying two heavy trays of drinks.

Back at the table, my mother and Louise were remembering Mum's childhood in Devonport in the 1920s. It sounded fun, with lots of cousins living in one big house. Things were very old-fashioned, however, with no electricity, just gas lights. There were trams in Plymouth and even a few horses and carts. My mother remarked that some children were so poor, they went barefoot. I was shocked.

Louise leant close to my mother and glanced at Ani. "That poor child," she said in an undertone. "Awful background. From a broken home. Thank goodness Hazel is nicely brought up."

I frowned at her. "She's very nice. Not like *some* people."

Louise gave a tinkly laugh. "Dear, dear – you are becoming teenage, aren't you?"

I fumed, but my mother said in a bright voice, "Has everyone decided what they want? The waiter's coming."

Ani laughed out loud at something Charles had said.

"God, what a racket," said my father.

The waiter appeared. He was Spanish. There seemed to be Spanish waiters everywhere in Plymouth in those days. This one was terribly good-looking and I blushed immediately, as if he could read my mind. We all started ordering, but he couldn't understand. My mother, who had a nice clear voice, took over and repeated it slowly and he understood her at once. She even seemed to know a few words of Spanish. It occurred to me, for the first time, that she may have done other interesting things before having me and being a housewife.

We all chose roast lunches. There wasn't much else available, certainly no vegetarian or vegan options. I hated red meat, so I asked for chicken and so did Ani. It came with boiled cabbage, carrots and peas, and a pool of gloopy gravy. The food was really filling but we all gobbled it up and had room for desserts too.

There were delights like Black Forest gateau, trifle or apple pie to choose from.

Looking back, I can't understand how we didn't put on weight with that heavy diet.

"Why are there so many Spanish waiters here?" I asked my father.

"The economic situation there isn't so good, so they need to go abroad for work," he said.

"Uh?"

"It's a poor country, that's what he means," interrupted Charles, patting my arm. Then he burst out: "We're so damn lucky to live in this country! Ted Heath is doing a grand job."

"Him," said Ani. "You must be joking."

"Well, really," squeaked Louise. Charles looked taken aback but then shook his head and seemed to laugh it off. Ani had worked her charms on him.

"Let's keep politics out of this, we're not in bloody France," said my father. No one had any answer to that, and we carried on eating.

I felt sorry for the Spanish waiters, having to go abroad for work. Ours looked sad and nervous. I wondered what Spain was like. The library might have some books about it.

"Oh – Isn't *Forbes* in Spain?" I asked. Mum gave me a warning look, before lighting up a cigarette. Forbes – he-who-must-not-be-mentioned. My father's younger brother, Forbes, was the black sheep of the James family. He was always kind to me but there was something odd about him. Recently, he had been living in Spain, doing some work or other.

Louise was instantly alert, evidently ready for gossip about my father's family. But we all clammed up.

The adults started boasting about their families and how all the children were getting on.

"Douglas and dear Meryl are doing so well! Of course, they are at top boarding schools," said Louise, pushing a lump of gateau into her mouth. I looked at her. She was wearing a pale-blue suit, with large black buttons. She had hideous dark-blue horn-rimmed glasses. She looked like our headmistress. Her breasts were quite big too. I wondered what they looked like without a bra, then regretted it.

"When you look at some young people now – well!" said Uncle, taking a large gulp of wine.

"Yes, what a disgrace," agreed my mum, blowing smoke everywhere. "Those Teddy boys are dreadful, aren't they? I just don't know what the world's coming to! And as for those hippies and free love!"

I perked up at this – free love sounded interesting. But unfortunately no one volunteered any other information.

The silence was punctuated by a little fart from my grandmother. My mother exchanged a glance with me and a slight smile.

"More wine, anyone?" said my father quickly.

Ani nudged me. "Shall we go to the toilet?"

"Yeah," I said.

We hurried out, arm in arm, and ran into the toilets. We collapsed against each other, giggling.

"You were hilarious, going on about Valium," I choked. I could hardly talk, I was so worked up.

"Your gran's fart!" Ani yelped. "What a funny old woman that Louise is!" she said.

"Yeah – she's awful!" I said. "I hate the meal! I hate this hotel. I want to escape from it all."

"Well, it *is* nice of your dad, taking us out," she said, which surprised me. Ani could be quite tedious and sensible at times. I changed the subject.

"What can I do about my tits?" I asked. "I need a bra but I'm too embarrassed to ask."

"We can ask Sarah for help," she said, frowning at her face in the mirror. "I'll ring her. We can see her one weekend, maybe."

"Has she still got a boyfriend?" I asked, to torture myself. I had made no progress in this area.

"Yep," she said. She looked at her reflection. "Christ! What a sight!" She reached into her bag and took out some green eye shadow, and started brushing it on. "Want some?" she asked.

I had never tried eye shadow. I experimentally poked a finger into the pot and rubbed it on to my eyelids. I looked really different, like a cat-woman.

"Ani," I said, "what about escaping? *Really* escaping? Like – going abroad?"

"Abroad? We'd need money for that. But there's a limit, isn't there? You can only take £36 or something. Dad was saying."

"Oh, God." I sighed. "We'll have to smuggle some money out then."

"Yep, we'll put it down our pants." Ani finished doing her eyeshadow. "I fancy France or Spain. Or India, even. Dave went to India last year, overland. Anyway, your Dad's going to take us to London in December. Let's see what happens there."

"Yeah, OK."

I sighed. There were so many things I wanted to do.

"I hate getting dressed up and going out for Sunday lunch," I said furiously. "I wish I could just slop around at home in old jeans."

"Well, you know we're quite lucky."

"What?"

"A lot of families don't have much money. Sarah told me about a girl at her primary school who had no pants, they were so poor."

"Really?" I found that hilarious and giggled, but Ani looked serious.

"Honestly, though, Hazel, we are quite lucky. Some girls at our school don't have phones."

That was true. I had another look in the mirror at my bright-green eyes.

I remembered a terrible incident that had happened a year earlier, at Plymouth Central Library. I sometimes went there after school, officially to do homework, but really to eye up boys. Once, a group of children surrounded me in the entrance hall, when I was wearing my smart school uniform. They were

Extremely Old-fashioned

in filthy clothes and stank like old cheese. They started asking me things, but their Plymouth accents were so strong, I couldn't understand what they were saying. I was so ashamed, sorry for them, but afraid. They chanted, "Snobbo, snobbo!" and I ran away into the library. I had never told anyone about it, not even Ani. I didn't want to tell her now, either.

"We'd better go back," I said, slumping against the sink and feeling dejected.

We trailed back to the dining room.

Everyone was drinking coffee and smoking.

"We ordered tea for you two – hope that's all right," said Charles. He smiled at us.

I muttered, "Fanks," and sat down. Ani stayed silent.

My father gave us a dark look. He knew we were being naughty.

"What have you done to your eyes? You look like circus clowns!" he suddenly said.

We giggled and blushed.

"I don't know if you should be wearing make-up yet," said my mother.

"Why not? Lots of girls at school do," I replied.

She raised her eyebrows. "When you're a teenager, you can start."

"Oh, goody, only five months to go," I said.

Charles leant over and gave us a pound note each.

"Thanks," we mumbled, and I felt slightly guilty about our behaviour. We drank our tea and kept quiet.

When we were leaving, my mother went over to the vicar and his family to say hello. She chatted to his wife for a few minutes and came back looking excited.

"Lorna was just telling me about the new amateur-dramatics group they're starting at the church," she said.

"Oh, God!" muttered my father.

"I thought it sounded quite fun," said Mum quietly. "Oh, well, I haven't really got time, I suppose."

I couldn't understand why she wanted to do something like amateur dramatics – she was busy enough looking after us.

My father drove us home – rather unsteadily, as he had drunk a lot of beer. Louise and Charles followed in their car.

Once home, Ani and I rushed into the TV room and grabbed the *Radio Times* to see what was on television.

"Hey – *The Man from U.N.C.L.E.* is on!" I exclaimed.

That was the biggest television programme of the moment, with sexy secret agents called Napoleon Solo and Ilya Kuryakin, who fought an evil organisation called THRUSH. The fact it was American made it even more alluring. We were obsessed with spies.

"I fancy Ilya," said Ani.

"And I fancy Napoleon Solo," I said. Most girls liked Ilya Kuryakin, but I was not going to follow the herd.

We switched the television set on, tuned it to BBC1, and lay on our stomachs on the carpet. I was still hoping my father would buy us a colour set next year, when he had more money.

Extremely Old-fashioned

They were about £250, which was terribly expensive. Needless to say, the Rydles had one already.

Louise and Charles looked in for a moment. "Ooh, that looks fun – what is it?"

"A spy programme," I mumbled, not looking round. They took the hint and went away. They were old people, our enemies, not part of our world.

We could hear them talking in the hall.

"Doesn't she watch a lot of television…children now… difficult age. Of course, Meryl hardly watches…such a gifted girl…" et cetera, et cetera. I scowled and thought poisonous things about Meryl.

We gazed at the action on television (men in black suits, guns and car chases) and forgot everything. I cheered up. This Sunday wasn't so bad after all. I looked at Ani, sprawled on the floor with her blonde hair spread out everywhere. My best friend.

"I'm glad you're here, Hippy," I said to her.

She rolled over, made a silly face, and grinned at me.

I said, "I'm sorry Mum and Dad are being so strict and borijng."

"Well, they are extremely old-fashioned, but my parents are nearly as bad right now. At least they're not as awful as your uncle and aunty," she said.

"I know," I said. "But why are my parents like that?"

"Sarah says they're suffering from a bad dose of middle-class respectability," said Ani.

"What? That's a bit rude of her! What does she mean?"

"I dunno, exactly. I think she means they want to look respectable and make you respectable. That's because they're older than my parents and not artists."

"Huh! They aren't *too* bad," I answered, feeling hurt. Perversely, I wanted to defend them now.

"Sarah said your gran sounds OK, though," Ani went on.

I said nothing but felt quite pleased about that. Life was so confusing and seemed to be getting worse as I grew up. I had always thought life would get easier when I was an adult, but now I wasn't sure.

Sometime later, the door opened and my father looked in. He looked annoyed.

"What are you two up to?" he asked.

"Nothing," we chorused.

"A word, please," he said. "Turn the television down for a minute."

We both sat up. Even Ani looked rather worried. He towered above us.

"You were both rude to Old Lou and Charles at lunch, as you well know," he said.

He said Old Lou, not Louise. A good sign. *Don't shout at us,* I prayed.

"I'm not going to ask you to apologise to them – I know she's ridiculous sometimes. But would you both come to the dining room and be pleasant and have some cake, please? I don't want any more nonsense. And I need to book the London trip next week," he added.

I relaxed. If he was doing that, things weren't too bad.

"Yes, of course, Ron," said Ani sweetly. "Thank you for a lovely day."

"Hmm, well…" he said.

"We're coming, Dad," I said.

We followed him into the dining room, like two good girls. The adults were sitting round a table laden with cakes and biscuits and teacups. Louise looked up at us and seemed a little sad. I felt a twinge of guilt. I wondered if we'd hurt her. I'd never worried about that before. She didn't say anything, but quietly drank some tea. We sat down.

"Yum," I said and smiled nicely.

"Yummy!" said Ani, grinning. She looked terribly innocent. We helped ourselves to mounds of sweet things.

"Oh, to be young again!" said Charles with a wistful look.

I never understood what old people meant by that. Being young was grim, like being prisoners. I couldn't wait to be an adult, doing what I wanted – having sex, staying up late, wearing what I wanted. I made myself a promise never to turn into an extremely old-fashioned person like my relatives. I would be attractive, fascinating and intellectual, even when I was really old (about forty).

CHAPTER 8
DON'T CALL ME REGINALD

Plymouth 2012

I made a to-do list today. It went like this:

> Tidy Mum's house
> Put house on market
> Talk to Tobi – our future?
> Contact Matti
> Go out for day to Dartmoor (where I went with Ani)

Big daunting things, except for the day out, which will be a treat. At least I've made a list, but I'm reluctant to carry most of it out. That takes me back to my childhood list…

* * *

Plymouth 1970

In late November I took out the secret list to review my progress:

My Top Secret List, to make me into an Exciting Girl

Go to London and get Levi's (flared) — Soon
Get a bra — Nothing!
Get new hairstyle — Nothing!
Meet some boys — Nothing!
Save money — Yes
Escape! Not yet. Bad
Make Ani my best friend — Yes!

I leant back against the bedhead and sighed. At least I had Ani. That was the most important thing of all. I had never adored a friend so much. My only fear was that she would get bored with me.

I was also saving money. But I had made no headway with the other things. Sometimes I felt as if I was swimming through treacle, getting nowhere. I didn't know how to move forwards; I lacked the knowledge.

For a whole week, I hadn't been allowed to see Ani in person. There was one more to go. I was sulking and upsetting the family. My father was irritated but Mum tried to be nice.

"I know what'll cheer us up," she said. "I've asked René round for lunch on Saturday."

"Oh, honestly, Mum!" I exclaimed. "I can't stand him!"

"What? You always get on so well with him, playing lovely games and things."

"That was when I was five! He always teases me nowadays."

René was a sort of friend of my mother, even though he was much younger than her, twenty-eight I think. She had met his mother, Gladys, absolutely years ago, during the Second World War. Mum really liked him, for some reason. His real name was Reginald, but he had changed it when he moved to London. "René is *much* more my thing, dear," he told us. He always teased me and made fun of me. Vile as he was, I was interested in seeing him because he wore unusual clothes and had managed to escape from Plymouth to London.

René arrived in his green MG Midget on the appointed day. Mum and I both looked longingly at the car. We loved sports cars. René came walking up the garden, lightly, like a cat. He had an earring in one ear, which I liked, but which Dad muttered was "effeminate", whatever that was. I looked at René. He was dressed well, in velvet jeans and a red quilted top. He had a nice tan. What I really liked was his hair – it was long, dark-blond, and cut in a very clever way, in layers. This gave me an idea.

He and Mum embraced like long-lost lovers, exclaiming "Oh, darling" and "You look wonderful."

Dad shook hands with him and then said, "Sorry, must do some gardening," (a lie as it was perfectly tidy) and he disappeared.

"Hello, Hazel, darling," René said as he breezed in. "Mmm, getting a little broad in the beam, aren't we?" he added, looking critically at my backside. I had been eating a lot lately as I was growing fast. But I certainly wasn't fat. I blushed furiously but controlled my temper as I wanted to keep on his right side.

"Come in and have tea and some coffee cake, Rens, dear," said Mum, showing him into our living room.

René put his arm around her waist. "Not one of your divine cakes, Fen…" he said. "Ohhh! Must watch my weight though."

His backside did look a little plump. He had a cheek, criticising mine.

Granny Lil appeared and he gave her a smacking kiss. We all sat down, cake was served, and Mum said, "Now, you must tell us about everybody – how is dear Gillian?" This was his sister, a weedy girl, who was surprisingly unlike René. The last time I had seen her, she was obsessed with doing jigsaws and puzzles in magazines. She liked wearing ginger tights and old-fashioned tweedy clothes.

"Gillian – well, you know she had that operation, don't you? Rather unfortunate, I'm afraid…"

He glanced at me and said to my mother, "*Pas devant les enfants,* dear."

I was better at French by then and understood this.

"It's OK, I'll go," I said, trying to look airy and indifferent. The dog got up to follow me. I plucked up courage. "Just before I go, can you tell me where you get your hair cut? It looks really good."

"This?" he said, flicking his hair about and shaking his head. "London – Sassoon's."

"What about in Plymouth?" I asked. "I want a new hairstyle."

"Yes, you could do with it," he said, bitchy as ever. "Best to avoid all Plymouth hairdressers, if you can! But let me see…I would say that Dino at Dingles is the least awful." He turned back to my mother and grandmother.

"Anyway, about Gillian…well, she won't be the same again."

Mum moved nearer to him, ready for a cosy chat. I wandered out with Hedley and we went into the kitchen, where pans were simmering away on the stove and the oven was sending out delicious meaty smells. Mum had left a half-done crossword on the table, and I sat and idly tried to fill in some clues, but they were beyond me.

* * *

After lunch, where René spent the whole time boasting about himself (my father and I exchanged several glances) he said, "Now, girls, would anyone like a spin in my car?"

"Ooh, yes," said Mum and I. Even though René was maddening, the offer of a ride in a sports car was irresistible.

"Beautiful Fenella first, then," said René, and they went off together.

I cleared up with my grandmother. My father had escaped to the living room with his newspapers.

"Gran, why does Mum like René so much?" I asked, wiping a large dish.

"Oh, she looked after him a lot when he was little, when his father…" She stopped short.

"His father what?"

"Oh, nothing, dear. She just likes him, because she knew his mother Gladys, you know. Poor Gladys. And he was a dear little boy. Pass me the new bottle of Fairy Liquid?"

"Oh," I said. I wondered what his father had done. Probably gone off with another woman or stolen the office money. Adults were so idiotic, thinking I didn't know about these things. I was nearly thirteen, after all, and an avid reader of women's magazines and watcher of television dramas.

René and Mum returned sometime later, smiling and chatting away.

"Where to, then, oh Great One?" René asked me as we got into his open-top car.

"Devil's Point?" I suggested.

"Don't see why not," he answered, revving the engine.

It was really cold outside, but the sun was shining. I huddled down into my old blue anorak. My mother was trying to wear down my resistance and get me a smart brown camel-hair coat, but I wasn't giving in.

We went roaring off through Plymouth to Devil's Point, a piece of parkland by the sea with views of Plymouth harbour. René's MG had the top down and I fantasised I was going out for a drive with a boyfriend or actor. I hoped people from school might see me.

During our walk, I asked, "Where do you live now?" I thought he would laugh and make fun, but he was quite pleasant.

"Still London," he said, looking out to sea. "I'm staying with friends in Earl's Court for now. Just doing a little work in an antique shop in Chelsea and making ends meet. It's parties all the time up there! And a few illegal substances, but you're too young to know about that!"

I rolled my eyes. I had read plenty of articles about drugs in magazines.

"I'll probably be going travelling in Italy soon, though. But enough of me – what do you want to do with your life, young lady?"

I bit my lip and said, "I think I want to be an artist or a writer."

"Do you indeed?" he said, turning to look at me. "Well I never. And how do you propose to do that?"

I had no idea. Of course I knew the Rydles, who were mixed up with the world of art, but I was too shy to ask how they had managed that.

"Umm, I don't know," I admitted.

"Let me give you some advice, then, for what it's worth," he said. "Get out of this city when you leave school. They say the sixties has only just got going, darling, well, Plymouth is still stuck in 1955! So parochial. All right, the sea's nice, but otherwise…ghastly, darling. No culture. Go and travel. Meet new people."

"Yes, but how?" I asked.

"University," said René. "For starters. In another city, like London or Exeter."

That sounded like a good idea. Perhaps that really was the answer, instead of silly ideas of simply running away. I knew next to nothing about university, though. None of our friends or relatives had gone and Plymouth had no university, only a technical college. I had only seen things on television or in newspapers – usually outrageous stories about protests or drugs. Photos of boys with sunglasses on, in black polo necks and duffle coats, and girls with long hair and flared jeans, protesting about things like the Vietnam War. But I didn't really understand any of it. My mother said that university was full of long-haired types who smoked pot and were usually Communists.

I blurted out, "My friend Ani's going to art college."

"Hmm, that's another option. Ani who?"

"Ani Rydle. They live in Crownhill."

"Rydle? The artists? The ones with swarms of children?"

"Yes," I said.

"Then you must know Sarah, the art student. She's quite a good friend of mine. Lovely lady."

"Oh, yes, I know Sarah. She's nice."

"She certainly is. They're an interesting family, but Sarah's the best of the bunch."

"No, Ani's the best," I said.

"The little one with fair hair? Quite a handful, if I remember. I predict trouble ahead."

"Why? What d'you mean?"

René shrugged. "Time will tell," he said.

"I wish you wouldn't tease me and make fun," I said, blushing.

There was a short silence. He stopped walking and looked at me.

"Sorry. I tend to forget that you're not a little child any more. We're all getting older."

For a moment, René looked old and sad. Up close, his skin looked puffy and yellow, rather than tanned. He seemed nicer at that moment, more honest and soft. He sighed.

"*I* went to university, you know. For one year. But things didn't work out too well. I had a bit of a breakdown. Don't tell your mother – she'll just fuss."

"OK," I said, enjoying this confidence.

"We're coming to London before Christmas," I said. "Can we see you there?"

"Great idea. I'll give you my phone number and address – well, it's Celia's number. She owns the house."

He scribbled it down and gave me the scrap of paper, which I pushed into my trouser pocket.

"Are you too old for ice cream now?" asked René.

"No, not yet."

"Then let's buy some and walk a bit more. There's a van over there, even in this weather. I'll tell you about where I live in London."

The afternoon just got better after that. I had never talked to someone like René before. He told me all sorts of things about London – how you could share a house with other people and have parties, go everywhere on the Underground, listen to pop groups in pubs and big halls, or go to coffee bars at night. And there were endless clothes shops and new little shops called 'boutiques'.

I wish this afternoon could last for ever, I thought. *Just talking to each other like adults.* But, of course, we had to go back to my family.

Back home, René reverted to his silly self again, and flirted with my mother. He put his arm round her and said, "You're like a sister to me, Fen!"

She loved it.

"Oh, Rens, what nonsense!" she said.

It was nauseating. Even Granny Lil looked unimpressed.

René finally went, blowing lots of kisses. My father had disappeared somewhere. It felt quiet and restful after he'd gone.

I had plenty to think about. I slipped out to the garden to be on my own. I would start buying a few teenagers' magazines like *Fab 208* and *Jackie*, to check what hairstyles were 'in', ready for my hairdo. René's looked good, but I wanted to be sure. Those magazines had articles about London too. Next month, I would be there with Ani.

After supper, I asked Mum if she could book me a haircut with Dino.

"Are you sure? You've always hated the hairdresser."

"Yes, I'm sure. I want to get a new haircut."

"Of course, I'll book it. Actually, I think I might get mine dyed blonde." She patted her grey hair and looked in the mirror.

"Really? Why?"

"Why not? You youngsters have all the fun. I want some too."

"Oh," I said, surprised.

That evening, when the others were watching TV and my mother was cooking, I crept in to the hall to phone Ani.

"Hello, Hippy – what are you doing?"

"Hi, Pony. We've been down to Falmouth, to see some artists we know. We went round their gallery and Dad bought some paintings and we had lunch in an old pub. It was super fun. What are you doing?"

"I saw this friend of ours called René. He's quite silly but very fashionable and lives in London. I went out in his sports car. He said he knows you!"

"Oh, yes, we know René."

"We had a talk. He said I should go to university."

"Yeah, well, why not?" Ani said, not sounding very impressed. "Loads of people *we* know are going."

"He said we can see him in London. I think he's going to help me escape."

She laughed. "Escape in London? Could do. Anyway, you can see me after next weekend. We're allowed out of prison then, aren't we? D'you want to come over for tea?"

"Yes, please. I've got to go now – *Morecambe and Wise* is on. OK, I'll see you in school on Monday." I decided not to say anything about my haircut. I would just surprise her with it when it was done.

I rang off and sighed. Ani always seemed to know more than me. I could never catch up. But still, I felt hopeful, thinking about René and our talk. He was all right in some ways. I was beginning to see that adults were changeable – one minute they were teasing you, the next they were nice. My mother seemed to be growing a bit strange, too, talking about having fun and hair dyes. Life was complicated.

CHAPTER 9
HAIR

Plymouth 2012

I know I should start tidying and emptying my mother's house, and contacting estate agents. But I'm overcome by nostalgia and inertia. I wander round Plymouth seafront, remembering those crazy days with Ani. The city's changed so much – a good university here now and it's more cosmopolitan. I need a haircut, must find a hairdresser. I still love having a hairdo. It's dyed red at the moment. Maybe I should get a tattoo.

I really rather like the new Plymouth. Could I live here now? Don't know. Vienna is a great city, but I've been homesick lately. No word from Tobi.

* * *

Plymouth 1970

I got my first proper hairdo that month.

At Dingles department store, we reported to reception and Dino the hairdresser came over to meet us. He was short and slim with black wavy hair and tight jeans. He wore pointed

Hair

boots. "Hello, young lady," he said. "And hello to the beautiful mother." He kissed Mother on the cheeks, which I thought was rather pushy. I supposed that he did know her. But she didn't object. She was whisked away by a woman to have her hair washed and then dyed.

After my hair had been washed by a sulky girl called Mandy, I sat in the chair and Dino looked at me critically. He grabbed a handful of hair and felt it. "Mmm, *very* dry. But good thick hair." He folded his arms. "What you want, then?"

"Long silky hair. In a feather cut," I answered, blushing.

He laughed. "You English girls, why you don't look after your hair, mmm? Well, we see. First, I use the thinning scissors. You want to keep it long, yes?"

Dino snipped away and piles of brown hair fell to the floor. After about twenty minutes, I could see a new girl in the mirror. A nearly teenage girl with wavy but well-shaped hair, not the old scruffy mop I'd had before.

At the same time, my mother had had dye pasted all over her hair and was now sitting under a giant dryer. She was old, so why did it matter what colour it was? At least she looked happy. While I was waiting, I read lots of women's magazines – *Woman's Own*, *Woman* and one called *She*, which had some very interesting articles about sex and how to enjoy it. I held the magazine up in front of me so nobody could see what I was reading.

Finally, my mother emerged, hair washed and dried and now a shining golden colour. It looked good, I must admit. She came over to me.

"My goodness, how glam Hazel looks!" she cried. "Thank you, Dino."

"You look great too, Mum!"

Dino stood back and considered his handiwork. "Yes, looks good now. You use this, OK?" He gave me a tube of Vitapoint hair cream. "You use every day." He regarded my mother seriously. "And you, Madam, you look beautiful now." He looked at me. "Your daughter is not classically pretty, but she has an interesting face," he remarked.

Huh, I thought. But I wasn't altogether displeased. Looking interesting was no bad thing. As we walked through the shop, one or two men looked at my mother. I felt proud.

"Now, shall we go and look round Dingles and get you some clothes?" she asked. The store had just opened a trendy clothes department.

"Ooh, yes!"

We explored the racks. It was the most blissful thing. Dingles didn't sell Levi's yet, but I found some fashionable red cord jeans and my mother bought me a warm anorak called a 'parka', which was green with a furry-edged hood.

"For the next time you go to the moors," she said. "But make sure you go with a group of people next time. We were so worried. I think you should join a youth club next year and meet some nice young people."

Hair

"Oh, wow, I'd love that," I said. She smiled.

When she wasn't doing housework or silly hobbies, she was quite fun. I assumed we were going to get the bus home then, but instead she said: "Shall we go to Dingles café now? I don't feel like going back yet."

"What about cooking for tonight?" I asked.

"Damn the cooking, everyone can wait for once," she answered with a shrug. "Come on, I'll buy you a piece of gateau and a cold drink."

So we went to Dingles café on the top floor and sat for ages and drank coffee and ate creamy cakes. My mother looked at me with my new haircut and smiled.

"My little baby is growing up," she said.

"Oh, stop it, Mum," I said. It was so embarrassing when she got like this.

"Now you're bigger, I want some new interests too," she went on. I wondered what she meant.

"I want to go out more. I get sick of staring at the bloody kitchen wall sometimes," she continued. "Dad thinks I'm happy being a housewife, but it's not all roses, you know. After the war finished, we were all glad just to be at home in Plymouth, but that's years ago now, and I want a change."

I screwed up my nose and said, "What d'you want to do then?"

"I don't know. Go out more, join a club, that sort of thing. I was thinking about those amateur dramatics that the vicar's wife does. You could come if you like."

"Oh, no thanks!" I said. The thought of being with a load of old people was too awful. I played about with my cake and squashed some bits flat with my fork. "But if you want to go to a club, why shouldn't you? Instead of being at home all the time."

For the first time, I saw things from her point of view. Maybe Mel had made me think. Or maybe it was reading that magazine, *She*, at the hairdresser's. They had an article about something called 'Women's Liberation'. Some housewives in America were complaining and saying they wanted to be free from housework and demanding husbands. Perhaps my mother wanted to escape, like me. The other thing that occurred to me was that I might have more freedom if she was out.

"Why don't you ring the vicar's wife when you get home, Mum?"

"Yes, I could do. I wonder what Daddy will say, though?"

"Oh, sod him! If I can join the youth club, why can't you join something?"

"Hazel! What language." But she giggled and we both smiled at each other in a conspiratorial way. "Yes, sod him. Here, go and buy another drink for us. You choose," she said, handing me a ten shilling note.

Rather than hurrying home afterwards, Mum said we should go down to the make-up department as she needed new nail varnish. I wandered about, admiring all the shining little bottles in shades of scarlet, crimson and pink. There was even an orange one, which I fancied.

Hair

As she was selecting a bright poppy-red one, I said, "Can I have one too? Ani's got some."

"You know I said you can when you're thirteen."

"Oh, please, Mum. Even Tallulah puts it on."

"Hmm, those Rydles are a law unto themselves. But, well, why not? If you just wear it in the school hols and at weekends."

Overjoyed, I chose a crimson one to go with my new cord jeans.

On the way to the bus stop, we chatted about what we would do in London, and what Ani would say when she saw my lovely hair. I felt rather guilty about my escape plans and didn't mention them.

Mum looked at her watch. "Is that the time? Gosh, we'd better get home."

Dad was taken aback at first by my mother's golden hair, but he said he rather liked it and it was a change. Nothing was said about amateur dramatics, and my mother and Granny Lil made supper and tidied up. I dragged myself upstairs to do homework. School was beginning to pile it on. I especially hated maths and history.

After dashing through the homework, I spent the evening modelling my new red cords and flicking my hair about, thrilled with the new style. Before bed, I fetched The List to review it. I could tick one more major item off, anyway – hair.

CHAPTER 10
NEW NEIGHBOURS

In September, our neighbour old Mr Gascoyne had died. I wasn't sorry, because he was always surly and unfriendly to children. His large house stood empty for some weeks and a 'For Sale' sign went up. Weeds invaded the front garden, choking the wallflowers and roses. Eventually, an estate agent in a suit came and stuck a 'Sold' sticker over the sign.

One Saturday in late November, a large green removal van arrived next door. A white estate car drew up behind it and four people got out. (I was spying on them from Granny Lil's side window.) There was a tall woman dressed in black, a tired-looking man and, most interesting, two teenage boys. A large yellow Labrador was barking in the boot and the woman shouted, "Shush!" I couldn't wait to tell Ani about this development.

I rushed downstairs to Mum, who was not in the kitchen as usual, but on the phone in the hall.

"Hey, Mum! There's a new family moving and they've got two b—"

She smiled and held up her hand to stop me. "All right, Lorna, fine," she said. "I'll see you at seven on Wednesday then, in the church hall. Super. Bye."

She looked very happy. "That was the vicar's wife. I'm starting at am-dram next week."

"What?"

"Amateur dramatics – you know, acting."

"Oh, really? Does Dad know?"

"Not yet. I'll work on him. What did you want to tell me, dear?"

"The new neighbours are moving in. They've got two boys and a Labrador."

"Have they? Let's give them a day to settle in, and then we'll go and introduce ourselves. I'll get Lil to make a cake."

The next morning, I mooned about in front of the mirror, modelling my red cords and flicking my hair back. The jeans looked just right for meeting the neighbours. I put on my black polo-neck sweater and scruffy tennis shoes to complete the outfit.

Mum and I trooped over to the new neighbours' house, holding one of Lil's fruitcakes. The tall woman opened the door. She had bright-red lipstick and a black polo-neck jumper, just like mine. She smiled, but it wasn't a gentle smile, more a firm, in-charge smile. The dog was barking and jumping around in the hall.

"Hello and welcome!" said Mum. "I'm Fenella James, or Fen, and this is my daughter, Hazel."

"Oh, come in, come in. Cake! How super. Sorry about the dog – do you mind them? I'm Judy Atkinson. I'll find my husband. He's just fixing the wine rack. ALAN!" she yelled.

I wondered if she was from up north. Her accent reminded me of *Coronation Street*.

"And my awful sons are lurking about somewhere, but they'll probably hide. They're at that terrible anti-social stage. RICK! CHAS!" she shrieked.

A head appeared round a door. A spotty face with longish fair hair. It withdrew again.

"For heaven's sake, come out, Rick, and meet our neighbours."

A lanky boy of about fourteen appeared, in old jeans. I couldn't see if they were Levi's. His hair was light-brown and messy, rather like mine before my new hairdo. He was really ugly. *Absolutely not boyfriend material,* I thought. He shuffled into the hall and stood with hands shoved in pockets, shifting from foot to foot.

He grunted something, possibly *Hello*.

"This is Rick. He's probably about your age," said Judy, giving me an assessing look. "A new friend for you."

I blushed. So did he.

"Super," said my mum. "Hazel could do with some male company."

I cringed.

"Gotta do stuff. C'mon, Custard," mumbled Rick, and slunk away, with the Labrador following him.

New Neighbours

But then another boy appeared. A tall boy who was around nineteen. With his mother's black hair and a tanned face, and sunglasses. Long legs. In a leather jacket. Holding an unlit cigarette. Heaven.

"This is Chas, my older one – he's eighteen," said Judy.

"Hi, folks," he said in a soft voice, taking off the sunglasses and looking my mother and me up and down. We were all introduced. My mother looked back at him, a strange smile on her face. I was struck dumb as usual and couldn't think of a thing to say. But I could imagine kissing him.

"Come and have a coffee in the breakfast room," said Judy. "It's chaos, but I'm sure we can squeeze you in."

A man was kneeling in the corner of the room, struggling with some shelves. "Bloody hell," he exclaimed and then turned to us and said, "Excuse my French, it's just this wretched wine rack." He stood and shook hands. I was interested to see that he blushed, too. I didn't realise adults did that.

"Alan Atkinson," he said. "Good to meet you."

"Alan, get us some coffee, would you?" said Judy, and we all sat down at a pine table, rather like the Rydles' one but more worn and scratched.

Judy told us all about her family. They had moved from Sheffield, the reason being that Judy had got a new job in Plymouth.

"I'm a psychiatrist," she explained. I gaped at her. Plymouth mothers didn't have jobs, at least not proper ones like that. "I research children's traumas," she went on, offering a cigarette to Mum.

"Goodness," my mother said. "I'm just a housewife."

"No, not you, Chas," Judy said, as he reached over for a cigarette. She smacked his hand, but he just laughed.

"Oh, come on, Mother, you know I smoke," he said, grabbing one.

Judy tutted but didn't stop him.

"And I'm going to teach geography at Devonport High," said Alan, handing out mugs and sitting with us. "But Judy's the career one. Chas is starting engineering at the tech college, and Rick's going to Plymouth College."

"Oh – a very good school," said my mum. "All the children are from nice backgrounds."

"That cuts us out, then," said Chas in a sniggering voice.

"Shut up, Chas," said Judy.

"Well, it's lovely to meet you all. You'll have to come to one of my coffee mornings, Judy, and meet more neighbours," said my mother, waving her cigarette around.

"Not much time for that sort of thing, I'm afraid," said Judy, "what with my clinical work, but I'll try." She had a deep voice. The type of voice that makes people do what you tell them.

There was a silence as everyone slurped their coffee.

"Gotto go practise my *geet-ar*," announced Chas in an American accent, extracting himself from the crowded table. I watched him stride out on his long legs.

"Aren't boys ghastly?" remarked Judy. But she looked at Chas adoringly.

"We'd better let you get on," said my mum. "Come on, darling."

"Thanks for welcoming us, Fen. We'll catch up soon," said Judy. "Alan – you can get on with assembling the bookshelves now."

"Must I?" said Alan.

"Yes, you must," she said.

After we got back home, Mum said, "You can see who wears the trousers in *that* household." *Yes*, I thought, *Judy is a scary creature*. But she seemed interesting too.

I went to find my grandmother and described the Atkinsons to her. After I told her about Chas, she said, "Hmm, I know that sort of boy. You want to watch him."

"Oh, honestly, Granny, you are boring," I shouted in her deaf ear. "You don't get it. He's great!"

"We'll see," she said, knitting away. "I've seen more of life than you. What about the younger one? He might be better."

"He's rubbish, really wet." The uncomfortable truth was, I could see myself in Rick. Similar hair, similar build and a diffident shy character. All too familiar and hateful.

"Give him a year or two. Boys grow up slower than girls."

"Yeah, well…Anyway, I'm going to ring Ani and tell her all about them now."

"That Ani – that's another one who'll come to no good, mark my words."

"Oh, don't be so silly!" I shouted, going out.

I went up to my bedroom before phoning Ani. I had something else to do. The List was hidden in the cupboard and I fished it out. I fetched a Biro and ticked off another item: *Meet some boys*. Things were coming on nicely.

But then I looked down at my chest. *Blast it. Still no bra. I should do something about that.*

I clumped downstairs to phone Ani and tell her all about the Atkinsons. She sounded moderately interested, but not as much as I'd hoped.

"Well, I can meet my brother's friends any time," she said. "Anyway, boys are usually stupid, always fighting and showing off."

"I think they're lovely," I said.

"Yes, well you're a sex maniac," she said.

"Oh, shut up! Anyway, Hippy, can I come round to you next week?"

"Yeah, just ring me first, in case we're doing something."

I felt at a loose end, and wandered into the front room to see if I could spy the Atkinsons doing anything. I looked through the net curtains, but next door all was quiet and the estate car had gone. Perhaps they were out shopping. It was exciting, having new neighbours, and I couldn't help thinking about Chas, the handsome, cigarette-smoking, sarcastic older one.

CHAPTER 11
A BRA

The moment had come to do something about a bra. I was twelve but looked about fourteen; I'd become tall and well-developed. It was getting embarrassing in school PE lessons, when I pranced around in my white Aertex shirt and brown pants, with my two bumps sticking out. People looked. Other girls had bras, even ones with flat chests. They were bitchy and teased me in the changing rooms. Ani was smaller than me but not bothered. "Mel says I'm flat as a pancake and won't need a bra for ages," she laughed. "Not like you, Pony. You're a woman!" I wasn't sure I wanted to be one yet. I wished I was like her.

I thought about Sarah and her advice. I must ask for things in an adult way. I made a plan to confront my mother. I had to get her alone. (If Dad was there, it would be excruciating.) I had worked out what I would say and would try to get it over with as quickly as possible. Mum never said much about bras or growing up; she was old-fashioned and embarrassed, although she was really kind to me in other ways. She wore large, white, complicated cotton bras called 'Playtex Control' and tight, high pants, which she called 'roll-ons'. It was impossible to imagine ever wearing such things. I'd seen pretty little trainer bras in the shops when I went to town with Ani. We had giggled over them, fingering them and holding them up in front of ourselves. There were tiny white lacy ones with padding, to make girls' chests look bigger, and nylon ones with pink or blue flowers on them, called 'Littlest Darling'. I longed for a blue one.

The next Thursday evening, my father was out working late and my grandmother was in bed listening to the radio. The moment had come. I practised my speech in my bedroom. My mouth felt dry. I was nervous. What would she say? Was I afraid she would be angry, or embarrassed, or laugh at me? This was like nothing I'd ever done.

I tiptoed out to the landing and listened. Lil's radio droned away loudly in her room. It was a play of some sort. I could hear sounds of washing in my parents' bedroom. I sneaked a look round their door.

My mother was there at her basin. I sidled in, in my spotty blue flannel pyjamas.

"Hello, dear," she said in a friendly way. A good sign.

"What are you doing, Mum?" I asked, standing awkwardly and fiddling with my hair.

"Oh, just freshening up – ready for an early night," she answered, swishing water round the basin.

This was it.

A Bra

"Mum, I just wanted to ask you something about…clothes," I began, looking away and feeling my face heat up. This felt unreal. It was more terrible and embarrassing than I had expected. I was blushing now. I thought I might even faint.

"Oh, yes?" she said, and carried on messing around with the washbasin and hanging up towels and flannels.

"Ermm, yes, I'm getting taller and growing up," I said, feeling stupid. "So I wondered if we could go and get a…a…"

She didn't look at me; she just started to rub some cream on her face.

This was bad.

"A…dress for parties," I blurted out. *Oh hell*, I thought.

She carried on rubbing in cream.

"Yes, if you want. Dingles have some nice ones. Time for bed now, though – it's eight o'clock."

"Yes," I said gloomily. "Time for bed."

My mother smiled at me and started brushing her hair.

I turned and trailed back to my bedroom. I was an idiot and a coward, but I was furious with *her* as well. Surely she knew what I was getting at, but she was too embarrassed to talk about it. She had failed too. How could I ask her again? I would have to have a crisis talk with Ani. Thank God for her. I would see her at the weekend.

I felt restless and irritated. An old toy, Bruno Bear, sat on a chair. I picked it up and cuddled it, half embarrassed as I wasn't a little child any more.

I said out loud to the bear: "What can I do? I failed."

Silence. This was the reality of life. There was probably no God, no talking toys, no magic answer. I threw the bear at the wall in a spurt of temper. It bounced off and rolled into a corner and I didn't care at all.

I got out The List and looked at the last item. *Escape!*

I wasn't sure what it meant any more. There was a sniffing noise in the doorway and the dog appeared.

"Hedley," I whispered. He padded over to me and I ran my hand through his soft fur. "God, what can I do?" He wagged his tail. Dogs didn't have to worry.

I got on to the bed and lay there, on top of the pink eiderdown. Life was hopeless. I rolled on to my side.

"Oh, shit," I said out loud. I felt my chest. The bumps were definitely getting bigger.

There was a *Fab 208* magazine discarded on the floor. I glanced at the cover. 'London,' it said. 'Where it's at.' At least we were going to London next month. Something might happen there.

CHAPTER 12
A ZIP-UP LILAC MINIDRESS

Plymouth 2012

Ten days since Mum's funeral. Tobi texted to ask when I'm coming back to Vienna. Does he want me or is he being polite? I don't feel like leaving Plymouth yet. Quite enjoying it here, surprisingly.

Also, have got going in the house – cleaned, made list of furniture to sell and went online to advertise. Carried some bags of smaller things to local charity shop. Not the lilac minidress, though! Want to keep that. Bought flowers and put in vases. Looks more homely now. Must email my translation agencies to ask for some work. There's no Wi-Fi here, but I could do it longhand and go to an Internet café to complete it.

* * *

Plymouth 1970

It was December and Christmas decorations were appearing everywhere. My father and I drove out to a garden centre to buy a tree and bundled it into our boot. The scent of pine drifted through the car and made me excited. Even more fantastic, our London trip was approaching. My first visit, and Ani was coming.

London was a long way away, but most places were a long way from Plymouth. ('Up the line', as my grandmother put it). It was five hours by train.

There were endless phone calls between me, Ani, my mother and Mel to arrange everything. There were questions like: how much money did we need? (Twenty pounds each, according to Ani. "Rubbish, fifteen," according to my father); what clothes to take ("Loads"); should we pack party dresses? ("Yes"); was it babyish to take a teddy? ("Yes, pathetic").

Ani had been to London a few times, but even so, she was extremely excited and kept talking about it. We both got very giggly the week before and drove Mel round the bend, talking in fake American accents and giggling together in the Rydle kitchen. Tallulah got jealous and moaned at us, asking why she couldn't go and pulling at Ani's clothes.

We thoroughly enjoyed acting like grown-ups, being cruel and saying, "No, you can't come with us, you're too young."

In the end, Tallulah had such a tantrum that Mel promised to buy her a space hopper toy and take her and Josh to a pantomime in Torquay.

The day came at last and we all met at Plymouth railway station, huddling together in the freezing wintery air. Ani appeared, wearing a black maxi coat and floppy orange hat.

A Zip-up Lilac Minidress

"What the dickens does she think she's wearing?" muttered my father, who was fussing with railway tickets and getting stressed. Mum and I smiled at each other. Ani had masses of luggage – bags, a case and a shoulder bag that looked as if it was made from a rug. I was wearing Sarah's old grey cords, which Granny Lil had said were a disgrace, but my mum gave in for once and said, "That's what the youngsters are wearing now, Mother." My gran was going to stay with our cousins. She said she was too old to cope with London.

We piled onto the train and found our reserved seats.

Dad outlined our plans like a Navy operation: we were going to see a pantomime (*Peter Pan*) and go sightseeing round London. We would visit Madame Tussaud's waxworks, the Tower of London, the Houses of Parliament and maybe London Zoo. But the most important thing for me was clothes shopping. Mum, Ani and I were going on a girls' outing to Carnaby Street – THE place for clothes.

Once settled in our seats, Ani and I spread books, comics and drawing stuff all over the table. Dad opened up *The Times* and began reading and muttering about various politicians.

"Time for a ciggie," said my mother, lighting up. She looked very nice that day, in new black trousers ('slacks', as she called them) and a patterned red and white jumper.

The train glided along, passing fields and farms and eventually crossing the chalk downs, where I saw a white horse shape cut into a hillside.

"Look at that horse!" I exclaimed. "Who made that?"

"Ah, that's the Westbury White Horse, an ancient monument," said my father, who knew everything. He looked about to give us a lecture, but we busied ourselves with our drawing and he didn't bother.

After a big lunch in the dining car, the scenery changed and we began passing endless houses and factories.

"This is the beginning of London," said my mother. "Start putting your things away now, girls."

At Paddington Station, we left the train, crossed the concourse, and as if by magic, we entered a dark passageway and went straight into our London hotel, The Paddington. There were red swirly carpets, hotel staff in uniforms, and hordes of guests who looked foreign and smartly dressed. We went up to our rooms, Ani and I in one, my parents next door. The first thing we did was to leap onto the beds and lie there giggling. Then we ran to the window to look out. I couldn't get over the height of the buildings and the crowds. Cars streamed by and there were people everywhere, walking, shopping, eating hot dogs, laughing, staring at the sights.

"We're here!" I said to Ani.

"Hooray," she shouted and grabbed me.

We danced round together and then leapt on to the beds again and bounced up and down as high as we could. We both collapsed and lay there, gasping for breath.

"Hippy…do you think we should escape while we're in London?" I asked her.

A Zip-up Lilac Minidress

"Uh? Yes, maybe," she said. She sat up and looked at me. "But let's wait a few days, get used to it first. Gotta buy clothes, anyway."

"OK," I said. In my trouser pocket I had a crumpled piece of paper with René's London phone number and address. I intended to get in touch with him.

We unpacked untidily, flinging clothes into the cupboard and tossing toothbrushes and flannels down anywhere in the big white bathroom. We ate all the free biscuits on the tea tray and then sat and looked at each other.

"Let's go and find my parents," I said.

Mum and Dad were unpacking carefully. The television was on loud so my father could see if it was working.

"Come and sit on the bed, girls," my mum said.

She boiled the kettle to make us all tea and handed out their packets of hotel biscuits. There was a party atmosphere and we fidgeted with excitement.

"Now, team," said Dad. "Plans for this afternoon – Tube ride and a quick visit to Trafalgar Square. Fish and chips at a Berni Inn tonight. Tomorrow we're booked for the waxworks."

"Groovy!" said Ani. She sounded like someone in *Fab 208*.

That evening when we undressed, I had a shock. As Ani pulled off her multi-coloured blouse, I saw she had a flat little bra on. It was pale pink and stretchy. Quite honestly, it was hardly worth it. But she had managed to get one, unlike me. I was deeply jealous. She hadn't told me, either.

"You got a bra," I burst out.

"What? Oh, yeah, I did," she said casually. She must have known how desperate I was.

"Did Mel buy it for you?"

"No, Sarah."

Of course, Sarah, the big sister. She was like a kind of mother. I wished with all my heart that I had a big sister. But it was no good; I was an only child. I had to face up to it. Perhaps I would get a bra here in London.

"Why don't you just ask Fenella for a bra, while we're here?" said Ani.

"You know I asked her at home and it was useless."

"Yes, but I'm with you here. I'll back you up."

"OK…thanks."

That first night I lay awake for hours in the huge white hotel bed, too excited and happy to sleep. Ani had fallen asleep quickly. I crept out of my bed and over to the window, sniffed the net curtains and parted them. They were grubby and smelt dusty. A London smell. It was past midnight, but the streets were still full of crowds, walking around, going in and out of nightclubs and bars, shrieking and laughing and enjoying themselves. Plymouth would be quiet by now. I saw some young girls, only a few years older than me, striding past, wearing ripped denim waistcoats and jeans, with chains hanging off the shoulders. They had long, wild, yellow hair. I had seen a few back home and knew they were Hell's Angels. I shivered.

A Zip-up Lilac Minidress

My mother had lived in London years ago, during the war, and still knew it well, better than my father who liked to be a know-it-all. I wasn't quite sure what she had done in London, but when we ventured out the first morning, some strange alchemy transformed her from a Plymouth mother into a force to be reckoned with, glamorous, decisive, and most of all, brisk. She led us through the Underground, saying, "Hurry up girls, keep up." I loved my new London mother. Even Ani followed her without protest.

My father kept giving Ani dirty looks. He thought she was cheeky. I was afraid there would be trouble between them as they were both so forthright. Ani was allowed to get away with more at home than me. Her parents called it 'expressing yourself'. My father would blow up if people went too far. When I was little, I would tell him to 'shut up' and got slapped hard for it.

I sent Granny a postcard of soldiers at Buckingham Palace:

London, 20th December 1970
Hello Granny, London is <u>fun</u>. We've been on the Tube. The names of the stations are so funny – Marylebone, Elephant and Castle and Waterloo. The electric Tube lines are scary. Have been to the waxworks, Tower of London and we're going to a pantomime of Peter Pan with Millicent Martin in it. Hope Hedley is behaving. Love, Hazel x

Naturally, the climax of the trip was the clothes shopping. My mother took us on day four. We took the Underground again, to Carnaby Street, the epitome of sixties (or now seventies) London. We wandered up the street and gaped at all the shops with peculiar names – Kids in Gear, I Was Lord Kitchener's Valet, Mary Quant. Crowds of people filled the street, some in incredible clothes – hippies, Hell's Angels, Jesus freaks or rich-looking women in fur coats and jewels. Even my mother looked impressed. I felt like a country bumpkin and prayed my red jeans looked fashionable enough. Ani strode along, at ease with it all. We had finally made it to Swinging London.

My mother bought me flared Levi's, my dream jeans, tutting at the price. I also bought some fawn cord Wrangler's and a jeans jacket with my saved-up pocket money. Ani had her own ideas and bought black flared trousers and a big belt, plus a floppy white hat. (Her parents had given her a large amount of money to spend.) There was more to come. Mum bought me two minidresses at Kids in Gear. One was lilac, with a huge zip up the front, and a large collar. It was the best dress I ever had. The other had a blue and green flower pattern on it, and we splashed out on some lacy white tights and white high-heeled shoes with a bar across. I was in a state of bliss. I wasn't a scruffy little Plymouth girl in old slacks and tennis shoes any more: I was With-It.

As we walked out of Kids in Gear with our carrier bags, I said to my mother: "Mum, can I have a bra while we're here?" Ani huddled against me and we linked little fingers.

Silence. My heart thumped. I felt myself blushing. But Ani was there by my side.

"Yes, all right. Let's go to Debenhams in Oxford Street," said Mum. A miracle.

So we all went there and I tried on wonderful, tiny training bras. It wasn't embarrassing, after all, but felt just right. My mother bought me two teenage bras. One had blue and white flowers, the other was lacy and white. I was in heaven. Finally, a chance to get rid of little-girl vests. Bras really did make a difference to how you looked. The only problem was that they felt so tight at first. I kept fiddling with mine and Ani laughed and said: "Spot the new bra-wearer."

"Well, you are as well," I pointed out.

The next evening, we went to watch *Peter Pan* in the West End. I had only been to small theatres in Plymouth or Torquay to see pantomimes before. This was so utterly different. The costumes, the acting, the music – everything was better. The actors flew about in the air, attached to almost invisible wires. It was a fabulous night for me, poor provincial child that I was.

But the next evening, things went downhill. My mother started a bad headache and went to lie down. She often had headaches, though I couldn't understand why. Sometimes she cried in her bedroom too. We left her in the bedroom and had a meal with my father in the hotel (steak and chips, followed by banana splits). Trouble began brewing because Ani and I wanted to go out alone the next day, to London Zoo.

"Certainly not," said Dad.

"Why not? We're nearly thirteen and we're mature," said Ani, shaking her hair back and looking very confident.

"Yeah, why are you being such a bloody pain in the arse?" I said, showing off in front of Ani.

Explosion! Dad dropped his spoon into the banana split and started shouting.

"You pipe down immediately, you little wretch! And you can behave too," he said, giving Ani a filthy look.

"There's no need to behave like that, Ron," said Ani, but she looked a bit shocked.

"Oh no? Well, you can damn well go to your room if you have that attitude!" he yelled. "Go on, up you both go."

We left our half-eaten desserts and got up. He herded us out of the restaurant. Other people stared at us. It was horribly embarrassing.

"Well! He's being a bit extreme!" whispered Ani, who had gone red, but was acting tougher than me. If you had divorced parents, you were probably used to this sort of thing. I was biting back tears. I couldn't understand why my father got into such bad moods, even though we had been rude to him.

We went up in the lift in silence and then Dad pratically pushed us into our bedroom and slammed the door. We both plumped down on our beds and looked at each other.

"Well," said Ani, "here we are, then."

I started to cry and sniffle in a babyish way.

"Oh, come on, cheer up, gorgeous. Don't let your old man get you down," she said. It was the sort of thing Sarah would

A Zip-up Lilac Minidress

say. "I know what – let's pretend we're going to bed and put the lights out, and then if we wait about fifteen minutes, we can sneak out again," she said. "We'll go out, get to know London. Good practice for our escape."

"Oh, Ani, I don't know…" I giggled a bit. It's the strangest feeling, giggling when you're crying.

"I know what," I said, wiping my eyes, "let's ring René. I've got his number here. And his address."

"Ooh, you little devil! Have you?"

"Yes, he said to ring if I was in London."

"Go on, then, if you dare," said Ani.

"Wait, let's put the lights out first and just lie there, in case my horrible father looks in."

It felt ridiculous, but we did just that and lay on our beds in the dark. We both stifled a giggle. But there was no sound from next door.

"I'm coming over to you," whispered Ani and crawled onto my bed. We snuggled up together. She smelt of scent and ice cream. Her silky hair tickled my face. With her beside me, I felt I could do anything.

"Sarah says your father suffers from an extreme case of middle-class angst," she whispered.

"What's that?"

"It means, he's always worried about what other people think, and wants to be all respectable."

"Yes," I said sadly, "that's what's the matter with him."

I rolled over on my back.

Suddenly, I scoffed. "Anyway, he can go to hell! Come on, Hippy, let's get out of here."

We got up, put on a lamp, and phoned René's number. I sweated with nerves. A woman answered:

"Hello, Celia speaking."

Celia – that was the lady who owned the house, I remembered now. What an awful name.

"Hello, could I speak to René?" I asked.

"Sure, who is this?" She sounded curious.

"Umm, it's Hazel, Hazel James. I'm a friend of his. I'm in London and I want to see him."

"Yeah? OK, I'll find him." I heard her put the phone down.

She yelled, "Ren! Ren! A girlfriend of yours on the phone! Hazel Something?"

I could hear René in the distance, saying, "Hazel? Oh. That one."

He picked up the phone.

"Hello, darling, where are you?" He sounded less than enthusiastic.

"At the Paddington Hotel with Ani Rydle. Can we meet you?"

"Good God! Partners in crime. I hope you two aren't up to something. Where are your parents?"

"In bed next door in the hotel. Mum's got a headache and Dad shouted at us at supper, so we left him to calm down." (I was proud of my quick bending of the truth there.)

A Zip-up Lilac Minidress

He laughed. "Oh, dear. Let me see, what could we do? It's a bit late for little girls to be out. I tell you what, why don't I phone the hotel in the morning? I'd like to see darling Fen too. We could meet for coffee. We'll have to get rid of Ron somehow. Say ten tomorrow? Can you tell Mum?"

"Can't we meet you now?" I asked.

"Gosh, it's too late for little girls now!" he answered in a bossy voice. "You two ought to be tucked up in bed. No, we'll all meet in the morning. I'll call Fenella. Bye now." And he rang off.

"Huh!" I said. "He just wants to meet us tomorrow with my mother."

"He won't help us to escape then," said Ani.

"No. He says we should be in bed, the meanie."

We both drooped with disappointment. I thought he might ask us over to a party, or meet us somewhere. But when you're twelve years old, no one wants you to have fun.

"Oh, what a load of rubbish," said Ani. "He's just as square as the rest of them. Tell you what, though, let's just go out on our own."

"What – now?"

"Yeah, why not? We can just walk." Ani stood up and ran her hand through her golden hair.

"Put on your new jeans," she ordered. "And put on some make-up."

I pulled on my new Levi's. They felt stiff but looked absolutely brilliant.

Ten minutes later, we were ready to go, wearing green eye shadow, long silky scarves of Ani's and a smear of red lipstick.

"Just up the road, nothing's gonna happen to us," she said. "Just act as if you do this every day."

So we went down in the lift and strolled through the hotel foyer and walked out into the thronging crowds. Nobody noticed or cared. All the world was here: religious Indian-type people dancing along, beating their drums and chanting, smart tourists, hippies, bikers, students, children with long hair, poor people, Salvation Army people, old ladies, girls in miniskirts, boys in psychedelic shirts and leather coats, nonchalant Londoners who were used to the big city, thousands of people all going about their business. And us, me and Ani, nearly teenagers, just walking along and not coming to any harm. No one bothered us. I felt good.

"Do you still want to run away?" I asked Ani.

"Yep, I think so," she said. "Do you?"

"Definitely, but I don't think I want to in London. It's too cold and big. I want somewhere warm. And I need to get a passport first," I said. I would ask my father soon, I decided.

"Give me your hand," Ani said. She took it and we linked our little fingers.

"This is our sign," she said. "We're in things together."

We were getting tired, so we turned round and went back to the Paddington Hotel and bed.

* * *

A Zip-up Lilac Minidress

The next morning, nothing was said about the row. My father was grumpy but polite at breakfast. I tried to forget the ghastly evening, and push away the pain and shock of it. I never told Mum or anyone else about it and Ani kept quiet. My mother looked better but still pale. After we admitted we had rung René, she agreed it would be nice to see him.

"I'd better ring him or we'll just be waiting around here," she said. "What's his number?" I gave her the paper.

She arranged to meet René at a coffee bar near our hotel and we three set off. Thankfully, my father had decided to go and visit some fusty old war museum. I was glad to see the back of him. It was relaxing just to be with my mum; she seemed more lively and fun on her own. She also knew the way to the café without a map.

Alfredo's coffee bar had a dark red front. Inside were giant hissing machines for making coffee. All the tables were red to match the outside wall and each one had a wine bottle with a candle stuck in it. René was already there, looking quite at home and sipping a large coffee. He looked very exotic, in a fur coat, long fluffy scarf and black velvet jeans.

He leapt up when he saw us and made a beeline for Mum.

"Fen! Darling – looking fabulous as usual!" he exclaimed, embracing her.

"Well, trying my best…" said Mum, rearranging her blonde hair in a self-conscious way.

"And the two girls – let's look at you." René stood back and examined us. I cringed, hoping he wouldn't say anything bitchy. But he just said, "Mmm, not bad at all. Nice jeans, Hazel."

Ani ignored him, and made me sit with her. René and Mum started talking about the old days, when Mum was young and he was a boy. Apparently he had visited her in London, in the school holidays. This was news to me.

"All those actors you knew, Fen, you were a real glamour queen," he said, putting his hand on hers. We both stared at them, not being invited to join in.

Mum smiled and said, "Oh, I know, René – it seems an age ago. I'm just a Plymouth housewife now. Although I have joined the Compton Players – the am-dram group." She sighed and got out a cigarette.

"That's marvellous," he said. "You'll never just be a housewife, though. I bet, once this one is grown up"—he jerked his head in my direction—"you'll take off and do something."

"Well, you never know," said Mum, lighting her cigarette and puffing on it. She looked thoughtful.

"And what have you two been up to in London?" René asked us.

"Oh well, the usual – buying clothes in boutiques, going to the pantomime, going on the Underground," said Ani, looking him straight in the face.

I didn't say anything. I was cross with René for not seeing us the night before. Now I could see that he was all talk and

A Zip-up Lilac Minidress

would never help me to escape, for he was too wrapped up in himself and too sensible.

He and Mum started talking about some actors they had known and ignored us again.

I drank my hot chocolate and thought about what Ani and I would do when we got back to Plymouth. At least I could go and hang around at the Rydles' house, where something was always happening, unlike at my own hideously quiet house.

* * *

Apart from René not coming up to my expectations, and my father's temper outburst, the visit to London was wonderful. Ani was wonderful, too, the best friend I had ever had.

"Did you like London, then?" Dad asked me on the train back.

"It was smashing," I said.

He nodded. "We'll have to go back next year."

"But I don't mind going back to Plymouth. It's nearly Christmas," I said. I didn't admit it, but I'd had enough of London for now. Although exciting, it was exhausting and frankly, rather dirty. I had achieved my aim of getting the right jeans and other clothes and was now happy to return home in triumph.

My mother was quiet and smoked cigarette after cigarette.

"All right, Fen?" Dad asked.

"Yes. I just wonder when I'll see London again," she said in a faint voice.

"Next year – Dad just said," I said.

She shrugged and got out a crossword. I wondered what was wrong.

I loved my lilac zip-up minidress from Carnaby Street and later wore it to all the birthday parties. Unfortunately, the large zip was too tempting and various girls tried to unzip it as a party trick. But I still loved it. And I had achieved my ambition to buy jeans and bras.

Christmas was the same as usual, apart from one big surprise: a colour television was delivered on Christmas Eve and installed in our front room. I was overcome with excitement and we all sat glued to it, marvelling at the vivid colours of fires, exotic birds, people's clothes and flowers. My father had his good side.

My cousins came for Christmas day from Exeter, we enjoyed a big roast, and my father told us not to open our presents before the Queen's Speech at three o'clock, his usual custom. But we were older and cheekier now. We ignored him and my oldest cousin, Sean, started tearing open his presents. I soon joined him and opened up my biggest and best present – a giant art box filled with poster and oil paints in tubes with assorted brushes. The names of the colours sounded incredibly romantic – cobalt blue, burnt sienna, cadmium yellow – and made me think of travelling to faraway places. I counted up all the Christmas cash I had got and dreamt about escaping from Plymouth.

I reviewed my escape plans. London seemed too big and dangerous. I didn't know anyone who would help us there, (except possibly Sarah Rydle) after that traitor René let us down. In any case, I wanted to see other countries now.

The following week, my father was in a good mood and I asked him if he had thought about a summer holiday for us. I was expecting to hear the usual old stuff about Cornwall, but instead he said: "Yes, I thought we could have a change next summer and try Ibiza. You know, the island off Spain. Apparently the Atkinsons went and they liked it."

Ibiza! I rushed to look it up in our encyclopaedia. Warm weather. Beaches. It sounded brilliant. It certainly had escape potential.

CHAPTER 13
THE PARTY

Nothing much happened in January, just weeks of dark mornings and school and cold rain. London seemed like a distant memory and I sank into a sort of depression. I kept fishing out my list and getting disheartened. I did finally have a bra (two to be precise) and better clothes and a good haircut. And I had Ani. But I hadn't escaped from Plymouth and nothing more had happened with any boys, not even the neighbours. I was twelve, but I was greedy and wanted everything from life, especially a boyfriend. A few girls at school said they had one. Maybe they were lying, but it worried me: supposing I never went out with a boy? I might end up like Miss Coles, the spinster up the road, who had stick-insect legs and a sour look.

I saw Ani every weekend, at my house or hers. We drew and painted, talked about horses and clothes, and tried to keep Tallulah and Josh at bay. Joshua was now walking and talking and they had become a pair of little pests.

At the start of February things got better. People began to shake off the winter blues and make plans. At supper one day, my mother said, "Let's have a party to cheer us up. I keep

The Party

meaning to ask our new neighbours in, and we should have some friends round too." She loved parties.

"Good idea, Fen," replied Dad. "Say Saturday in two weeks?"

"Right. I'll start planning the food," said Mum. "Lil – can you do your pasties for the party?"

Despite being boring most of the time, my parents gave good parties, with plenty of food and drink. My gran liked to tell naughty stories about the old days, my mother loved dancing and my father could be relied on to pour out enormous alcoholic drinks.

The Atkinsons were phoned and said they would love to come.

I felt excited inside – this could be *it*, a boyfriend at last. My sights were set on Chas. Now I was wearing a bra and looked more adult, I reckoned he might be more interested in me. I completely discounted Rick: he was too young and ugly.

On the day of the party, we pushed all the furniture back and put out ashtrays on tables. Hedley was taken to a neighbour for the night as he behaved badly at parties, barking at people or trying to climb on to their legs to do 'embarrassing things', as my mother put it. Ani wasn't coming; she was going to Manchester for the weekend with her father. A mean little voice in me said, "Just as well or she might get off with Chas."

"Are you going to the off-licence now, Ronny?" Mum asked, in a happy mood.

"Yes, Fenny, and taking my assistant with me," said Dad, smiling at me.

We got in the Vitesse and drove to an off-licence on Mutley Plain to buy the drinks. I loved those trips with him. He chatted to me like an adult for once, instead of checking up on my homework or preventing me from doing things. He had the same routine every time – buying cans of pale ale and bitter, Mateus Rosé wine, red wine and white wine ('plonk', as he called it), lemonade, whisky, brandy, soda, orange juice, Coca-Cola for me and ginger ale. He also bought twenty packets of crisps. We drove home, the boot clinking with all the bottles. Meanwhile, my mother and grandmother were busy in the kitchen preparing mounds of food – pasties, salads, sandwiches, trifles, mousses and strawberry flans. My job was to stir the mousses and pour them into bowls, and then put out crisps and peanuts. *Only four hours to go. And then – boyfriend time!*

As the evening approached, I put on my Carnaby Street lilac minidress and white high-heeled shoes. I was getting more and more excited about the Atkinsons. I kept checking that my dress looked good and hitching up my white tights. My hair was freshly trimmed by Dino and lovely, not like the old days when I looked like a shaggy dog.

Mum looked very glamorous in a black cocktail dress and high heels, and Gran was resplendent in her red velvet dress and a silver brooch.

Guests began to arrive and light up cigarettes, while my father poured out enormous drinks for everyone and made his usual comments. "Would you care for a glass of red plonk, Doris? A whisky for you, Vicar, or are you on the wagon?"

The Party

The Atkinsons suddenly arrived. I had a paralysing attack of shyness and fled into the living room. Someone had left a glass of white wine on the table. On impulse, I took a gulp for courage. Judy came in first, with Chas. She had got thinner and was wearing a tight red top and black miniskirt. Chas had a black leather jacket on and ripped denims. Gorgeous! Rick came last, looking miserable, although marginally better as he had grown taller and his hair was longer. He ignored me and mumbled, "Yeah, ta," when Dad offered him a pale ale.

I hung round near my grandmother, who was sitting by the window. She nudged me and whispered, "Your young man's here – go and talk to him."

"What, Rick?" I hissed. "No chance."

"Yes, go on!" She gave me a little shove and I went through the crowd of guests towards them. I decided to give it a try.

Rick and Judy had sat down on a little sofa. Disappointingly, Chas had wandered off. Judy was already puffing away on a cigarette and knocking back red wine.

"God, I needed that," she said loudly to no one in particular. "Such a mad day I've had. Terrible problems with the architect and our new bathroom."

Rick was drinking his beer, head down.

Judy spotted me.

"Ah, Hazel, come and chat to me and Ricky and tell us all about yourself," she commanded in a deep voice.

I sidled over and sat on a chair.

Rick and I looked at each other. He still had a few spots, but his eyes were a nice blue. *Could I actually fancy him? Or ever kiss him?* I felt myself growing hot and flushed. "I…umm," I said.

"What?" he answered irritably.

"Errm, well…" I said.

Silence.

In desperation, I blurted out, "What music do you like? I like T. Rex. Do you like them?"

"Oh, them! Can't stand them," he said.

More silence.

"What about The Beatles?" said Judy brightly. "They're groovy, aren't they?"

"They're finished, Mother," drawled someone in a lazy voice. Chas. He had reappeared, holding a glass of what looked like whisky.

"And who does this little dolly bird like?" he said, staring at my legs.

"Um, I like David Cassidy and Nancy Sinatra and The Beatles and T. Rex. I don't know any others," I said, going scarlet again.

"Christ! Well the last one is halfway decent. Got any records?"

"Shut up, Chas," said Judy. "Go and get me another wine." He took her glass and went, smiling in a superior way. *So sexy, though,* I thought.

I sat miserably near Rick, looking at the carpet, saying nothing, while all around us, people gaily chatted and got

The Party

drunk. I just couldn't think of anything else to say. He had dried up as well. My brain had shut down. This was horrendous. I had never known anything like it. He seemed exactly the same – paralysed. It was far worse than I had imagined. I was a failure. I would never be able to talk to boys. He hated me. Chas hated me. I was going to end up like Miss Coles.

Even worse, Mum came over.

"Hello, Judy, lovely to see you. Hello, young man. How have you settled in?"

Rick mumbled something inaudible.

Judy spoke up: "Fine, thanks, Fen. We love it. Now, I meant to ask you – are you interested in amateur dramatics? I've got a leaflet here…" Judy rummaged in her big shoulder bag and handed a leaflet to my mother.

"How funny – I already go! Why don't you join us? We're doing *How the Other Half Loves* at the moment – you know, Alan Ayckbourn. So funny."

"I'm terribly busy with work, but still, I could do with some light relief. All right – what time do you meet?"

"7.00 p.m. on a Wednesday. I could call for you?"

"You're on! Alan can make supper for once."

They said nothing to me and Rick. I looked at him. He was looking away.

Judy got up. "Fen, would you mind showing me your bathroom? I'm getting ours redesigned and wanted some inspiration."

"Of course, I'll show you now. Also, Judy, I meant to ask you…"

Rick was still looking away. *Oh, God.*

I finally leapt up and escaped, mumbling that I had to get a drink. I took refuge in the kitchen and stuffed myself with leftover crisps and cakes. Some other neighbours started chatting to me. They were old and unfashionable, but that was fine; I'd had enough of being trendy – it hadn't got me anywhere.

I heard a record start up in the living room. 'Things We Said Today', by The Beatles. I longed to go in but couldn't face anyone.

For the rest of the party, I avoided the Atkinsons and hung round the kitchen or sat by my gran, who was having a great time in the dining room, telling naughty stories to a circle of admiring people.

Later, about eleven, I sneaked back and looked into the living room. People were dancing away. Chas was dancing with Mrs Linton, who was much older than him and really tarty. My parents were doing an excruciating disco dance. Even the vicar was jiggling about. Rick, Chas and Judy had disappeared. Ani should have been there with me; she would have sniggered at them all. But she was in Manchester. I crept away.

I went up to my bedroom and looked at myself in the mirror. I stuck my tongue out and said, "That was shit!" Tears started leaking out of my eyes. I tore off my lovely dress and pulled on my pyjamas. I flung myself on the bed and stared at the ceiling.

The Party

It was the worst party ever. My plan had failed. I would never meet a boy and I would probably end up a spinster. And never have sex. A few tears ran down my face. But then I imagined what Sarah Rydle might say:

Rick and Chas aren't the only boys, you know? There are other boys about. And you didn't look ugly tonight; you looked good.

But I didn't believe it, so I got into bed properly and cried into my pillow.

I could hear people leaving, shouting in drunken voices.

"Lovely party, darling."

"Thanks so much, Fen."

"Super food!"

I switched the light out.

Much later, my mother looked in. She whispered, "Are you all right, darling? You disappeared."

The thought of describing the ordeal with Rick was too terrible.

"Had a headache," I mumbled in the dark.

"Poor girl, sorry. You looked so nice tonight too. I'll bring you some Disprin and warm milk."

"Yeah, OK." I pulled the covers over my face.

My life was ruined. I was still stuck in Plymouth and had no boyfriend. I couldn't even *talk* to boys the right way.

I finally drifted off to sleep, feeling miserable about Rick and Chas. I would never be able to face them again.

CHAPTER 14
BLACK SHEEP

I was tougher than I thought, however. The next morning, when I heard Dad shaving and Hedley running round and Granny singing some old music hall song, I cheered up a tiny bit.

My mother came in and put a cup of tea by my bed, saying, "Morning, darling. We thought we'd go out to Tavistock later, to look at antique shops and have a cream tea."

"Yeah, that'd be good." I sat up and reached for the tea. She said nothing about the party or Rick. I was sure she had witnessed some of the disastrous encounter. But she was kind at heart and tactful. Hedley came running into my room (still forbidden by my father but encouraged by me).

"Up, boy," I said and he jumped onto my bed.

I decided to make a mini-list of goodish things. I got a Biro and put my other arm round the dog:

1. I am nearly a teenager
2. I am not fat
3. I have got the right jeans (hooray)
4. Ani is still my best friend

Black Sheep

Outside, I heard a motorbike rev up. I tiptoed over to the window and peeped out. Chas was just getting on his Honda and saying something to Judy, who was in the doorway.

"Sod you," I muttered. I was going to ignore him and Rick from now on, or try. He roared off in a cloud of blue exhaust fumes.

We all cleared up after the party, and my mother opened the outside doors wide to get rid of the cigarette smoke. Everyone smoked in those days. My father started asking me about Rick, but Mum gave him a furious look and he shut up.

After lunch I made a decision. I went up to my bedroom and shut the door. Then I took out all my clothes for inspection. It reminded me of when I'd shown them to Ani, on her first visit. I had moved on since then. I had some decent jeans and tops now, as good as any adult like Sarah or Mel.

First I sorted the clothes into two piles on the bed – 'cool things' and 'square things'. Items like my navy-blue dress with a white collar, stretch Ladybird trousers, pinafore dresses and frilly party knickers went onto the reject pile. Acceptable things like my new jeans, minidresses and white high heels went on the keeping pile. I then called my mother in and said that I was getting rid of most of my clothes.

She picked up the navy-blue dress and held it up.

"What a shame. I loved this little dress," she said. "Can't you just keep it for best?"

"Nope," I said. "Anyway, I'm too tall for it." That was true, I was shooting up. If there was one thing I was sure of, it was this clothes clear-out. "It's going to the jumble sale."

She gave in and took the rejects away.

That afternoon, I refused to go out. I wanted to be alone. Dad fussed but my mother said I would be all right.

"After all, she's nearly thirteen," she said.

"In twenty-one days," I pointed out. I was counting down.

"That's fine, Hazel, you don't want to trail round antique shops – you do your own thing here." She smiled at me.

I didn't know what was happening to her, but there was a mysterious transformation going on, which meant she sided with me more and more.

"Mind you take Hedley out, though," said Dad.

"Yeah, OK."

With that, they went. The house fell silent.

I felt bored. I went and fetched a biscuit and ate it as I wandered round, dropping a trail of crumbs. The dog followed, hoovering them up. I felt tired, heavy, not like doing much. So I lay on the sofa for five minutes.

I must have dozed off because a loud noise woke me. At first I couldn't think what it was. Then I realised – the doorbell and the dog barking. Could it be Chas? Saying he wanted to ask me out? I leapt up and hurried to the door.

It wasn't Chas. Standing there was a grey-haired suntanned man, holding a small duffle bag. A taxi was just pulling away.

"I'm glad someone's in," he said, laughing. "My Lord, you've grown!" He glanced at my chest.

I looked at him. "Uh…*Uncle Forbes*?"

"The very same. Are you going to ask me in or not?"

"Sorry, come in. Everyone's out and I was asleep."

I led him into the TV room.

"Umm, do you want a cup of tea? Or something?"

"Thank you, darling. Actually…have you got anything stronger, like a beer? And bring me an ashtray while you're about it." Forbes sank into an armchair and patted Hedley, who was wagging his tail frantically.

"OK." I went and got one of Dad's cans of pale ale for him, and made a cup of tea for myself. We sat and regarded each other. I felt very shy. I hadn't seen him for years. He looked a little like my father, same voice and way of walking, but more arty-looking and scruffy. Quite good, really. Even good-looking. But then I felt appalled and thought, *You shouldn't fancy relatives.* Ani had educated me about incest recently.

Forbes took out a pretty pack of cigarettes with the word 'Gitanes' on it and lit one. It stank.

"Aah, that's better. Yep, sorry I just turned up here, but I was back in England at a loose end and thought, why not? Catch up with the family and all that. Now, tell me about yourself."

I told him nearly everything, about Ani and Plymouth and art and wanting to travel. About how we had just had a party. (I did not include the part about Rick and Chas, however). He looked very interested. Oddly, he had heard of the Rydles.

"From my art days," he said, and left it at that.

"You should come and visit me in Spain," he said. "Broaden your mind and all that. Although you're so young…"

He looked me up and down, which made me blush slightly.

"I've got a nice little place near Barcelona. Interesting artist friends…" he went on.

"Oh, thank you. But I don't think I'd be allowed."

"Whyever not? Oh, I see, I'm the black sheep and a bad influence." He laughed and took a swig of beer.

I wondered: *Does he mean it, that I could visit?* But I hardly knew him. There was something odd about him, too.

"We might be going to Ibiza this summer," I said.

"Perfect, I live near pretty near there."

We both considered that for a moment.

I spoke up. "Would you like a chocolate digestive biscuit?"

He burst out laughing. "What a very English thing to say! I would love a chocolate digestive, dear," he said, lighting up another cigarette. I fetched the packet and we shared it, not bothering with plates. My mother would have disapproved.

Forbes sat back and looked round the living room, with its gleaming antique tables and ornaments. He got up and walked round the room, picking up vases and silver trays and examining them thoughtfully. I had a strange feeling he might pocket one and take it away to sell.

"Old Ron's done well," he said to himself.

"What was Dad like as a boy?" I asked.

"Wild," said Forbes, chuckling.

"Really?" I was shocked. I couldn't imagine my father being wild.

"You remind me of him, although you look like your mother, too, a lovely woman. And a little like your grandmother Mary. My mother. She was an unusual lady, very artistic. But unhappy. An unhappy ending, oh yes. Depression – and more," he said cheerily.

"Oh," I said, dying to know more. My father never said much about her.

"You should really come to Spain; it's a different life out there," he said. "I haven't got much time for England, to be honest. Too uptight and bourgeois for old Forbsie."

"I'm sick of England too," I said.

Forbes laughed and said, "You must take after me." He stubbed his cigarette out in a pretty china saucer, which he had taken off the mantelpiece. "Be careful you don't end up riding The Middle-Class Conveyor Belt, Hazel," he said.

"The what?" But he just laughed and shook his head.

I had an inkling of what he meant, in any case. People like Uncle Charles and Aunty Louise sprang to mind. That got me thinking – could he help me to run away? Next summer, in Ibiza? René had been useless in the end. I thought he was a friend and would help me, but he had turned out to be just a typical adult – too sensible. He had sided with my mother and wasn't going to help me with my plans. But perhaps Forbes would be different.

"Got a boyfriend yet, have you?" he asked.

I blushed. "Not really," I said.

"I think you might be rather beautiful in a few years, darling," he said, lighting another cigarette. "The boys had better watch out!"

I was pleased at that but couldn't think of a witty answer.

I was saved by the return of my family. They came in and stopped dead when they saw who was there.

Forbes jumped up and said, "Ron, old man! Good to see you! Just thought I'd drop in, see the family, et cetera. Your Hazel's been entertaining me."

"So I see," said my father, glancing at the beer can and general mess.

There was an awkward silence, then my mother made a sort of lunge at him and babbled, "Forbes, darling, welcome! What a surprise! Has Hazel been looking after you? Thank you, sweetheart"—a smile at me—"I was just saying to Ron yesterday, wasn't I, Ron? *We haven't heard from your brother for a long time*, and here you are in Plymouth, my goodness!"

She went on in this vein for a few minutes while Dad looked him up and down. Granny Lil laughed and Hedley went mad and ran around barking because he thought there was trouble brewing.

"Are you staying long?" asked Dad, once Mum had finished.

"Oh, well a few days perhaps, if it's all right with you good folks, of course. I'm doing a bit of journalism work now, for my sins, and I wanted to do a piece on post-war architecture in Plymouth, you know…"

"Yes, well, we're very busy actually," said Dad.

"Of course you can stay," interrupted Mum. "Now, I'll go and make up the guest room, and we'll think about supper. Do you like chicken pie? Is that your duffle bag? Hazel, take it upstairs for your uncle and then you can get us all a cup of tea."

"Let's have some cake," piped up Granny, who was trying to work out what was going on. She always gave people cake as a default.

So we all sat round and ate fruit cake and drank tea. Even my father relaxed a little, and it was decided that Forbes must stay for a few days.

"We can chat about the old days, in London and Malta – ooh, and we could go out to some country pubs," my mother said.

"Did you all live in those places?" I asked, surprised.

"Oh yes, Hazel, my love. We did have a life before you came along, you know," Forbes said, taking another slice of cake and looking for a cigarette. My mother held out the lighter for him.

"Is it too early for a drinkie?" she said and the adults all agreed it wasn't. My father fetched glasses and we all had something. Mum looked happy. It was turning into a bit of a party.

I decided to ring Ani – I was sure she would be impressed by my freewheeling uncle. But when I got through, Jim answered and said, "Sorry, love, Ani's not feeling too well this evening.

She's not going to school next week. Can you ring back on Saturday?"

I was taken aback – Ani always wanted to talk to me. I put the phone down and roamed around the house, quite lost. But then my mother came and found me, to tell me we were all going out to the seafront for ice creams, and I forgot about her.

During his visit, Forbes spent a lot of time doing crosswords with my mother, both of them tossing ideas for words back and forth and roaring with laughter. I wondered if they actually fancied each other, a repulsive thought. Dad didn't seem overjoyed but was at work for some of the time, anyway. Every evening, we all went out to pubs or had drinks at home. Forbes offered to help in the house, doing messy washing up or some approximate hoovering.

"I can't take to him," my gran told me on the quiet. She had strong feelings about people.

But I thoroughly enjoyed having Forbes around. I almost forgot about Ani that week, and why she wasn't at school, and then felt guilty. Forbes seemed to know about a vast range of subjects. He helped me with my French homework and advised me about my drawing. We took Hedley for walks, usually via the corner shop so he could stock up on cigarettes. He didn't seem to have much money. Once I walked in on him asking Dad to lend him twenty quid.

"I will *give* you twenty pounds, Forbes," my father said. "But you'd better try and get on your feet again."

"Oh, absolutely, Ron," Forbes said sincerely, taking out his cigarette packet. "I've got a few things in the pipeline back in Barcelona, never worry."

On Forbes' last day, he gave me a scrap of paper with his address and phone number.

"If you ever need to get in touch, just ring there and ask for Maria. She's my landlady. And girlfriend, sort of." He winked at me. I put it away carefully.

Dad and I took Forbes down to the bus station on the Sunday so he could catch a coach back to London. We waved him off.

"Blithering idiot," said Dad.

"I liked seeing him. He's lively," I said.

"Yes, well, he is family, I suppose. He's all right in small doses. Come on, back home now. Have you got any homework?"

"Yeah," I sighed.

"Don't say, 'Yeah'. Say, 'Yes'," said Dad.

Back to the usual nagging.

A week went by, and Ani still hadn't rung. I had to do something. I sat in our hall and called her number. It rang for a long time before Mel answered.

"Oh, hello, I wondered if Ani was there," I said.

Mel said, "Sorry, sweetheart. Ani doesn't feel like seeing anyone today. She's still upset."

She sounded rather upset herself.

"Oh," I said. I thought I might faint. "Doesn't she want to see me any more?"

The Rydle Year

What had gone wrong? I was also quite angry with Ani for neglecting me.

"No, no, it's not you. She adores you," she said. "Ani's just feeling like being alone; she's had a difficult week. Try in a few days."

It was agony, not seeing Ani. I couldn't understand what was wrong. But I waited and rang her a week later.

"Hi, Pony," she said. She sounded tired.

"Hippy…are you OK now?" I asked, longing to know what had happened.

"Yeah, I'm all right now. It was just to do with Realmum. I don't want to talk about it. But I'm OK now. Sorry I didn't ring you."

"That's OK. Do you want to come out for my birthday? We're going to the Silk Tent – it's a new wine bar."

"Yeah, I know. Oh, lovely, yes please."

Thank God. She still wants me.

CHAPTER 15

HAPPY AND UNHAPPY FAMILIES

On March 12th I was thirteen. Finally a teenager. I didn't want a party that year, not after the humiliation in February. I asked to go out for meal instead, and only with my parents and Ani. My mother took me shopping and bought me a dark-blue velvet jacket at the Etam boutique, which went with my red cord jeans. One or two better clothes shops were appearing in Plymouth by then. I tied a tiny blue velvet ribbon in my hair to complete the outfit.

I chose the Silk Tent wine bar for my meal. It was a new thing in Plymouth. Instead of old-fashioned hotel food, like roasts, they served continental food like savoury flans (or 'quiches') and salads, French bread and huge delicious gateaux, all washed down with a huge choice of wines, not that I knew the first thing about wine. According to Ani, there were already a lot of wine bars in London, but it seemed they had reached Plymouth too. We were both allowed a tiny glass of Mateus rosé. I felt terribly sophisticated, sipping away and observing the other diners.

They looked very interesting. They wore black clothes and talked loudly about French holidays, jobs in television and clever children. *Just like in the colour supplements.* It was definitely my sort of place and I gazed at them longingly. Ani looked happy too. She hadn't said anything else about Realmum and I hadn't asked. Next weekend she was going up north somewhere to visit cousins, and I wasn't invited.

"I'll miss you," I whispered to her as we sat close together on a long padded seat in the Silk Tent. She was playing with her wonderful, soft hair.

"I'll miss you too, Pony. I don't want to go, really. I'll see if you can come with us next time. It's just that Dad's been so busy, I haven't had a chance to ask him."

"Look – I've got you a birthday present," she said, pulling a large flat package out of her shoulder bag. It was wrapped in shiny silver paper with a blue ribbon, much better than the cheap flowery paper I usually bought from the newsagents.

I ripped it open. It was an LP. It had a strange greenish cover, with pictures of planets and stars and swirly watery patterns.

"Sarah thought you'd like it – it's called *A Saucerful of Secrets* and it's by Pink Floyd," Ani said.

"Very nice," said Dad, peering at it. "Are they like The Beatles?"

Ani gave him a withering look. "No, they are not like The Beatles," she said.

I had never heard of Pink Floyd, but I loved the name.

Happy and Unhappy Families

My father raised his glass and said, "To your good health, my darling. Happy birthday."

"Yes, darling Hazel – happy birthday," said my mother. But she seemed rather distracted, and kept glancing at the other eaters and listening to snippets of their conversations.

Perhaps she was tired; she was busy at home, learning lines for her part in the am-dram group, as well as doing all the usual cleaning and cooking. She called her lines her 'homework' and she worked hard at it.

Ani raised her glass and said, "Hey – you're a teenager."

"Hooray," I said, and took a big gulp of wine. "You next month," I added. She gave a thumbs up.

It was a big moment. Time to leave silly childish things behind and start being an adult. A handsome, older dark-haired man at the next table watched us and smiled. He was wearing a denim jacket. *I think he fancies me*, I thought. I nudged Ani and looked over at him. We both had an attack of giggles.

"What's up with you two now?" asked Dad. He didn't have a clue what was going on. My mother did and gave me a knowing smile.

I smoothed my velvet jacket front down and sat there like a queen, enjoying my power.

After we had dropped Ani home, I went straight into our living room and put on the Pink Floyd LP. It was like nothing I'd heard before. It began with eerie music, like something from a ghost film. Then there were other songs with words. The best one was called 'Remember a Day', all about being a little child.

I loved that one and played it again and again, staring out of the window. It made me sad. I could easily remember being really little, but then I thought – *One day I'll be old, too old to remember it.*

My father ruined this by looking in and saying, "What super music," but I ignored him. You couldn't talk to parents about music.

* * *

Meanwhile, all was not well with the Rydles. At the end of March, Mel rang and asked if Ani could stay the weekend with us.

It was a rainy miserable weekend, and Ani and I spent hours shut up in my bedroom, avoiding the adults. I had got a little cassette recorder for my birthday from my grandmother. I hoped Ani would like it, but she was much more intent on relating the latest happenings in the Rydle household. I pushed the recorder aside. Hedley lay on the floor next to us, gnawing at a dog chew and making occasional retching sounds.

"I think they wanted me out of the way, Pony," said Ani, looking depressed and biting her nails, "so they can get on with having rows."

"Why?" I asked, wanting to be kind, but bursting with curiosity and wondering what drama was going on now.

"Well, Mel has been fed up and moody lately. And she yelled at Dad."

This was a surprise. Mel complained about things and smoked her roll-ups and was messy but rarely shouted.

"Were you there with them?" I asked.

"No, I listened at their bedroom door last night," she explained, not at all guilty.

"I couldn't sleep and I got up to get some food from the kitchen. But as I went past Mel and Dad's room, I heard funny sounds, like gasping or heavy breathing. I thought they were having sex, at first!"

We both said, "Yuck!" and made vomiting noises. The thought of parents having sex was disgusting. Hedley shifted and looked at us, not sure what was going on. I patted him and said, "It's OK, boy."

"Anyway," she said, "I carried on listening…yeah, I know it's wrong. But then I heard Mel crying and them talking or arguing. Dad sounded angry and was saying stuff like, 'Aren't you happy just having this beautiful house and the kids?' and she shouted, '*No, I'm fucking not.*'"

We both giggled at the 'F' word, but it wasn't funny really, none of it.

"Then Mel said she wanted to be a proper artist, not a bloody housewife."

"Oh," I said, "that's strange. Does she want a job then?" I thought about my own mother, who was a housewife and seemed to like it. On the other hand, she liked going out to am-dram and getting away from it. My father didn't seem very happy about it. I supposed she couldn't do housework *all* the time. Other mothers seemed happy enough. My father frequently said it was a shame when mothers *had to go out to work.*

"Yup," said Ani. "I think things are going to change at home. And I'm worried about it. S'pose Mel leaves us?" She chewed at her fingernails.

I'd never seen Ani worried before. It made *me* worried. Things were changing, moving. Our little world felt less safe.

"But she gets on your nerves, so won't it be better?"

"No, I don't want Daddy to be alone. And what about Tallulah and Josh?"

"Oh, I see. Well, we should plan our escape and get away from them all," I said.

But Ani said nothing.

I swallowed and decided to be daring. "Do you remember your dad divorcing your real mum?"

She didn't answer for a while, but messed around with a strand of hair, pulling and twisting it. I wondered if I'd gone too far.

Finally, she said, "I can only remember a bit, Pony. I was so little then. We were living in Dorset, me and Sarah and Dave and my parents. There was lots of shouting and crying and Realmum would go out for hours. I didn't understand what was going on. I got fat, you know. I ate and ate. Sarah looked after me, mostly. She was thirteen, I think."

Our age, I thought.

"Then Dad told us we were moving to Plymouth without Mum," she went on, "and we moved here to a cottage first.

Happy and Unhappy Families

At Cremyll in Cornwall. I can't remember it much. Sarah looked after me. Then Dad met Mel when he was teaching at Plymouth art college, and she married him. But I still see Realmum sometimes."

I nodded, longing to ask more. I was afraid of looking young and stupid, or being unkind.

"What's Realmum's name?"

"River. She was called Janet, but she changed it to a more modern name. I might see her soon, anyway." Ani turned and looked at me, but there were tears in her eyes.

River – what a ridiculous name. But I kept quiet.

She shrugged and said, "It's just the way things are. I can't do anything. Let's do some recordings and see how they sound."

I was lost for words. She sounded so adult. *Thank God I have a real mother*. I would try to be nicer to her.

On impulse I said, "D'you want to come to Ibiza with us, in August?"

"Really, Pony? That'd be fantastic." She started crying again.

"Well, you're my best friend. I'll ask Dad and see," I said.

She turned and hugged me, without saying anything, and wiped her eyes on her sleeve. I held her and stroked her hair, the first time I had really shown my deep feelings for her. She looked so small and defenceless.

"It's OK, Hippy, I'll look after you. Who cares about silly parents?" I got some tissues and handed them to her.

I went on. "Hey, if we still feel fed up when we're in Ibiza, we could find my Uncle Forbes and run away with him. He lives in Barcelona, you know. I'm getting a passport and saving money, just in case."

"I've got loads of money, so we could survive," she said, wiping her eyes and sitting up. She held out her hand and we linked our little fingers. Our sign.

"D'you want to have a go with my cassette player, then? We could do different accents. My mum's doing a Scottish one in the am-dram play."

"Your mum's really clever, doing that. Yeah, let's have a go."

* * *

It was still raining the next day. Our cousins had invited us to lunch, but I wanted to stay at home with Ani. So Dad drove my mother and grandmother to them, then came back himself, not trusting us unsupervised in the house, I suspected. He disappeared to the garden, leaving us blessedly alone.

We gravitated to my bedroom again, after making some doorstep sandwiches for an indoor picnic. We dumped the sandwiches on my bed and sat down. After we had chewed our way through the inedible sandwiches, we wondered what to do.

Ani had forgotten her family troubles for the moment and looked mischievous.

"Shall we do some art? Let's draw each other."

"Oh, yeah, good idea."

We got our charcoal and drawing pads and began. We drew each other's faces first. It was harder than I expected. I just could not get a good likeness of Ani. She looked like a cartoon picture. Her sketch of me was pretty good, though.

But we grew bored with it and looked about for other projects.

"I know," she said. "Have you ever done *life* drawing?"

"No, what's that?"

"It's drawing naked people."

"That's disgusting!"

"No, it's not, it's a very important part of art."

"Like the one in your bathroom?"

"Exactly."

"Not likely. I'm not stripping off for you!"

"Oh go on, you coward. Aren't we best friends? If you won't, I will."

And she started pulling off her T-shirt and jeans to reveal her curvy white body. I noticed that her breasts were growing at last.

"I'll leave my pants on," said Ani, evidently having second thoughts. She stretched out her legs. Her toenails were red and the varnish was chipped.

"Now, I'll relax on the bed, and you draw me," she said, reclining and looking very professional, as if she did this every week.

I felt uneasy but got my drawing pad and began. It was extremely embarrassing, but I covered this up by giggling. I was a British prude to the core.

"It's no good. I can't draw your…you know."

"Oh, you're pathetic! Let's give up then. Shall we go and call on your boyfriends next door?"

"They're not my…"

We heard footsteps on the stairs.

"Hello." My father's voice. "Anyone there?"

We stopped dead.

"Do you two want to come to the garden centre with me?"

Ani grabbed a blanket and covered herself.

He opened the door and looked in.

"What are you two up to now?"

"Umm, doing art," I said. He looked from one of us to the other. *Thank God I'm not the naked one*, I thought.

"Just practising for art college," said Ani.

For a second, he looked quite amused, then snapped back into parent mode, and said, "Well, I don't know what you were doing, but you've been shut up in here long enough. Let's go to the garden centre and café."

"Ooh, yes please, Dad," I said. "Come on, Ani."

When we were all in Dad's Triumph, with the dog between us, Ani said, "Hazel and I are both going to be artists, so we need to work on our drawing, Ron."

I grimaced, hoping he wouldn't get cross with her, but he just said, "Hmm, well when you're both eighteen, you can go off to Paris or New York and lead a dissolute lifestyle. Meanwhile, you're in Plymouth and you're still children, so I hope you're going to behave."

Ani raised her eyes to heaven and I grinned at her. No more was said.

* * *

One evening, I asked my father about Ani coming to Ibiza, and after some initial resistance, he caved in.

"As long as you don't have any funny drawing sessions," he said, from behind his newspaper.

"Yeah, well, I want to be an artist one day," I said.

"There's no money in art," he said. "Concentrate on academic work. Art's a nice hobby. And don't say, '*Yeah*'."

I made a face. This was the usual attitude in my house.

"It's company for Hazel, having Ani in Ibiza," said Mum, who was sometimes sad I had no brothers or sisters.

"I'm afraid you'll have to share a hotel room with Lil, though."

"We don't mind," I said.

Granny Lil was fun to be with, but as she was deaf, we could talk about secret things at night and she wouldn't hear.

I went upstairs and wrote a letter to Forbes in Barcelona, giving our holiday dates and the name of the hotel in Ibiza. He didn't answer.

I also asked my father if I could get a passport. He was suspicious.

"Why do you need one when you're added to mine?"

"It might be handy for school trips – to France and places," I said innocently. "Ani's got one already."

"She would! Well, all right. I'll take you down to the big post office to get passport photos and get the forms."

Victory. Escape seemed nearer.

* * *

The next time I went to the Rydles', things seemed to have calmed down, although it would soon become clear that things were changing. Mel was tidying out her old clothes and gave me a white embroidered smock. Smocks were 'in'. It looked great over my denim jeans. Mel was always kind to me and seemed to like me.

Ani and I were still drawing but concentrating on animals or fully dressed humans, much to my relief. Mel asked to see our latest drawings.

"Oh, brilliant," she said, looking at Ani's work, a pony by a gate. It was very good, anyone could see that. "Keep going, and you'll get to art college."

"Very nice," she said, viewing my efforts (a rather shapeless pony). But deep down I knew I was only quite good, nothing like Ani or the other Rydles, who all seemed to be natural artists. It depressed me.

"Has Ani told you that I'm going to do more painting at home?" said Mel.

"Oh?" I said.

"Ani's probably told you that I've had enough of being a housewife," she went on.

I blushed. This was very embarrassing, but in true Rydle style, Mel was horribly open about it all.

Apparently, Jim had grudgingly agreed to this, but there was the question of who would do the cooking and cleaning. They decided to engage an au pair, but while they were looking, Ani had to do some more cooking and help in the house. I thought that was awful, but she took it on quite cheerfully. Her father was giving her some extra pocket money for it, which she thought was a good exchange. She said she was just glad that Mel was staying. So I was glad too.

"You're a bit spoilt, Pony," she said, "with your mum and gran doing everything."

I was hurt by that but went away to think it over. Was I? Should I offer to do more? I would ask Mum.

I told my mother all about the Rydles' latest problems when we were watching the colour television one day (omitting the part where Ani eavesdropped at her parents' door). She was a bit disapproving but interested too.

"Hmm, Melissa seems to want a lot of things." She lit a cigarette. "But who can blame her? She's still quite young. Children need their mothers or stepmothers, though."

She looked thoughtful. I was afraid she would say I shouldn't see Ani any more, if there were family problems.

"Am I still allowed to see Ani, then?" I asked.

"Well, yes, I suppose so. She seems a nice girl, with good manners, even if they are Liberals and all that. You're probably a good influence on *her*," said Mum and smiled.

Phew, I can still see her. Was I a good influence? That had never occurred to me. I didn't swear *too* much and I was neat and tidy and worked hard at school. I still wanted to have a more interesting life and escape from Plymouth at some point, but I suddenly saw how much my mother did.

"Mum, can I help you more in the house? Will you teach me to cook?"

She laughed and said, "Why not? I'll teach you to make pastry at the weekend."

"What about cleaning? How do you work the Hoover?"

She laughed. "Mrs Mill does most of it, of course, but why not do your bedroom? Start tomorrow."

"Yes, I will. And now I'm going to take Hedley out."

"You're a good girl, Hazel. Thank you. Oh damn – is that the time? I need to think about supper. Perhaps we can all have beans on toast tonight, as I've got am-dram. You can help."

"Will Dad mind just beans?"

"Oh – stuff him! He can put up with it for once."

"Mum!"

CHAPTER 16

AN ESCAPE

Before I could do any more about escaping, someone else did.

Ani came rushing over to me in school break the following week. We were in different classes, so only met in breaktimes. She looked flushed and worked up.

"Pony," she said, "can I talk to you somewhere private?"

"'Course you can, Hippy," I said. This sounded exciting. "We can go round the back of the tennis courts to the bins."

We squeezed behind the bins, a popular place for illicit cigarettes and clandestine meetings, and Ani said: "Mel has run away with Josh!"

"What? You're joking!" I exclaimed. "When? How?"

"Last night," Ani said. "When we were in bed asleep. She took some luggage and Josh and went off in her Mini. She left a note. She's gone to the commune on Dartmoor, but she said not to get in touch. You know, the farm we found. Dave got to know them."

"Wow!" I said and quickly added, "Sorry, I know it's awful news, but it's just such a shock. Erm, how do you feel? How's Jim?"

"He's really upset, obviously. And Tallulah is being terrible, screaming and being babyish. I don't blame her. Dad had to drag her into the car to go to nursery school, and he had to tell the teachers. I'm OK at the moment. Well, I think I am."

"I thought Mel was happier nowadays, with her art and everything."

But when Ani continued, she said Jim had been getting on Mel's nerves and she'd seemed restless.

"I'm worried about things at home. Pony – d'you think you could come and stay with us for a few days, to kind of help me and keep Tallulah company? She says she wants you."

I liked that. To be loved by Tallulah was a big thing, since she took violent likes or dislikes to people.

"Yeah, I'll come and stay, of course I will. I'll need to ask my boring parents, though, so I'll phone you after school, OK?" I said.

We separated and went back to our classes.

I decided I'd better invent a story so my parents wouldn't know the whole truth about this situation. They might prevent me from going if they thought there would be rows and tears. *'Pas devant les enfants,'* as René said. Of course, that was exactly what I was hoping for – adult rows and dramas. I would just tell them Mel had gone away on a 'little break' and that Ani and Tallulah were lonely.

My lies worked and I was allowed to go. I packed a big shoulder bag and caught the bus to Crownhill, to the Rydle house.

An Escape

I hardly got through the door before Tallulah came hurtling downstairs, yelling "Pony! Pony!" Unfortunately, she knew about my secret name. I hugged her and took her grubby little hand.

Ani appeared and hugged me.

"You OK?" I asked.

"Yeah, yeah. Dad's in his office on the phone to a friend. We're not allowed to say anything to Mel's parents yet. Or anyone."

All I could say was "Oh dear."

"Can you come up and help me cook dinner? We're doing spag bol."

"Sure," I said, although I had never made it. "D'you want to help us, Tal?"

"Yes, yes, yes!" she shouted, grabbing at my T-shirt and clinging to me. I struggled upstairs. It was like having a human limpet attached.

"When's Mummy coming back?" she said to Ani in the kitchen.

"Soon, probably," said Ani in a reassuring voice. She whispered in my ear, "She keeps asking this every five minutes." I guessed Ani was used to disruptions, after her own parents getting divorced and all the changes afterwards.

I stood helplessly, and Ani said, "Right, you can chop these onions up and then do the mushrooms. I'll grate some cheese." We worked fast, with Ani showing me what to do. My mother's cooking lessons hadn't extended this far as yet.

Tallulah hung round, whining, so I went to the giant fridge and got out a bottle of Pepsi Cola and poured glasses for the three of us. Then we all helped to make the meal, in a rather chaotic way. We cooked the bolognese sauce and Ani and Tallulah boiled a mountain of spaghetti.

It felt good to be in charge of a household with Ani. It was a change from being told what to do at home.

"Hello, girls – gosh, well done!" said Jim, when we were ready. He sat Tallulah on his lap, for a treat, and chatted to us quite normally, as if nothing had happened with Mel.

After we had eaten and Jim had gone back to his office, we loaded the dishwasher and sat around the table, chatting. Ani got some playing cards and we played Snap with Tallulah.

A bit later, Ani asked me if I could help with Tallulah's bathtime.

"Yes, yes! Pony help me!" yelled Tal, jumping up and down. I noticed she had become rather toddler-like, probably a reaction to the difficult situation.

Tal led me down to her bedroom. I liked her room – in some ways it was cosier than Ani's, which was tasteful but rather bare. Tallulah's room was full of little girlish toys and soft colourful blankets and bean bags, in pink and white and red. Her white wooden bed was up on a platform with a ladder leading to it, and underneath was a marvellous den, strung with fairy lights and filled with cushions, colouring pens and cuddly toys. Tallulah ran into her den and threw herself onto a giant toy tiger in the corner. She lay across it, sucking her thumb. I felt very sad for her. She must have felt so confused, with her mother gone.

She stood up. "Help me," she demanded, struggling to take off her red sweater. I didn't know how to look after little children. But she stood there looking forlorn. She could probably undress on her own, but I realised she needed babying. She held her arms up and I pulled off the small sweater, being careful not to catch her tangled hair. Then she pulled down her pink dungarees, leaning on me and lifting each leg like a little horse. Next came a blue T-shirt and white socks. Finally she tore off her little white vest and pants. I found her blue fluffy dressing gown and wrapped it round her.

I had never liked little children much before this, but for a moment, I felt a surge of love, and had a funny thought – *I might have kids one day.*

"Shall we run your bath and put lots of foam in it? And we can sing sea shanties," I said.

"Yes, yes, yes!" she said. Then suddenly she collapsed against me in tears, crying, "Want Mummy, where's Mummy?" I nearly cried myself.

"She'll come soon," I lied, cuddling her. "D'you want a piggyback upstairs?"

We struggled up slowly to the bathroom, with Tallulah wiping her face in my hair.

I thought back to September, when I'd first come to the Rydles' house as a silly shy girl and sat in this bathroom while Josh had a bath. It felt like centuries ago.

For five evenings, Ani and I worked hard, like little mothers, keeping Tallulah, Jim and ourselves fed. Jim tried to help in the kitchen but was fairly hopeless. Once we had done all the chores, we did some hurried homework at the kitchen table. I had never been so busy. Jim was kind to us in a vague way, but mainly shut himself in his office, phoning people or silently doing mysterious things in there. Tallulah would be put to bed, but then wake later in tears, and ended up in bed with Ani every night. I was in Sarah's old room. We were tired at school, but we managed.

I worried most about Tallulah and hoped that Mel would get fed up with the commune and come back soon. Life in the Rydle house didn't seem *too* bad to me. It was more easy-going than my house. Was Mel fed up because Jim was older than her? Ani reckoned that Mel had got into Women's Lib. I knew something about it, as there were numerous articles in my gran's magazines. I wondered if my mother would get drawn into it. I could hardly imagine it, but then again, she did seem restless lately.

By the following week, Mel still hadn't rung, and when Jim got exasperated and phoned the commune, the others said she didn't want to talk to him. He decided to just drive there the next weekend. He also told their friends the Tremaynes about it. (I know because we were listening outside his office.) It seemed they were going to come to the Rydles' house and take over.

"Oh, God," said Ani. "Their mother is a total pain."

"Why?" I asked.

An Escape

"She's mad and hysterical, and she talks to trees."

"Oh, God. What about the father?"

"What, Henry? He just flaps around in the background, being useless. He's an auctioneer."

"I see."

"But Tallulah likes their kids, Esther and Freddy, so that'll be good, anyway."

Mum rang me the next evening. "Hello, darling," she said. "Are you having a nice time with the Rydles?"

"Well, actually…" I paused. Then I told her what was really happening. She wasn't as shocked as I expected. Quite a few of their friends were getting divorced, so it wasn't too scandalous. And Mel had only been gone a week or so. Ani sat across the kitchen table while we were talking, making funny faces at me. I mouthed 'shut up' at her and grinned. Tallulah was in Ani's bed.

"It's OK, Mum – Jim isn't becoming an alkie or anything and we're all fine," I said on the phone. My mother laughed. Ani gave me a thumbs up.

"You sound very grown up," Mum said. I could hear her talking to my father in the background. *Uh-oh!* He sounded displeased.

Mum came back. "Listen, Hazel – we think we'll come and collect you."

"Oh, no! I'm having fun here!"

Ani nodded like mad.

"Let me just talk to your father," my mother said.

Her voice grew fainter, then she came back.

"All right, we'll wait till tomorrow evening. Can you get Jim, please? I want to have a word with him."

"Can you get your dad?" I asked Ani. She made a rude face and shook her head. I started laughing. "Go on, you idiot!" I had to push her out of the kitchen.

Jim came in holding a glass of wine, with Ani in tow. His hair was on end and his shirt buttons done up unevenly. He raised his eyebrows at me.

"Parents?" he asked. I nodded. He took the phone and sat down.

"Hello there, Fenella? Yes, yes, she's fine. She's being wonderful. The girls are brilliant. Oh, well, Mel will probably come back soon. Just one of those things. Mmm? Yes, of course, do drop round tomorrow evening. Hmm? No problem. Eight o'clock, then? Great."

Jim took a swig of wine and sighed.

"How do your parents manage it, eh? Staying together, I mean."

I thought about it. Nobody had ever asked me such a thing.

"I don't know, but they do get annoyed with each other sometimes," I said. "I think my mum gets fed up."

"There you are, then," said Jim. He laughed, but not in a happy way. "Welcome to the adult world, girls! It's downhill all the way from now on," he said, getting up and going back to his office.

Ani and I looked at each other. She pulled a face.

"Let's not be adults yet," she finally said.

An Escape

"No. Shall we see what's on TV?" I said, and we went out.

* * *

I was dreading the parents' summit meeting, but it wasn't too horrendous. Mine turned up and then the three adults shut themselves in the living room with drinks, to have a serious talk. Of course we eavesdropped, with Tallulah wedged between us. We had to put our hands over her mouth, to shut her up and stop her bursting into the room. She thought it was great fun, which cheered us up.

The adults all seemed to be getting on well, which surprised me, as I had thought my parents were hideously old-fashioned compared to the Rydles. But we could hear a perfectly normal sounding-conversation and even some laughing. We rushed back to the kitchen when they got up to leave, and pretended to be busy there.

"Well, it sounds as if you two have been doing a sterling job here, running the house," said my father.

I smiled and felt wonderful. Finally we were being taken seriously.

"But we think you'd better come home for a while, and get on with things like homework and looking after Hedley," he added, which spoilt it all.

I went off to pack in a sulk, with Ani and Tallulah trailing after me and moaning.

On the way home in the car, I scowled and grumbled. "Why did you have to drag me away when we were managing so well?" It was back to childhood now.

"Hazel, they need time alone to sort things out," said my mother. "You did really well there, but it might be an idea to leave the Rydles alone for a few days, to have some time together."

"Well, they won't be alone, because the Tremaynes are coming," I said angrily.

"Oh, God, not them," said Dad. He knew nearly everyone in Plymouth. "They're a useless pair."

I had to laugh.

"There you are, then, the Tremaynes can help. Just for a few days," said my mother. "Listen – we were thinking of driving to Exeter tomorrow, for a shopping trip. You might want some more jeans."

I couldn't resist a day shopping in Exeter, where the shops were better and more trendy than Plymouth. Traitor that I was, I agreed to that and forgot the Rydles for a little while. I had to admit, it was nice to be home and be looked after, instead of rushing round cooking and fitting in homework afterwards.

The Exeter trip was a success, and I added to my jeans collection. However it took an age, driving up the A38, which was the only road to Exeter and clogged with traffic.

"They're going to build a by-pass and a motorway soon, thank God," said my father. "Called the M5."

"Oh, no," said my mother, who worried that the countryside was being ruined by roads. But my father thought it was a good idea: better roads for his beloved Triumph.

* * *

An Escape

In school the following week, Ani found me and told me that Mel was going to come back. She looked relieved, even if Mel did annoy her at times. I guess she was glad for a return to normality and for Tallulah to have her mother back.

"Mel thought the commune was too dirty and disorganised," she explained.

I agreed with her about that, remembering the squalid farmhouse and grim bathroom. I felt grateful to my mother and gran for our clean and beautiful house.

"I'm glad, 'cause Tallulah will be happy," I said. "She missed her mum."

"That's true. Anyway, Pony, thanks for helping. You were amazing. Can I come over to your house next Saturday?"

"Of course you can, Hippy." We linked our little fingers.

CHAPTER 17
I KNOW A BETTER PARK

Plymouth 2012

A shock today – Tobi called me. Said, "Servus. When are you coming back to Austria?" I felt a huge reluctance to commit. "I don't know yet, there's so much to do here." I didn't add that I'm happy here. Weather getting hot and I'm off to a beach today.

A row ensued. Began with me saying, "Hey, Eva phoned me on Sunday and said she'd seen you with Helga at the Naschmarkt. What's going on?"

"Yeah, Helga's been helping me with some research, that's all – the stuff on post-war recovery and people's needs."

More likely research on Tobi-needs.

"Oh, yeah. You think I believe that?"

And on and on, with lots of shouting and accusations and an abrupt end. But I didn't feel sad, I felt angry. To think I loved him once! Or was I in love with Austria? Must be honest. What a mess it all is! I cried a bit, but soon recovered. The thing is, I don't want to go back yet.

When I look back on the Rydle Year, I was stronger than I thought. I can be strong now. I see a way ahead.

* * *

Plymouth 1971

After all the drama of Mel's escape and helping the Rydles, I felt dog-tired. I wanted to be alone for a while. So when Ani phoned to ask me to tea, I said, "No, I have to help Mum with some things."

"What things?" she demanded.

"Um, decorating the toilet," I said, improvising.

"That sounds boring," she said.

"No, it's fun."

"OK, boring old fart, see you around." She slammed down the phone.

I didn't care. Something inside me said, *You don't always have to do what Ani wants.*

I slopped around at home or took Hedley for long solitary walks. It was good; I could think while I was walking. April had come and the weather was warm enough for jeans and T-shirts.

One day I took the dog to Mutley Park. There was a big field there and an old log where I liked to sit and daydream. I settled on the log and Hedley went off to sniff round in the long grass.

A boy appeared in the distance – it looked like Rick. I hadn't seen him properly for a long time. He was with Custard the Labrador and seemed to be heading for me. *Help! What can I say?*

Rick had changed since the terrible party in February. He'd grown taller, and as he got near, I could see that his skin was looking better. His hair was even longer than before. He still wore ugly baggy jeans, though, not Levi's. I pushed my hair back and waited.

"Hi," he said. "What you doing?"

"Just, umm, out with Hedley," I said, pointing at the dog and feeling silly. That was stating the obvious.

He stood there, shifting from foot to foot and not saying anything. The dogs raced towards each other and Hedley growled.

"Shut up, Hedley," I shouted. "Sorry about him, he's naughty." I hid my embarrassment by holding on to Hedley and making him sit.

Rick gave a small smile, then looked as if he would walk away, but turned and mumbled, "Wanna come for a walk? I know a better park than this."

"Yeah, OK," I said, feeling flushed. Was he asking me out? I didn't want to look too keen; all the magazines said you shouldn't act too keen with boys. But I couldn't resist it, even though I still preferred Chas.

We set off in silence. I racked my brain for something interesting to say, and found myself asking, "How's school?" *Oh God!* That was the sort of useless thing parents asked.

"OK," he said. "Doing O levels this summer. Sixteen in June."

I was impressed.

"I'm thirteen and I want to be an artist, but my Dad won't allow me," I blurted out.

"Oh, yeah, parents! Art's good, though. Hey – uh, I'm sorry about the party."

I was shocked at this sudden confession. But pleased.

"It's all right."

"I was pathetic with you. Sorry."

"I was pathetic too."

"I wanted to talk to you cos I think you're interesting. Most girls just giggle all the time."

I made a mental note not to mention my frequent giggling fits.

"But I'm no good at talking and I hated my mum being there and watching us. And Chas makes fun of me. He calls me Baby Boy and says I'm crap." He gave a clump of grass a vicious kick.

Hedley was trying to eat something disgusting in the gutter. I clipped his lead on and dragged him away. We were coming to a big park with lots of trees.

"I'm just an only child, so that's crap too," I said.

"No, you're quite lucky," said Rick.

"Why?"

Most people were sorry for me or said I was spoilt. It was embarrassing admitting I had no brothers or sisters.

"Yeah, really. My mum's one, and she says they're strong people and they're good at getting things done. You know, she's a psychiatrist, so she knows about it. And you're lucky not having a prick like Chas around all the time."

This was great. No one had ever said only children were OK. I did a little jump for joy.

Rick laughed. "You're a bit mad," he said. "But you're OK. Look – this is the other park."

We walked and walked and opened up about ourselves – what we liked doing and how sick we were of school and parents telling us what to do. Rick liked art. He did a lot of drawing at home. He also liked reading about history. Custard and Hedley were getting on well, after Hedley's bad behaviour at the beginning. I wondered, though – did Rick want me as a girlfriend? He didn't try to hold my hand or kiss me, but he seemed to like me. I imagined kissing him.

I sneaked a look at him. He was walking along, swinging his arms. He saw me.

"What?" he said.

"Nothing." I blushed.

I wondered if I should grab him and try to kiss him, but I didn't dare. Could we just be friends, like Ani and me? It was a strange idea, but not a bad one. It was the first time I had really talked to a boy who wasn't a relation. I liked big boys – their tallness, their long legs, their deep voices and tougher view of the world.

When we got near home, Rick reverted to his shy self again and muttered, "See you around, then," and strode into his house, as if he didn't want anyone to see us. Boys were so curious. I didn't think I'd ever understand them, or maybe I would when I was an adult – at least twenty-one.

I had a lot to think about. Life was getting nicely complicated. I wondered what Ani would think of Rick and our walk. Perhaps she would be jealous. I was starting to miss her and wanted to boast about going for a walk with a boy.

I couldn't contain myself and rang her that evening.

"Hi, Hippy – guess what? – I've been out with a boy! Well, for a walk."

"Oh, yeah. Who?"

She sounded a bit put out, no doubt because I turned down her tea invitation.

"Rick, who lives next door. I told you about him."

"What, the drippy one? Or the sexy one?"

"The younger one. But he's not drippy really. We went to Peverell Park with our dogs."

"Wowee. Did you kiss him? Are you in love? You're such a sex maniac, you probably tore his jeans off!"

"Don't be so stupid! I told you, he's not a boyfriend."

"You can tell me more soon. Anyway – Mel's back and they're all lovey-dovey."

That was good. I knew Tallulah and Jim would be so happy, but I wasn't sure exactly how Ani would feel. Would she mind being bossed around again?

"What's it like then? Is she being nicer now?"

"Yeah, well I haven't seen her much actually, 'cause she's mostly in her new art room. So it's OK. How's the decorating going?"

"The what? Oh, that. Yeah, OK, thanks."

"I don't believe you did any decorating, did you?"

"Umm, well we cancelled it. Mum was too tired."

"What a pity! Well, see you soon then."

"OK."

Ani put the phone down. I was all hot and bothered. Things felt a bit odd. Ani was still my best friend, but I had a new feeling – *Is she enough?* I pushed the thought away.

I went to look for my mother, who was walking up and down, practising her lines for the play.

"Mel's back, Mum."

"Hmm, well so she should come back. On the other hand, I can sometimes understand women wanting to run away. Cooking and cleaning aren't the be-all and end-all. I'll have a quick break from my lines, then I must get on. What are you up to?"

"Don't know – think I'll look for Granny and see if she'll play Ludo."

"That's nice."

My mother fetched a cigarette and sat down with *She* magazine. She opened it and began reading something.

"What's that?" I asked.

"Oh, nothing, just a silly article in one of Lil's magazines," she said, and turned it away from me.

"OK, see you later."

As I walked away, I looked back. At the top of the page, it said: 'The New Generation of Women. They don't want Marriage, they want Freedom.'

CHAPTER 18
AMATEUR DRAMATICS

"The first thing Mel did was kiss Dad and Tal and say hello to me, then she rushed into the spare room and said, 'Right, I'm making this into a proper studio. You've got your design room and I'm having a room too.'"

"Wow." I was curled up on the window seat in our hallway, on the phone to Ani.

"But is she bossing you about?" I asked.

"No – she seemed sort of uninterested in me. In a good way, I mean. So that's OK."

"Yeah, it is."

"And since then, she's been in her new art room most of the time. I'm still doing some cooking and helping. I'm all right, anyway, and the Austrian au pair comes soon. Hey – I was thinking we could go out to town at the weekend and go to cafés and clothes shops. We don't have to stay home *all* the time."

"Ooh, yeah, great. D'you know what – my mum wants Mel to come to the church theatre group with her! She never used to go to anything. Now she's on about this am-dram all the time."

Amateur Dramatics

"It's Women's Lib, Sarah was telling me," said Ani, knowledgeable as ever. "Wives want to be free! Anyway, we can look after ourselves now, after Mel being away. If they go out more, we can do what we want."

At that very moment, my mother appeared in the hall. She was wearing a blue and white scarf wrapped round her head, like a gypsy. She looked happy and excited.

"Is that Ani? Don't ring off, I want to talk to Mel," she said, grabbing the green phone receiver from me. I backed away, wandered into the TV room, and leant against the door to listen.

"Mel? Hi there. How are you? Oh, of course, yes, I can understand that. Well, never mind, you're back now. Actually, I wanted to ask you something – are you interested in amateur dramatics?"

They nattered on for a while and I could hear Mum arranging to meet Mel one evening at the church hall. I was astonished – surely those two wouldn't get on.

I decided to go to my bedroom and review The List. It was a long time since I'd checked it.

Go to London and get Levi's (flared) – Yes
Get a bra – Yes
Get new hairstyle – Yes
Meet some boys – Sort of – Rick?
Save money – Yes
Escape! No
Make Ani my best friend – Yes!

It was nearly complete. The only two things outstanding were to meet more boys and escape. Escaping was the biggest thing, but also the most uncertain. I still didn't know how or where I could do it, and sometimes I was too afraid to do it. But the thought of spending the rest of my life in Plymouth was unbearable. Surely there was more to life.

The following Wednesday evening, Mel arrived in her Mini and she and my mother went off to the am-dram group. My father was restless and stomped around the house, complaining and huffing. I sat with my grandmother in the kitchen. She was making his favourite stew, and I was trying (not very hard) to write a history essay about the Cavaliers and Roundheads. I was wearing Sarah's hand-me-down faded grey jeans and a stained old T-shirt.

We sat down to eat. Gran served the stew.

"Do you want potatoes?" she asked me.

"Yeah, all right," I mumbled.

"Don't say 'Yeah', say 'Yes'," ordered Dad, appearing in the doorway. The dog growled.

"Yes, then!" I snapped, scowling. They were both getting on my nerves. I longed to take the food up to my bedroom and hide there.

"I don't know what's come over you, since you stayed at the Rydles to help," he said. "You've become so offhand. And what are you wearing? You look like a down-and-out!"

Granny Lil agreed, muttering about disgraceful clothes and what other people would think.

We all chewed our meat in silence. Afterwards, my father went to watch the news.

I looked at my mother's empty chair. It felt depressing not having her there. She was always around, keeping things together, cooking, chatting, having a cigarette. She held us all together.

On impulse, I said, "I'll help you with the washing up, Gran."

I had to repeat it at top volume as she didn't hear.

As we were washing the dishes, she said, "Seen Rick, have you?"

"Not lately," I shouted.

"He's all right, he is. I should get friendly with him, if I were you. You could do with some male company. A kiss and a cuddle does you good."

"Granny!"

She laughed.

Dad looked in and said, "Have you done your homework?"

"No. Just going – no need to keep nagging me!"

As I dragged myself upstairs, followed by the dog, I could hear snatches of their talk:

"…like amateur dramatics at home too…don't need to go out for it…"

"…getting teenage moods now…"

"…so rude, can't seem to get through to her…"

"…not as bad as that Chas, though!"

I smiled at that. That was my grandmother talking. She had it in for Chas. I'd gone off him, anyway. I wondered what Rick was doing. I'd worked out that his bedroom was opposite hers. I went into her room – she wouldn't be coming up for a while. Rick's light was on. I tapped on the window and looked across. *Yes!* He was in there. He looked up, startled. I waved and he looked surprised. I beckoned.

Rick opened his window and stared out at me. I opened mine.

"Hi," I said.

"Oh, hi."

"What are you up to?"

"Just homework – maths."

"I hate maths! I've got to do some geography, but I don't mind that. My mum's gone to her drama class."

"Oh, my ma's gone to that one too! Dad had to cook and he made a right mess of it."

We laughed. Rick seemed quite friendly that evening. I decided to be bold.

"D'you want to come for a walk again?"

"Yeah, OK. I can call for you one day – say Friday at five?"

I went red hot with excitement. He was going to call round! It was a proper date. But then I heard footsteps – my father was coming upstairs. The last thing I wanted was him to catch me talking to Rick – he would probably tease me. I wrenched the curtains together, grabbed a random magazine off my gran's table, and sat on her bed.

Amateur Dramatics

"Hello, you all right? What are you doing?"

"Just reading," I mumbled.

"Was that the boys next door?"

"Sort of."

To my relief, he didn't ask any more. Instead, he said, "It's strange without Mum, isn't it? I don't really see why she wants to do all this amateur dramatics stuff."

"Well, it makes a change for her, from being here all the time."

"Why? She can go out shopping and to her coffee mornings."

"That's not very exciting, though, is it? Maybe she wants to meet new people."

"I don't see why – I like being at home with you three."

"Yes, but you go to work every day."

He frowned and hesitated. "D'you think it's this Women's Lib nonsense?"

"No, I don't think Mum would like that."

That wasn't entirely true, but I felt somehow loyal to her and didn't want to get her into any trouble.

"Well, don't be too late to bed, will you?"

I sighed. "No."

To my surprise, he said, "You're a good girl. Thanks for helping Gran." He even kissed me.

I went into my room, lay on the bed with my clothes on, and stared at the ceiling. Outside it was dusk and my room was shadowy and still. I wondered if I would feel like this when I was thirty. Or fifty. Or sixty. It was impossible to know. Too far off. What was it like, being old? Like my gran or Miss Coles up the road. Would I have children? I hoped not. They were a nuisance. Tal and Josh were cute, admittedly. But Mel had found it hard, running after them, cleaning them up, entertaining them, playing with them. Perhaps I was a nuisance too? Lots of adults didn't seem happy. What was the answer?

But I had a date! Nothing else mattered. I lay there for an age, until it was dark. My gran came up to bed and put on her radio, loud as always. I still lay there, languid, luxuriating, stretching my legs. It was like lying in a bath full of warm treacle.

Our front gate opened and shut with a clang and I heard my mother coming into the house. My father said something to her. He didn't sound very pleased. She was laughing and talking back to him. I caught a few words.

"…Wonderful, really interesting people."

And I caught his words: "…be like this every week?"

And she said, "Probably. I'm going to get a drink."

Stupid parents, I thought. *Why can't they just be happy?* I decided never to get married but travel round the world and meet unusual people. And wear interesting clothes.

* * *

The next morning, my mother looked happy and hummed to herself. She was making a pie for that evening, rolling out dough and chopping meat.

"What was it like, Mum?" I asked.

Amateur Dramatics

"Sorry, dear?"

"The am-dram."

"Oh – super. Such lovely people, real characters. Even the vicar's wife is in it. After this play by Ayckbourn, we may do a musical called *Pajama Party* and I might sing a part."

"You? Sing?"

"Oh, yes. I was a good singer at school, you know. Anyway, I'll have a go."

She did sing at home sometimes, when she was cleaning, but I didn't realise she was that good. My mother seemed to be changing into someone new. I watched her as she wiped the draining board and put dishes away. She was humming a little tune to herself. I waited, hoping she would talk to me, but she seemed far away.

I grabbed my school bag and ran to catch the bus.

CHAPTER 19
THE SISTER I NEVER HAD

Plymouth 2012

A surprise visit today! My old school friend Pat turned up on the doorstep.

"Pat! How did you know I was here?"

"Oh, you know Plymouth – everyone knows what everyone's doing. My sister Christine spotted you in town. So I guessed you were back from Austria. And we saw the announcement you put in the paper about your dear mum."

She came in for coffee and we caught up on ten years of our lives. So great to see a friend; made me stop obsessing over my problems. And she remembered things about the Rydles, which was extremely interesting. She knows Ani isn't in Plymouth any more, but thinks Josh is around. He'll be about forty now! Makes me feel old. We promised to keep in touch and she'll see if she can find out more about them.

* * *

Cornwall 1971

It was the Easter holidays and we were in the Rydles' new Range Rover, driving down to Polperro in Cornwall. They had asked me to a holiday house there, as a thank you for looking after Tal when Mel was at the commune. And it was Ani's birthday on 13th April.

Ani had piles of luggage, which did not please Mel, but we all squashed in together somehow. Sarah was due to join us a day later in her own car. Tallulah and Josh were over-excited. He could talk a bit now and was very chatty in the car.

"Pony come, Pony come with us!" he said to me, grabbing at my sleeve.

"Yes, Joshy, I'm coming with you," I said.

Tallulah squeezed next to me, wanting attention too.

"Pony – will you teach me swimming?" she asked.

"Well, I'll try," I said. I wasn't a very good swimmer.

"There's an indoor pool there," said Mel, looking back at us.

A pool – gosh. Like in a film.

"Hey, let's play I spy," said Ani. "I'll start. I spy with my little eye…"

* * *

We arrived in Polperro at midday and all piled out of the car. The house looked really new and futuristic, like something from American TV. One wall was all made of glass and the rest was like giant cubes all pushed together. My family would have hated it; they liked crumbling old houses full of antiques.

Jim unlocked the front door and we raced inside to explore.

"Let's choose our bedrooms," shouted Ani, already halfway up the stairs. Tallulah and Josh pursued us. We raced around and found a large room at the front, with a view of the sea through the glass wall. The little ones went out.

"Bags I this room for us," Ani shouted. It had two double beds on a platform and a huge bath. I was amazed. But the Rydles had a bath in every room in Plymouth, so they probably weren't impressed.

At that point, Mel appeared and put some luggage on one bed.

"Right, this is our room," she said. "Yours is at the back, girls."

I started to go out.

"Don't go, Hazel," Ani ordered. "We have a right to this room."

"Oh no, you don't," said Mel. "This is the master bedroom, and we're having it."

I hovered near the bed, watching them both.

"I'm talking to Dad," said Ani. "Dad!" she yelled.

Jim appeared, carrying Tal on his shoulders. Josh was running round his feet.

"Mel won't let us have this room," said Ani.

"Absolutely not," said Mel.

"Now come on, Ani love, there's a lovely room at the back. Off you two go."

He dumped Tallulah on one bed and she started bouncing up and down, and saying, "I want this room."

"No, darling, you're with Josh in the back bedroom," said Mel.

I backed out, not wanting any part in a row. Ani followed me, swearing under her breath, "Bloody stepmothers…"

Tallulah started screaming – "Want this room, want this room!"

"Tal, come in here with us," I called and held out my hand to her.

But Mel said, "No, leave her there. It's important she expresses herself."

Tallulah started rolling round and crying.

Then Jim said, "Tallulah May Rydle, I know a lovely ice cream shop near here. I wonder if anyone wants a super-giant strawberry ice cream sundae?"

Tallulah stopped screaming and went quiet. Then she leapt up and launched herself at Jim.

"Ice cream, ice cream, me want raspberry ripple!" she chanted. Jim picked her up and carried her out.

Mel murmured, "Thank God for that." I felt the same.

Sometimes the Rydles were too much.

Things calmed down and Ani and I settled into our back room, which was just as good as the front one and had its own bathroom. Jim gave her two pound notes to spend and she cheered up.

That evening we had a barbeque on the patio and all stayed up late, playing Charades and eating ice cream. Ani and I got very giggly and played silly games, trying to balance sausages on our heads and throwing bread at each other. But no one was that bothered because the Rydles thought everyone should express themselves. The little ones were so tired they fell asleep on the sun loungers and had to be carried to bed at around midnight.

We overslept the next day, when Sarah was due to arrive. When I finally got up, I became terribly excited as I hadn't seen her for ages. I really wanted to ask her for advice again and just be with her.

A smart red sports car drew up and Sarah got out. Still sleepy in our pyjamas, we went outside to meet her. Sarah was thinner than before, and had a new shorter haircut, so you could see her silver earrings. She was as pretty as ever.

"Hello, trouble, how's it going?" she said to Ani, kissing her.

"How are *you*?" she asked me and smiled. "We'll have to have a good chat."

"We're going to the beach," shouted Tallulah, dancing around in a frilly red swimsuit.

Josh followed her, shouting, "Beachy, beachy."

"Shall we three stay here by the pool?" Sarah suggested.

Ani and I got dressed and we all sat together and had a late breakfast of sticky cakes, which Sarah had brought with her, and big cups of coffee. It was beautifully quiet without the little kids.

"I'm thirteen now," I told Sarah.

"Wow, and you look good," she said.

"And I'm thirteen on Tuesday," Ani reminded us. "Do I look good too?" she said, shaking her hair and pushing nearer to Sarah.

"Of course, you're as gorgeous as ever," said Sarah.

They both looked similar, the same freckles and faces, despite Ani being chubbier and fairer.

"I've got some news for you both – I've got an exchange place at an art college in Paris and I'm going in June."

I stopped dead. This wasn't good news – it was bad news. Sarah would be going further away. I always thought she would be around and visiting Plymouth and that I could get friendlier with her. But things always seemed to change. Now Sarah was going abroad. She would probably forget me.

I hung my head and said nothing.

"That's fabulous," said Ani.

"I don't want you to go," I said in a small voice.

"What's that, Hazel? Oh, don't worry, it's only for a year. Hey – you two could visit me once I get a flat."

I was dubious. People always said that sort of thing, like René in London, and then they didn't keep their promises, or just ignored you and sided with other adults.

Ani stood up. "Just going to the toilet," she said.

Sarah got some cigarette papers and tobacco out and started to make a fat cigarette. I watched her.

"Sarah," I said, "I just wanted to say that I'm glad I know you. I haven't got a sister. You're like, like – the sister I never had." I blushed, afraid of being laughed at.

"Oh, sweetheart," she said, and smiled at me. I was afraid I would cry. "It's hard for you, isn't it, being the only one? But I've got a feeling you're going to do great things one day. Just keep on going."

"Thank you," I said. *Does she mean it?*

"Can I ask you something, Sarah?" I went on. This was horribly embarrassing. "The thing is…well, I've started periods, but I don't like to ask Mum for help."

"Jesus, you poor girl," she said, shaking her head. "Aren't you finding it easier with her?"

"Oh, yeah, I've done a lot since I saw you. I think I've grown up more. But this is, well, awkward. My mother never says anything about it."

Ani reappeared now. She had heard this.

"She has to run around in gym lessons with no pads, just tissues, and her pants get soaked with blood," said Ani. "At least she's started, though; I haven't properly."

"OK, OK," I said, flushing dark red and wanting to hide.

Sarah said, "Look, no hassle, I'll give you some pads of mine. And I'll take you to buy some, all right?"

She was so wonderful.

Later, Sarah drove us to Polperro and we found a chemist where she bought me some thin pads. I was so relieved, I could have cried. She bought Ani some, too, ready for when she started. Sarah said I should just buy them myself in future without asking my mother. Incredibly, that hadn't occurred to me, but I guessed I didn't need to ask my mother for *everything* any more.

Sarah wanted to see some friends, so Ani and I were let loose in Polperro and behaved appallingly, running in and out of shops and knocking into people and being cheeky to them, buying vast amounts of sweets and make-up, giggling a lot and eyeing up the local boys. She was worse than me, for once, and egged me on, saying I should go and talk to two boys who were lurking by the harbour wall.

The boys had seen us. They were leaning against the wall and smiling. One was tall and dark and good-looking. The other was of medium height with nice brown hair but some spots. They were wearing denims and looked very cool.

"I'll have the dark one," I whispered to Ani.

"No you won't," she said.

I pushed her. "You go."

She strolled over.

"Hi there. "

"Hi, girls," said the dark one. "You on holiday here?"

"Yep. Are you from round here?"

"Yeah, 'fraid so."

The dark one was confident. I walked over, feeling terrified. I could feel a blush coming on.

"She's blushing. You afraid of us or something?"

"No," I said. *I must remain cool.* Thank God I had put on my Levi's.

We waited. I really wanted to get to know them. I'd talked to Rick in the park and it was fine, so why shouldn't we talk to these boys?

The two boys moved away a few yards and talked together. I caught snatches:

"Nice tits…pretty…tall one…the little fat one…sexy…nice blonde hair…"

Ani looked annoyed. "I'm not bloody fat," she said, looking down at her waist.

"Well…" I said, "you're just a bit…curvy."

She scowled at me. "Thanks for nothing. Anyway, I don't fancy either of them; it's just a laugh."

"Want to go for a walk and we'll show you round?" said the dark one, coming back towards us.

We shrugged.

"Yeah, could do," said Ani.

We set off and exchanged names. The dark one was Steve; the spotty one was Piran, which we all giggled at nastily. Unusual names didn't go down well. You had to be a Tracy, Dawn or Kevin to succeed.

"It's a Cornish name. His dad's a Cornish nationalist," said Steve.

"Oh, we like them, and we're fans of John Pardoe," said Ani.

"You what?" said Steve.

"The MP, stupid."

We set off in a gaggle, all quite shy. When we did talk, it was all about what schools or colleges we were at, what music we liked, what we did in Plymouth. Piran attached himself to me. I fancied Steve much more, although I soon saw he was actually quite stupid and big-headed. Piran was less good-looking but nicer and more intelligent. *Typical*, I thought. *Why can't he be good-looking AND clever?*

Piran and I talked about our pets. His mother had two Persian cats. I described Hedley. We wandered along the coast path, not noticing the pretty scenery or anyone else. Piran was in his last year at tech college in Saltash and would be leaving that summer to train as a mechanic. He even had his own Honda motorbike. He seemed impossibly adult.

We stopped and looked out to sea. I was secretly watching Piran like a hawk, wondering if he would touch me. I wouldn't have minded. He moved a little closer and slowly put his arm round me.

"Want a kiss?" he asked.

"Uh, OK," I said. *Might as well give it a try.*

He turned and pulled me gently to him. We had a bumpy kiss, just lips against lips. He tasted quite good, like chewing gum. I pulled back.

"Thanks," he said, nothing more.

"That's OK," I said.

We walked a while in silence. Ani and Steve had disappeared ahead. God knows what they were doing. We chatted a bit more, about what Polperro was like ("boring") and what Piran thought of Plymouth ("a dump").

I checked my watch. It was four thirty already. Time had flown by.

"We should go back. It's getting late," I said.

"Oh, come on, don't go yet," said Piran.

"Ani," I shouted. "Ani! Where are you?"

She and Steve appeared, looking red and flustered. "Hi there!" said Ani.

"We should go, it's getting late," I said.

"Oh, hell, we should," she said, looking at her watch.

She hurried over to me and we linked arms.

"Meet us later, back here? We've got lager," said Steve.

"We'll try, at seven," she said.

I knew we wouldn't.

Piran looked keen. He wasn't too bad, really.

"See you," he said. The boys turned and sloped off along the coast path.

We clung to each other, giggling triumphantly.

"What a laugh," said Ani. "Did you get a kiss? I did, and more."

"Yeah, I did," I said, sounding nonchalant. I felt a bit bad about Rick back in Plymouth, but he wasn't exactly my boyfriend.

We walked down to Polperro and spotted Sarah in the distance. She waved to us and we started running.

"Oh – where have you two been? I was looking everywhere," she said.

My father probably would have blown up, and I thanked God he wasn't there.

"We were on a date," I said.

"It wasn't a proper date!" said Ani.

"Yes, it was." I glared at her.

"No it wasn't."

Sarah smiled.

"Well, whatever it was, I'm glad to see you both. Are you OK?"

"Fine," said Ani. "We just went for a walk with two blokes. Nothing happened."

Nothing and everything. I felt brilliant. I wasn't going to tell Rick, though. He still had potential.

We spent the rest of the week with the whole family and I wasn't in the least homesick. There were trips to the beach, clothes trying-on sessions in our bedroom, whispering in bed late at night and playing in the luxurious pool with Tal and Josh. I wasn't a very good swimmer, but because of that I was patient with Tallulah and even got her swimming a few strokes by the end of the week. Mel was impressed.

"You're so good with her, Hazel," she said. "I can see you being a teacher one day."

I was thrilled to be good at *something*. I wondered what I would do for a job, in the future. I still wanted to be an artist, but my father was opposed to it. Perhaps there were other interesting things out there, like teaching or doing something with languages. It all felt a long way off.

After swimming, we joined Josh and Tallulah, who were sprawled on the floor in the lounge, watching *Gus Honeybun's Birthdays* on television. This was a ridiculous slot on local TV, where a puppet rabbit accompanied a TV presenter reading out birthday cards to young viewers. Gus bounced up and down, winked and wiggled his ears for everyone. Officially, Ani and I scoffed at it, being sophisticated teenagers (or nearly), but secretly we enjoyed it too, and we lay on the floor and watched with them.

When Ani turned thirteen, I gave her a little box of eye shadows in blues and greens and lurid blue nail varnish I'd bought in Plymouth before the holiday. She loved it all. Jim had arranged a surprise pony-riding day for us both. Mel had secretly brought our riding clothes and produced them with a flourish. She could be very kind sometimes, although it occurred to me that this also gave her a break from the demands of Tallulah and Josh. She drove us to the stables and we spent a blissful day, riding with a group along country lanes. We returned that evening, stinking of horses but tired and happy. We headed straight for the swimming pool. Jim, Sarah and the other children were out somewhere.

"Well, teenager, what d'you want to do when you're older?" I asked Ani as we floated in the shallow end.

"Be rich and have fun," she said promptly.

"Oh yeah, how will you do that?"

"Well, I've got money already. I'm going to look out for a wealthy man. He must be handsome too," she said. "And I'll probably go to art college."

She had it all worked out, unlike me.

"What about you?"

"I don't know," I said. "I just want an interesting life. No kids. I want to travel and do artistic things. We should still think about you-know-what…I mean escaping…I know – maybe you can come to Ibiza with us.

"Sounds good, thank you," she said, but didn't expand on this. "Come on, let's do some swimming."

Sarah appeared in a black bikini and dived in. She was a great swimmer. I splashed around in the shallow end, trying to improve. Ani wasn't very good either. But Sarah didn't make fun of us. We had a happy time, chatting, swimming in the shallows and laughing.

I loved those days with Sarah. Being an only child was so hard in some ways. You had to fight for things alone. I will always remember Sarah saying that you could change things if you wanted.

At the end of the week, she asked me for my address and said we should keep in touch. I gave it to her but wondered if she would.

As we headed home in the Range Rover, I thought about the coming summer. Ibiza sounded amazing. I had a feeling that something big was going to happen there.

A few days later, my father rang Jim Rydle and arranged for Ani to come to Ibiza with us. Or, as Ani put it, "Dad has given your dad a big cheque, so it's all on!"

Being rich had its advantages.

CHAPTER 20
REALMUM

It was May. Time to dig out summer dresses and shorts and sandals (and see if they still fitted). I took the dog for long walks in the park and eyed up boys. I still liked Rick but I hadn't seen him lately as he was closeted at home, revising for O level exams. I was determined not to chase him. All the magazines like *Jackie* and *Fab 208* said you shouldn't appear too desperate with boys.

One Saturday in May half term, I was slopping round in my pyjamas. My mother had arranged to go to an am-dram course that day in Exeter. Even more surprising, she and Mel had become friends and Mel was driving them there. Granny Lil was away at our cousins and I had been instructed to make beans on toast for supper later. My father was in one of his tetchy moods, feeling neglected and deprived of proper meals. But no one else was bothered and he was ignored. I longed to get out and escape the atmosphere at home, so I rang Ani to see what she was doing.

Sarah answered the phone, not Ani. That was a surprise.

"Hi, Hazel. Yeah, I'm just on a flying visit to Plymouth. Hey – d'you want to meet me and Ani for coffee somewhere?"

"Oh yes."

She called out to Ani. "Hey, little sister, shall we get together with Hazel for coffee?"

I could just about hear Ani saying, "Sure," since Josh and Tal were making such a racket in the background.

"OK, honey, meet us at ten thirty. Shall we say Fuller's café?"

"OK."

Fuller's sounded great. I was getting bored, always meeting at my house or Ani's, and she felt the same. We wanted to spread our wings. I went to choose what clothes to wear. My Levi's were getting rather faded with all the washing, but that made them look even better. I chose a blue T-shirt to go with them. My father had dashed out to the shops and the house was quiet.

I left a note saying where I was going and fetched my shoulder bag. The dog looked at me hopefully, but I hardened my heart. "No, you're not coming. I'll take you out later." I slid out of the door, keeping him in with my foot, and caught the bus to the shops. I felt alone and free, sailing down the hill to the town centre, with no parents to supervise me.

Sarah and Ani were in the café already, chatting away. Sarah was all in black and Ani was wearing a red shirt and jeans. I sighed and wished I had a sister. But it was pointless thinking this.

Sarah got up and hugged me and Ani blew me a kiss.

"What are you having? We've got white coffees."

"I'll have that please," I said. Ani went to buy one.

Sarah pushed her hair back, as she always did, and asked, "What have you been up to, Hazel? Doing any more drawing?"

"Yep, and reading loads of books. But it's nice to come out. I'm sick of being at home."

"Me too," said Ani, returning with my coffee. "Mel isn't being so bossy now, anyway, and she looked happy about going off with your mum today."

"I can't believe they're friends now. I thought they were so different," I said, stirring my coffee.

"I know!" said Ani, laughing. "I thought your mum was a bit square…but she's quite cool really."

That annoyed me, but I shrugged.

"Well, it's great they can both have a new interest and get away from domestic things," Sarah remarked.

That was a good point. I now accepted that our mothers needed more freedom.

"Anyway, how about your real mother?" I asked Ani. "When are you going to see her in Dorset? Or is she coming to Plymouth?"

There was a silence and then Ani went bright-red, then white. Sarah stared at me in a strange way.

"What's the matter?" I asked, suddenly nervous.

Ani was looking down at her drink. Sarah stared at me with an unreadable expression.

"I think you've got the wrong end of the stick, Hazel," said Sarah.

"What d'you mean? Ani – what does Sarah mean?" But Ani wouldn't look at me.

Then she jumped up, knocking over her coffee, and fled. Some other customers looked at us.

Sarah mopped at the mess with a napkin, then reached across and took my hand.

"Hazel," she said, very serious, "the thing is…our mother died four years ago. Of cancer."

"What? Why? I mean, why did Ani tell me she lived in Dorset? Why did she lie?"

"I don't know, honey. I'm as confused as you." Sarah reached for her leather shoulder bag. "Look – let's drink up and go after Ani, and make sure she's OK."

I nodded, blushing and fumbling for my shoulder bag. I looked out of the window but Ani had gone.

"Don't worry, hon, it's not your fault. Ani didn't tell you, for some reason. We'll find her and try to sort this out. OK?"

We got up. A few people were still staring at us, enjoying the drama, but we ignored them. We weren't sure which direction to go in but decided to walk to Royal Parade and look for her.

We spotted Ani in the distance, walking slowly past the shops. We ran after her and I shouted, "Pony, wait for us!" I was afraid she would be angry with me.

"Are you OK, honey?" Sarah called.

Ani kept walking, keeping her distance.

"Let's go to the Hoe and have a walk there," said Sarah, loud enough for her to hear.

Realmum

The Hoe was quiet. It was a cool windy day and people were sheltering in cafés. Ani stopped and gazed at the sea. We joined her and both stood, waiting.

"Let's get an ice cream," said Sarah, after a while. She walked away to find a kiosk.

Ani finally opened her mouth and said, "Sorry, Pony." She still wouldn't look at me.

"It's OK, Hippy," I said, "I'm sorry about your mum, I really am. But it's all right."

She mumbled something.

"What?" I asked.

"I said – I was trying to impress you," she blurted out. She started crying. "You're so lucky, having a real mother. I was jealous of you, that's all. I know it was stupid of me and childish."

I was shocked to the core. I never thought Ani was jealous of me. She normally seemed so confident and strong. She must really miss her mother. Realmum would never come back. It was terrible. I tried to imagine my mother dying. She annoyed me at times, but to lose her would be unbearable.

I reached over and linked my arm in Ani's.

"Don't worry, we're still friends. It doesn't matter. It's better if I know the truth. Look, Sarah's coming back with ice creams."

We walked along, looking at the sea, licking our freezing ices. It was a good place to be after the shock and upset. The salty wind blew in our faces and seemed to help.

"Life is full of ups and downs. You just have to keep going," said Sarah finally. Realmum had been her mother, too, after all.

"We're going on holiday to Ibiza in July; that'll be good," I said. Ani nodded. She was still quiet, but she kept her arm in mine. Usually, Ani was the strong one. I felt extremely sorry for her, but simultaneously found it a heady experience, being the more adult one.

I kept mulling over what had happened and trying to understand it. Why had Ani lied for so long? It was just as well I had found out the truth. I wondered what Sarah thought about it all, but I couldn't really ask her, not in front of Ani. She was subdued too.

We all caught the bus home and I got off before Ani and Sarah.

"I'll see you soon," I said. Sarah waved and smiled. Ani nodded and waved.

I had seen a new side to Ani – a vulnerable one. When I got home, I took Hedley for a long walk so I could think about it all. People seemed to be all mixed up – not totally happy or totally confident or totally bad. I thought about my own mother too. Perhaps I should be nicer to her. She spent lots of time looking after me, and I wasn't very grateful sometimes.

When I got home, my grandmother was back. I tidied up the kitchen and started getting out the baked beans and bread for supper. Then I laid the table.

My grandmother said, "Oh, good girl. I was going to do that. Your mother will be pleased."

I smiled. "I'll make you a cup of tea, Gran," I shouted. I decided to be nicer to her, too.

"Thank you, I feel a bit poorly today," she said.

I noticed how slowly she was walking, in her old pink slippers. She suffered from arthritis and rarely complained. It struck me how unpleasant old age might be.

Soon after, my mother arrived back from her course in a flurry. She radiated excitement and happiness, saying it was fantastic and such a liberation. I wondered if she really meant *like Women's Liberation.*

"Mel loved it too. She really is a nice girl," said Mum, helping herself to a glass of red wine. She spotted the ready-laid table and pan of beans.

"Oh, you angel. Thank you."

"Do you know what, Mum? Ani made it all up about her real mother. She died four years ago. Sarah told me."

My mother stopped and looked aghast. "My God, that's terrible," she said. "What a thing for a little girl to go through. You must mean a lot to her."

"I suppose I do," I replied. It was a sobering thought. I stroked Hedley, who was sitting by my feet.

I asked myself – *Do I really want to escape? Or am I being a stupid little girl?* But at that point my father came in and started complaining about the meal, wanting meat and vegetables, and I thought, *Yes, I have to escape – one day anyway.*

CHAPTER 21
UNDER THE BLANKET

The truth about Ani's mother changed things for me. My world tilted and shifted: I had learnt that things were not always what they seemed, and that we lie to impress, to protect ourselves, to give the right impression. I didn't blame her, though; if anything, it brought us closer and I felt protective towards her.

I had my period. It was really beginning to hurt me every month, but at least I had pads now and Sarah had given us tampons to wear for sports lessons. But periods were still taboo in many ways and we kept them secret from other girls and parents. Something extremely humiliating happened that weekend, which brought this home.

Ani had come for a sleepover. My mother was encouraging me to invite her over more, after the revelation about Realmum. She thought Ani needed special attention and some mothering. We were playing round upstairs trying on make-up when the doorbell rang. It was Rick. He looked rather sheepish and said, "Hi. I'm gonna have a party tomorrow. Two of my cousins are staying. Mum and Dad are going out. D'you want to come?" He looked at Ani.

Under the Blanket

"She can, too, if she wants," he said.

"Oh, this is Rick from next door," I said.

"Hi there," she said. Rick nodded.

"Yeah, we'll come, thank you," I said. "Shall we bring a bottle?" Bottle parties were the in-thing, according to my teen magazines. My father probably wouldn't notice if we removed one or two bottles from his beer collection.

"Yeah, bring some drink. We'll have records too." He stood there, shuffling his feet, looking awkward. I still liked him, but just wished he wasn't so shy. I could see myself in him and didn't like it. The same build, same colouring, same maddeningly awkward manner. His skin was clearing up at least. *One day he could be handsome.*

"OK, see you at seven tomorrow," Rick said and loped away.

"He fancies you," said Ani.

"Oh yeah? D'you think so?" I asked, feeling pleased.

"Yep. Of course, he's a bit of a drip," she added, ruining it. I made a face at her.

"Well, d'you want to go? It could be a laugh. We could get drunk."

"Yeah, let's go. Will your parents let us, though?"

"I'll think of something," I said. I thought I would burst. *A party! With boys! Well, one boy.* Maybe more were coming.

My mother thought the party was a great idea. My father was more suspicious.

"Will his parents be there?" he asked.

"Oh yes," I assured him.

"All right then. They seem a good family." He was obsessed with that sort of thing. I suspected he was already worried about me getting pregnant. He was always harping on about unmarried mothers.

"You can take a bottle of sherry."

"Oh, Dad, honestly! No one wants sherry."

"All right, all right, what then?"

"Can we have some cans of your beer?"

"All right, don't drink too much, though. Take some Coke too."

"I think it sounds lovely fun," said my mother. "Think of all those *dishy* boys you'll meet."

We giggled. No one said 'dishy' any more.

"They're only next door, they can't come to any harm," said my mother. She seemed to worry less about me these days, which suited me perfectly. Perhaps it was the effect of the amateur-dramatics classes, where she was meeting all sorts of unconventional people.

We spent a long time preparing on the Saturday evening. Ani got out purple eye shadow which we'd bought in Boots, and put it on me, and I made up her face. We both applied her blue nail varnish and waved our hands around to dry it. I wore my lilac zip-up minidress, with white tights. It was getting a little short and tight as I was still growing fast. Ani put on her long, black lacy dress. I felt unbelievably excited. I'd never been to a teenager's party before.

Under the Blanket

We rang Rick's doorbell, clutching our beer. The house seemed quiet but then I heard laughing from upstairs.

He answered the bell, wearing his usual scruffy jeans and check shirt.

"Hi," he said. Two girls appeared in the hall. The cousins. They were wearing scruffy jeans too. I instantly realised we had got it wrong and shouldn't have dressed up. But it was too late. I fidgeted with my too-short dress and handed Rick the beer.

"Lager? OK," he said. I don't think he noticed our clothes.

"And Coke," I said.

Ani was already going in and saying hi to the girls. I could see them scrutinising our party dresses.

"I'm Elaine and this is Pam," the taller one said. They were both pretty in a robust way, with black curly hair and round faces. Unfortunately, they looked very confident.

"Is anyone else here?" I asked. I had thought it was going to be a proper party with lots of people.

"No, just us," said Rick. I wondered if he minded being with all these girls, but he looked quite happy.

"We live in London," said Pam. "It's much more fun than Plymouth," she added, looking bitchy. I decided I didn't like her.

"We go to London sometimes," I said, on the strength of one visit.

Pam laughed and said, "Come on, Rick, let's get some drinks and go upstairs."

We followed them all into the kitchen. It looked a mess. There were bottles everywhere and dirty plates and food and teenage magazines lying on the table.

"So where are all your parents?" I asked.

"Gone to some boring old theatre," said Elaine. "They don't know we're having a party. We got rid of Chas, too, 'cause he would just spoil it. He's gone to his girlfriend. Probably going to try and sleep with her."

I was relieved.

"How did you get rid of Chas?" I asked, knowing how intractable he was.

"I bribed him with two quid and lent him my Emerson Lake and Palmer LP," said Rick.

Rick got some beer cans and handed them round. There was no food. I decided to get drunk for the third time in my life. The first was the peaches in brandy meal with the Rydles; the second was my thirteenth birthday.

"Come on, let's go up to my room and play records," he said.

I'd never been in his bedroom before, only seen it from our house. It was interesting: the walls were painted dark-blue and the curtains were purple. Two big candles burnt on a saucer, but that was the only light. He had a black bedspread and cushions on his large bed. There was a record player in one corner, which made me jealous, and posters of rock groups on the wall.

The girls flung themselves on his bed and sprawled about. Rick sat on the floor by the record player. Ani plumped down on the floor, leaning against the bed. I sat next to her. I suddenly felt horribly shy and tongue-tied. Rick was less shy though, with his cousins there. He seemed to know them well and was showing off this evening.

Ani nudged me and pulled a face. That made me feel better.

"I don't like his cousins," I whispered in her ear.

"They're cows," she whispered back.

I took a long swig of beer from my can and winced at the bitter taste. Rick put on a record. It was wailing electric guitar music, with no singing.

"What group is that?" I asked.

"Don't you know? Oh, man," said Elaine.

"I know loads of groups, just not that one," I said.

"It's the Pink Fairies," said Rick. "Don't be a know-all, El," he said. He smiled at me and handed me the record sleeve. It was called *Uncle Harry* and was pink with a picture of a pig on it.

"Who do you like, then?" said Pam.

"We like Pink Floyd, T Rex, Velvet Underground and the Stones," announced Ani, and burped.

"Not bad for *Plymouth* girls," Elaine said.

I bristled at that. I also felt scared of her. She looked older than us – about fifteen. I thought Pam was more our age.

Ani and I both downed some beer and I began to feel more relaxed. No one did anything, just played records and drank. A pleasant blurry feeling overcame me. Pam and Elaine had gone quiet.

Rick went to change the record and turned it up loud, and then, instead of sitting by the record player, he came and sat next to me.

"What d'you think of the music?" he said.

It was so loud, I had to move nearer to him, so our legs touched. "It's good. You've got a lot of LPs." I could smell his hair – it had a fruity scent of shampoo and I thought he had aftershave on too. We looked at each other for a moment. His hair had grown again and it looked better. He had slight stubble on his chin. I had a sudden urge to kiss him, but didn't dare.

"Can you get me more beer?" I asked him.

"Yeah, one minute," he said and heaved himself up. He seemed quite drunk already. He disappeared out of the room. I sneaked a look at Elaine and Pam, but they were still lying on the bed, whispering together.

Ani moved over to me.

"Do you fancy him?" she asked me in an undertone.

"Yeah, I think so," I said. "Do you mind?"

"Nah, he's not my type. I'll just get drunk. I fancy one of Dave's friends actually – he's called Rod and he's in a group. Plays guitar."

"Oh, do you?" I was glad she didn't fancy Rick. I felt floaty and excited.

Rick reappeared with more beer and sat back next to me.

"Let me feed you some beer," he said. He held the can to my mouth and started pouring it in. Some spilt down my dress, but I didn't care. We both laughed.

Under the Blanket

"Let me do it now," I said. I held my can to his mouth. He put his arm round me. I could feel him trembling and had a feeling he hadn't done this before. We sat jammed together, enjoying the music.

"I like your dress," Rick said in my ear.

"I like your shirt," I answered, trying to pull the dress down over my knees.

I turned to look at him. He leant towards me. Our mouths made contact and we kissed for a while, and then our teeth clicked together and we pulled apart, flustered.

A voice interrupted somewhere above us – "Hey, excuse us, lovers – we're bored. Can you stop snogging and play some games with us?"

It was the odious Elaine, hanging over the edge of Rick's bed. She and Pam were ready for trouble.

"Not now," said Rick.

"Oh, come on, Ricky, you're supposed to be the host," said Pam.

"OK, all right then," said Rick but he kept his arm round me.

Ani looked quite drunk, but sat up and said, "What are we going to play then? What about Charades?"

"Are you kidding? That's for babies. We know a much better game, don't we Pam?" said Elaine.

"We do," said Pam. "Have you ever heard of Under the Blanket?"

"No," we all said. I had a feeling it wouldn't be fun.

"Right, one person has to sit under a blanket," she said. "And they have something ON them that we all want. The one under the blanket has to guess what. If they get it wrong, they take it off."

I shuddered. This sounded ominous. I struggled to sit up.

"Gotta go the toilet," I mumbled. I hoped that if I spent an age in the toilet, I might miss the game. When I stood up, I felt dizzy. I must have been more drunk than I thought. But as I had never been very drunk before, I didn't know what it was like.

I staggered out into the dark hall and looked for the toilet. One part of me wanted to get back to Rick soon, to be close to him and carry on kissing him. The other part wanted to hide from those terrible cousins. I found the toilet and sat on the cold seat. I weed and then just sat there, in a half dream. My period was hurting. I got a clean sanitary pad out of my bag and put it on. Nobody knew except Ani; everyone always kept periods secret.

I must have had a little nap in there, as I was woken by voices and giggling.

"Is she still in there? Come on out, Hazel, *dear*, we're ready for you."

The cousins were in the hall.

"What?" I said.

"You're going to star in Under the Blanket!" they exclaimed. I groaned. They started hammering. I forced myself up and spoke through the door.

"Why have I got to?"

Under the Blanket

"Because Rick's the only boy and it's not fair and Ani's too drunk and we know what happens already. Come on, it's a laugh. Are you afraid?"

I came out cautiously.

Pam said, "It's the wildest game you'll ever play and you won't forget it, will she, Elaine?"

"No, she won't," said Elaine, coming right up to me. "Come on, Hazel," she said in a false-nice voice, "you'll be brilliant at it."

"OK," I said, wary and still quite drunk. Maybe we could get this over quickly.

"Everyone – Hazel's going to play," announced Elaine. "You all sit in a circle on the floor, and Hazel goes in the middle."

Ani and Rick looked tired and drunk, like me, but they did what Elaine told them and she pulled a blanket off Rick's bed.

"Right – Hazel – you get under it and sit down," she ordered.

"Now, you've got something ON you, but you have to guess what," said Pam.

"My necklace?" I said.

"No, take it off and throw it out on the floor."

"My shoes?"

"No." The two girls cackled, like a pair of evil witches.

This continued for a while, with me stripping off my clothes till I was down to my pants. I was desperate. The pad inside felt damp and hot. What on earth did I have on that they wanted? Did they know about the pad? It was zero hour. I blushed and sweated and felt I would never escape.

I heard Rick say, "I'm gonna put another record on. Wait a minute."

A song started up and Ani asked what it was. "'See Emily Play'," Rick told her. I knew that one, it was Pink Floyd.

I sat still under the blanket, almost in tears. Did the girls know I had my period? Did they want my pants? Why didn't Ani say something? I couldn't face being naked. And they would see my pad. This was a horrendous game.

The girls started shaking the blanket up and down, roaring with laughter.

"It's ON you," they kept saying. "It's ON you."

I tried to be tough – I would have to take off my pants. It was the worst game I'd ever played.

Ani said, "Come on, this is pathetic, let Hazel out. We don't know the answer."

Rick joined in – "This is crazy – stop it now, El."

Finally Elaine said, in a smooth voice, "OK, darling – do you give up?"

Thank God this is going to finish, I thought.

"Yes, I give up," I said. I curled into a little ball, terrified they would tear the blanket off me and show everyone my naked body with the pad under me.

"OK," said Elaine. "So the answer is…it's the BLANKET! Harharhar!"

The two cousins rolled round on the floor in hysterics.

Under the Blanket

She chucked all my clothes at me under the blanket and waited a few minutes while I dressed in a desperate hurry. Then she tore the blanket off.

I crawled out slowly, totally relieved the ordeal had finished, but angry with her and angrier with myself at being so thick and compliant and not guessing it was the blanket.

"Wot a laugh!" said Elaine. "I'm gonna get more drink now." She went out. Pam followed.

"That was a rubbish game," said Ani and came over to me on all fours.

"You OK?" She offered me a drink from her can.

"Yeah," I said and pretended I was fine. "That was crazy," I said. I collapsed on my back to recover.

"Sorry about them, they're a pain," Rick said and crawled over to me.

I lay there, hating the cousins but deeply happy it was over. "I'm hungry," I said.

"I'll get some food," said Rick and disappeared.

"What a pair of cows," said Ani.

"You could have done something," I pointed out.

"Sorry, Pony, I was sort of paralysed and drunk. I didn't know what would happen."

"You know I've got my period? I was afraid they would tell everyone, I mean Rick."

Ani stroked my hair. "Sorry, Pony, I forgot that."

I lost track of time but Rick came back eventually and waved some Ritz Crackers and cheese above my face.

"Feed me," I mumbled.

Rick slowly pushed bits of food into my mouth and I chewed it all up. But as soon as I'd finished, I began to feel ill.

"Feel sick," I muttered and started crawling to the toilet.

"I do too," said Ani. We both made for the toilet on all fours and I just got there in time before puking up. It was disgusting but I instantly felt better after it. I washed my face in icy water and went back to the bedroom. Ani was sick after me.

I wanted to be with Rick again. The drink had made me more daring.

He was sitting by the bed, his head between his legs. I threw myself down next to him and leant on him.

"Are you OK?" I asked.

"Feel ill," he said.

"I'll look after you," I said and put my arm round him. He leant against me.

"D'you want to be sick?"

"No, just lie down." He stretched out on the floor and I lay next to him. His check shirt felt soft and smelt of clean cotton. Although I had just been ill, and been humiliated in the blanket game, I felt happy just to be with Rick. I could tell he liked me. We both lay there, cuddled up together in the warm darkness, and I thought, *I'm with a boy who likes me and I never want this to finish.*

But things never last. I must have slept but was woken by lights being switched on and adults' voices. I tried to think what was going on. Then I remembered I was next door, at Rick's house. It was Judy and Alan Atkinson, back from the theatre, and there were voices of other adults – the cousins' mother and father, I supposed.

I heard Judy say, "Look at you, like the Babes in the Wood. Have you been having a party?" She didn't sound cross, just amused. I felt extremely embarrassed.

The two cousins had disappeared a while ago, probably to their room. They would no doubt pretend it was all our fault, later on. Ani sat up, blinking.

"There's another one there," said Alan. "Hello there. Who are you?" He didn't seem to mind.

"Oh, hello," said Ani. "I'm Ani, Hazel's friend." She was never shy. She actually got up and shook hands.

"We'd better go," I said, moving away from Rick. It was too late, though; his parents had seen us cuddled up. Judy was smiling and staring at the two of us.

I stood up unsteadily and said, "Thank you for the party," in an idiotic voice to Rick, as if we'd just had an eight-year-old's birthday party with cake and little games.

"It's OK," he said but didn't budge from the floor. "Go out with the dogs next week?"

"Yeah. Shall I ring you?"

"OK."

"Come on," said Ani, dragging me by the arm. I was glad we only had to stagger next door as I felt distinctly queasy again.

"Bye, girls," Judy called out. "Come back another time." She watched us go back to my house.

We had to ring the bell to be let in. I had no wish to see my parents. I was afraid they would be angry with us, or nosy. All that happened was that my father smelt my breath and said, "Have you been drinking?"

I felt proud and said, "Yes, we have actually."

All he said was "Go and clean your teeth."

My mother was in the background, holding a drink. She looked rather cross, but not with me, with him.

"Everyone deserves to have fun," she said to him in a funny tight voice. "Up to bed, girls, now. See you in the morning."

We said goodnight and staggered upstairs. I was in a state of shock, after all the events at Rick's party – being with Rick, kissing Rick, getting drunk, the blanket game. But most of all, I felt happy about Rick. He liked me. Would he be my boyfriend? He hadn't asked me out exactly. But other people had been there. I would have to wait and see.

"Did you mind me being with Rick?" I asked Ani as we got into our pyjamas. I felt guilty about ignoring her.

"No, it's OK. I'm glad you like him. But I want you to help me get off with Rod. Problem is, he's eighteen. So he probably thinks I'm too young."

We got into bed and put the lights out. My head was still spinning. We both chatted about the party and about how vile Elaine and Pam had been.

"That was a hideous game," said Ani and yawned. "Still, you survived it."

"That's easy for you to say! I'm the one who had to do it!" But I had indeed survived and was more worldly-wise. Next time I would refuse to play any such games.

"His cousins were real bitches," I said, stretching out in bed and wondering how Rick was. Probably asleep. I hoped he wasn't too ill.

"I'll help you get Rod," I said, feeling generous now I had a boyfriend of sorts. "We'll think about what you can do and look at your clothes. You might need to wear more make-up to look older."

But Ani didn't answer. She was already asleep.

CHAPTER 22

LATCHKEY KIDS

Things went into overdrive in the next few weeks. First, my mother got a job. She didn't tell anyone she was applying for it, simply announced to us one lunchtime that she was starting as a part-time secretary at the new theatre in Plymouth.

"Well, I think I'll be a general dogsbody really," she told us, smiling. "But I don't mind because I'll be in the thick of theatre life, meeting actors and creative people, that sort of thing."

My father didn't look pleased. "Are you serious about this?" he asked, putting his knife and fork down. I watched them both with interest.

"Quite serious," she replied, and wiped her mouth with her napkin. "Hazel's old enough to be more independent, and I need a change."

"What about me?" he asked.

"You'll manage, Ron – Hazel and Lil can look after you when I'm out. Or you can look after yourself."

"I see," was all he said.

"You can open a tin of baked beans, can't you?" she added.

"Yes, but that's hardly the point."

"Well, it's too late now," Mum said, getting out a cigarette. "I start on Monday." She got up and went out to the garden to smoke. The dog followed.

"What's that, what's going on?" said Gran, who hadn't heard any of this.

"Mum's got a job at the theatre," I shrieked. "But we can look after Dad."

"That's right, we can. She needs a change," said Gran.

My father made a scathing "Chuh!" noise.

It was all very exciting. I thought it was nice for my mother. I wanted to escape somewhere and she did too. I could now see that women did quantities of boring housework and stayed in more than men. Except for Judy Atkinson next door. She was different, being a psychiatrist. She did what she wanted and ordered Alan around. Granny Lil didn't like her and said she wore the trousers in that house.

It also occurred to me that I might be less supervised, with one parent out of the way. Things were working out well.

I fetched Hedley and went out for a walk. There was a lot to think about. I wondered if Mum and Dad would split up, given the tension between them. I was slightly worried, but then I thought, maybe I could live alone with my grandmother, or (wonderful thought) even go and live with the Rydles. At least I still had a real mother, unlike poor Ani. She had to make do with Mel, who was nice but preferred her own two kids.

When I got back, my mother had gone out to am-dram and I found Dad in the kitchen, struggling with a tin opener.

"How does this blasted thing work?" he asked, banging a tin of baked beans around.

"Give it to me," I said and opened it at once.

"Thank you, Hazel, you *are* clever," he said.

I shrugged.

"Are you cross with Mum, getting a job?" I asked, leaning against the draining board.

"Not exactly, but I just don't understand her. She used to be so contented, running the house. Now she seems to have been infected by all this ghastly Women's Lib nonsense. Can't see the point of it myself."

He looked sad and puzzled, not like his usual self. I didn't know what to say to cheer him up. I inspected my fingernails. They had green nail varnish on today and it was chipping.

"Can we still go on our holiday to Ibiza?" I asked.

"Oh, yes. I promise you we'll do that," Dad answered. "In fact, shall we drive down to Mutley Plain today and book it at the travel agents now?"

I danced round with excitement. "Hooray! Yes please," I said.

So we went out and booked it. Two weeks in a hotel in Ibiza in August and a flight from London. It was called a 'package tour', a new type of holiday where everything was booked in one go. Even my father looked happier after that, and we drove home singing silly songs and smiling. For a short time, he even started making jokes about my mother's job.

Latchkey Kids

"I suppose you'll be a latchkey child now, you poor creature," he said.

"Yes, I'd better get a piece of string to wear round my neck with a key on it," I said. But really I knew that it would be all right. My grandmother was still there to keep things going and I wasn't a little child any more. I might learn some more cookery from my grandmother. And I was glad my mother was having some fun. I didn't believe my father was a hundred per cent happy, but I couldn't help that. He became moody again when we got home and went off to mow the lawns.

That evening I checked The List. I had done everything on it except for escaping. It was hard to know how to achieve it. I didn't like the commune on Dartmoor, so I wasn't going to run away there. René had let us down in London and hadn't helped us – he had just sided with my parents. But Ibiza could be a good place for running away, if only Forbes could help us. I got out some writing paper and wrote him a secret letter, then hid it in my shoulder bag. I would post it later that day.

With my mother out three days a week, I was left alone more, which was a pleasant change. I started dropping in on the Atkinsons and seeing if Rick was there. We got quite friendly and took our dogs out for walks. It was a strange relationship, because he wasn't exactly a boyfriend, although we had a kiss sometimes. He was more like a type of low key boy-Ani. Sometimes if Rick was busy with homework, I would just talk to Judy. She encouraged me in all my hopes and dreams, being an only child herself and having struggled to have a career.

"Follow your ambitions," she said, "and don't be put off by other people's negative comments."

Even Ani went round with me and Rick occasionally, at weekends, as Mel wasn't so interested in her now, what with all her art work and the impending Austrian au pair. We were all latchkey kids and I loved it.

It was Ani who had an idea for getting our revenge on Chas, who treated us disdainfully and called us the 'little schoolgirls and boys'. She hated him from the start when she first met him at their place and he'd said:

"What's your name – Ani? You sound like a Victorian parlourmaid!"

"Yeah, well," she'd answered. "You sound like a failed pop singer."

Ani could always think of something cutting to say back and never blushed.

We decided to play a trick on him. The idea came when Ani, Rick and I were sprawling in his bedroom one afternoon in the early summer. Judy and Alan were out, and Chas was probably at the café, where he spent more time than at college, with his biker friends, who had ridiculous names like Soz and Gaskit.

"He's gone all soft lately, 'cause he's after a girl," said Rick, lying on his back and dropping a whole biscuit into his mouth.

"Who is she?" asked Ani, reaching for the packet and getting one out.

"She's called Sharon and she lives down at Mutley in a flat with other girls. I think he met her at the Tech or something.

He's written her name on his arm in Biro – well, it's hidden but I saw it when he took off his shirt. I said, 'Who's Sharon?' and he got all touchy."

Ani sat up suddenly and said, "I know what – let's write a letter to Chas, pretending it's from her!"

"Oh, you can't do that," I exclaimed.

"Oh, Hazel, you're too soft," she said. "Let's have a laugh! He needs taking down a peg or two."

"Yeah, let's," said Rick.

"You tell us what she's like, and then I'll write a fake letter – I'm good at writing," said Ani.

"Shall we have a sneak round his bedroom while he's out?" asked Rick. "No one's allowed in – not even Mum."

We all thought that was a laugh, so we went in there. I had never seen such an astonishing room, not even at the commune or the Rydles' house. The walls were painted pure black, the carpet was black and the bed had a black and red check blanket. There were clothes everywhere – on the bed, on a chair and on the floor. An overflowing saucer of cigarette butts was balanced on a pile of books. On the walls were pinups of groups, but also ones of naked women.

Ani and I had a good look at them and giggled. I supposed it was daring, better than being a goody-two-shoes and dressing like a nun. But I wasn't sure if I would want to have photos taken of me like that.

"Oh, yeah, my brother Dave likes that sort of thing," Ani said casually and didn't seem very bothered.

"Look – here's his diary – he might have written something about Sharon in it!" said Rick, picking up a small black notebook.

We all sat down and pored over it, sniggering a bit. I was nervous, in case Chas suddenly came home and caught us. I kept looking at the door.

"What's up with you, got ants in your pants?" asked Ani, nudging me.

"Here you are," said Rick. "He's written things about her in there…here we are: '*I want to go out with Sharon, but she ignores me. How can I impress her?*' Or this one, this is good – '*I want to touch her face and hair and beautiful breasts!*'"

"No! Let me see!" I said and grabbed the diary.

We all collapsed laughing and lay on Chas' bed. I knew it was despicable but I was enjoying it.

"OK – shall I write a letter pretending to be from Sharon, saying she fancies Chas and wants to meet him?" suggested Ani.

"No, I've got a better idea – you write one from her saying she *doesn't* fancy him any more and she's going out with another bloke," I said.

"Genius!" said Rick. "Let's do that. Can you write it, Ani?"

"Yeah, of course. Better go back to your room and find some felt pens and paper," said Ani.

So we rearranged the room as it was and went back to Rick's bedroom, and Ani wrote a really fiendish fake letter, with some brilliant drawings of leaves and Greek goddesses at the top. It said:

Dear Chas

Hi, this is Sharon. This is kind of difficult to write because I've been trying to get my head sorted out and work out my feelings. But I had to tell you the truth.

I know you fancy me and I did fancy you up till now in a way, but I've met a guy from France who is a ski instructor and he's in love with me and we're probably going to go off to France and live. I always wanted to explore France and I love outdoor types of men, so I have to do this. I don't really get why you want to do engineering and I couldn't be a good little girlfriend who just goes along with it. I want to expand my consciousness and do my art and travel. I don't think we were meant for each other. I'm sorry if this hurts you, but I'm leaving next week. Don't try to contact me, Chas.

From

Sharon xxx

Rick and I sat and read Ani's letter. I had a twinge of guilt but ignored it and felt pleased, thinking how upset and humiliated Chas would be after reading this.

"That's brilliant, just brilliant," said Rick. "How are you going to get it to him?"

"I'll just drop it through your letterbox before I go today," said Ani with a shrug.

Over the next few days, I wondered what would happen when Chas got the letter but heard nothing.

Then on the Friday evening, a note dropped through our letterbox. It simply said 'Hazel' on the front. I whisked it away to my bedroom before my family could intercept it.

Inside it just said:

He read the letter. Really freaked out. Won't come out of room.
R.

I grinned to myself. *Great,* I thought. *Now you can see what it's like to have things going wrong, you mean swine.*

I was also frightened that Chas would guess it was us, but why should he? I don't know what happened with Sharon in the end, whether Chas actually confronted her or just accepted it. Rick told us he was miserable for a while but then cheered up. Chas was so vain he probably didn't worry about Sharon for too long. He would have found other girls to chase.

However, I avoided the Atkinsons' house for a few weeks, to make sure that Chas had no suspicion of us being the fake letter-writers. Ani and I went downtown to cafés or did our homework in the library, officially to find useful books but really to observe boys from Sutton High School, who tended to do homework there. When I looked back on this episode a few months later, I cringed with embarrassment at our juvenile and idiotic behaviour. I was growing up fast and putting aside childish things.

More importantly, the summer holidays were nearly upon us and we were all going away. Rick was going camping in France with his parents. Chas refused to go away with his family as he said it was too square. He was going to hitchhike to Italy with some friends. And Ani was coming with us to Ibiza.

CHAPTER 23
IBIZA

Plymouth 2012

Ibiza – the name still conjures up a tangle of memories – the Mediterranean heat, the light, my new daisy flip-flops, the foreignness of it all. Ani and I finally had freedom to run wild. Until it went too far.

* * *

Plymouth 1971

On July 23rd 1971, I came home and tore off my ugly brown uniform for the last time that school year. I put on some soft washed-out shorts and a Pink Floyd T-shirt and wandered around barefoot, followed by Hedley. I was free for six weeks.

I went alone to the post office the day after and withdrew thirty pounds, which I hid with The List. My new passport was in there too; it might be needed if my plans came to fruition. In my diary I crossed off the days till 7th August and our holiday.

We took a night flight from Heathrow. The lights on the runway shone like little beads. Granny Lil was with us; incredibly, it was her first flight. She stayed calm and resolute, only tutting at the antics of the young people on the plane who

Ibiza

were making a racket – singing, drinking and shouting messages along the plane to their friends. My parents were stressed by flying and reacted in their own ways – by doing crosswords and drinking brandy or gripping the seat arms and grimacing during take-off. Ani and I adored flying. As the plane took off, we leant over and gazed out of the window, watching the lights of London recede as we headed south into the night.

We arrived in Ibiza in the early hours and stepped out into velvety warm darkness. I caught a scent of dry herbs and grasses. A coach took us to our hotel, The Els Pins. We checked in, half dazed, staggered into our room (shared with my grandmother) and fell into bed.

* * *

"Wake up, you lazy woman!" Ani was looming over me, already dressed. It was morning and our room was bright white with the sunlight.

"Wha—? Where am I? Oh – Ibiza." I groaned and threw back the covers.

Within minutes, I was up and grabbing clothes from my case. We had that incredible teenage ability to sleep for hours but then launch ourselves into manic activity. We woke my grandmother in a cruel way, by dripping cold water on her face. She gasped and came to, spluttering, "You little beggars! Stop that!" We giggled and raced off to find my parents and food.

Breakfast consisted of sticky cakes and pastries, washed down with coffee. There was no sign of cornflakes or other familiar cereals. We screwed up our noses at the strange food, but my mother loved it and said it reminded her of her Navy years when she had travelled abroad. We weren't really interested in food; we just wanted to explore.

"Can we go off alone?" I asked.

"I should think so, if you stay in the hotel grounds," said my mother. "But meet us back in reception at eleven." Like most old people, she and the others simply wanted to sit by the pool and do nothing, a pathetic attitude, in my view.

We walked through the reception area. Two teenage boys in hotel uniforms gave a low whistle. We grinned and ignored them.

Outside there was a huge swimming pool with a fountain in the middle. Guests were already lying around it or splashing in the turquoise water.

"Look at that – people are climbing up the fountain steps and jumping off," said Ani.

"I can't wait to go in there," I said. "It looks a lot warmer than the Hoe pool back in Plymouth!"

We carried on, through gardens full of palm trees, cacti and plants with huge fleshy flowers. I recognised nasturtiums, but they were gigantic, like monstrous vines. We approached a strip of pine trees and saw a white sandy beach beyond. A few people were lying there, sunbathing. We broke into a run and dashed across the sand, kicking it up and screaming with happiness.

"I love it here!" I shouted.

"So do I, Pony!" said Ani. We sat down, breathless, and ran the hot sand through our hands. I looked down at my pink and white sundress and flicked back my recently cut hair. *Not bad,* I thought. *I'm like a girl in the Sunday colour supplements.*

Ibiza

We returned to find my parents ensconced by the pool. My grandmother was sitting indoors in the shade. The heat was too much for her.

"It's smashing here," I said. "Can we go swimming?"

"Yes, darling, go and fetch your things," said my father, who seemed very relaxed and pleasant today. He was wearing a straw hat and reading *The Times*.

But once we were in our bedroom, I had a crisis of confidence about my red bikini. It was my first one and I didn't want to reveal my stomach, which I thought was white and ugly.

"Honestly, Pony, why are you so hung up about that bikini?" Ani said.

I looked down at my stomach with disgust and squeezed it viciously. "I just hate my stomach."

"For God's sake, I don't know why you worry." She laughed and pulled on a knitted yellow bikini held together by wooden rings. She looked pudgy but wasn't bothered.

"Oh, shut up," I said, and (ridiculously) felt like crying. I bit my lip.

I put my red bikini away and got out my saggy old blue school swimsuit. I was furious with myself. Ani shrugged and shook her head.

"Come on, girl, let's get down to that pool," she said.

Most guests had already bagged seats round the pool and were lazing around in skimpy clothes or swimwear. Some were unbelievably tanned already. Ani and I were both pale as lard. We were determined to get brown as fast as possible, and greased ourselves up with Ambre Solaire oil, before stretching out in the burning sun to get to work, at a distance from my parents.

"Lost your clothes, have you?" A voice woke us up. It was my gran, who had finally ventured out. She disapproved of bikinis and most modern fashion, which she thought were 'disgraceful'.

"Hello, Granny," I shouted. "Are you going swimming?"

"Not ruddy likely at my age," she said, sitting down heavily in a plastic chair. She got out some knitting.

Ani laughed. She was fond of my grandmother, even though the feeling wasn't mutual.

"Look, Granny, we're getting a tan," I shouted.

"Silly fools."

"Do you like my leg?" said Ani, sticking up one leg in the air.

"I'm very fond of your leg. Pink's my favourite colour," said Lil.

We giggled at her.

Naturally we got horribly burnt that day and had to spend the evening languishing on our beds, with my mother ministering to us and gently applying Savlon cream to our bacon-coloured skin. She was very forgiving.

"I did just the same thing in Malta, as a girl," she said. "You don't realise the power of the sun here."

Ani suffered more than me, with her white freckly skin. I was sorry for her and sat with her in the darkened room. But by the next morning she was healing. It was blissful to be in Spain together anyway. We had secret talks about what we would do when we were twenty. We were always changing our minds.

Ibiza

(Ani: live in France and find a wealthy boyfriend. Me: go to university and travel round the world and paint pictures. We didn't ever want children.)

We soon settled into a dreamy Ibizan lifestyle. We explored the hotel grounds, ate garlicky food, got properly tanned, tried to learn Spanish, giggled and stuck together like twins. We were even taught to swim properly by my father, who went into the sea with us and coached us.

After being nagged endlessly, my mother caved in and bought us cheap pairs of flip-flops decorated with plastic flowers from the local supermarket. Mine had daises on them; Ani's had a row of pink blossoms.

"I'm sure they're bad for your feet," said my over-protective mother, but we were sure they weren't.

My parents relaxed and became more lenient than usual. We avoided them as much as possible, however. I didn't know what they did in the daytime and didn't really care. They were old. I was only interested in Ani and me.

Sometimes I looked at Ani, when she was splashing round in the pool or greasing herself with sun oil, and wondered if she thought about Realmum. It was terrible for her, having no mother. But she never mentioned it and I didn't want to stir things up.

* * *

On the fourth evening after dinner, my father suggested we go to the bar for drinks. Unlike Britain in 1971, bars in Spain were easy-going about children. We sat in the spacious bar in our best clothes and my father went off to order drinks. There was a party atmosphere, with my gran telling funny stories about her young days in Plymouth, and my mother doing imitations of accents. It was late but no one said we should go to bed.

Suddenly, my mother said, "Good Lord – look everyone – I think that's *Forbes* over there."

We all stared, and sure enough, a familiar sunburnt figure was making his way across the terrace to us and waving.

"Ye Gods," said my father. "How the hell did he find us?"

I kept quiet. Nobody knew about my letter.

"Hell-o, *mis amigos,*" said Forbes, doing a sort of jig and blowing a kiss.

"Well, this is a surprise," said Mum. "How on earth did you find us?"

"A certain young lady told me you'd be here," he answered, winking at me.

Everyone looked at me and I blushed.

"I wrote to Forbes, actually," I admitted, hoping they wouldn't be cross. Forbes wasn't exactly popular with Dad. But he was kissing all the women and slapping Dad on the back by now, and it was hard to be hostile.

"You two look very lovely," he said, eying up me and Ani in our strappy sundresses. "What's your name, dear?"

"Ani Rydle."

"Aah! A Rydle, eh? I knew your father years ago, at art college. Anyway, it's my round, everyone. What do you want?"

Forbes came back, bearing a tray of drinks. He said he was over from Barcelona for a few days "to look up some friends in

Ibiza

San Antonio, the capital". He was just dropping in on us this evening. My father looked relieved. He probably had visions of Forbes getting drunk and sleeping on their bedroom floor that night.

We stayed up really late and the adults got tipsy. Forbes left about 1.00 a.m., but not before arranging to meet us in town the next day.

* * *

"Why did you tell Forbes we were here?" asked my father the next morning at a late breakfast.

"I thought it would be interesting, him knowing Spain and everything," I said innocently, chewing on a sticky bread roll.

"I see. Shows initiative, I suppose. Well, we're meeting him and his friends today for lunch, in San Antonio, for our sins," he said.

"Great!" Ani said. "Whoopee!" I said. San Antonio was supposed to be ultra cool and full of hippies. We dashed up to our room to get ready and fetch our shoulder bags.

We all caught the little passenger ferry across the bay to San Antonio. After our self-contained hotel in the pine woods, it was a shock. A crowded, coffee-scented, noisy town, overrun with young people from all over Europe, or so it seemed. Nearly everyone looked fashionable, wearing flowing Indian clothes or patched jeans. I thanked heavens I had put on denim shorts and Mel's white smock top, which looked perfect with my flip-flops. Ani's purple patterned minidress was perfect, too. We waited at the San Antonio ferry port, a little over-awed.

"I hope he damn well turns up; you never know with Forbes," said my father, looking dubious.

But a short figure was pushing his way through the crowds to us – Forbes. He was clutching his usual cigarette and grinning.

"Welcome to the big city, folks," he said, coming up and giving the womenfolk smacking kisses. "Let's get out of this madhouse – come on Lilly, sweetheart…" He took Gran's arm and helped her along.

Forbes led us up a side alley and away from the mayhem. I caught a smell of good cooking coming out of a flat and heard someone strumming a guitar. We followed him, and he turned into a courtyard with little palm trees in pots and a white marble floor. A buxom young woman with red-blonde hair was laying a table there.

"Here we are – my friends' abode," he said with a flourish. "This lovely lady is Fiona."

"Hi, everyone," drawled Fiona in a posh voice. "The others are still out – had a bit of a party downtown last night."

After introductions, we all sat down and were brought drinks by Forbes. His friends were all artists apparently (I noted this with interest) who were living in San Antonio for the summer. After a drink or two, the adults relaxed, even my father, and the conversation flowed. I listened intently while the others talked about living abroad, their painting, what was wrong with England (no feeling for art, apparently) and how good and cheap life was in Ibiza.

Ibiza

"You all ought to move out here, get a change of scene, Ronny," said Forbes, lighting up a cigarette for my mother and handing my father another beer. He winced. He hated being called Ronny.

That would be amazing, I thought. But predictably, my father reacted in a boring way.

"And live in a dictatorship? No thanks. And we wouldn't want to take Hazel out of her high school," he said, and I scowled. "Although Ibiza's got its good points – the locals are friendly and your money goes a long way."

"This money? Oh, it's awful!" piped up Gran, who had the wrong end of the stick, as usual. She fiddled with her hearing aid, which wasn't working properly. She had never got used to the new decimal money system at home, and still converted everything back to the old pounds, shillings and pence. Now she was struggling with Spanish pesetas.

"It's OK, Granny, I'll help you with the money," I said. I felt sorry for her, always mishearing and being left out.

"Let's have lunch," said Fiona, and hurried away to fetch some food.

While we were eating Spanish omelettes and other delicious dishes (I was getting used to the food and finally enjoying some of it), Forbes plumped himself down between me and Ani and put an arm round each of us. He smelt of garlic and cigarettes.

"How are you two girls enjoying it here, then?" he asked us.

"Oh, we love it," said Ani.

"I wish we *could* stay out here and live," I added.

"You'll have to come and see me in Barcelona some time," said Forbes, winking at us. "I'm renting a big flat at the moment. Super lifestyle."

"Oh, I'd love that," I said. I glanced over at my parents to see if they had heard any of this. Obviously they would stop us. But they were chatting away with Fiona.

Forbes got up and said, "Just fetching a ciggie; don't go anywhere."

I nudged Ani and looked at her.

"Escape?" I mouthed. She nodded.

Forbes returned and wedged himself between us again. I watched with fascination as he lit a cigarette on the stub of the old one.

"D'you know lots of artists here?" Ani said.

"A fair few," said Forbes. "I was at art college myself for a while – Camberwell. Soon dropped out, though."

"I'm going to art college," announced Ani. "Shall I show you some of my drawings?"

"Oh, please do, darling," said Forbes, leaning close to her. She took out a little sketch pad from her shoulder bag. I had seen her latest horse drawings and they were good.

I felt a sour little stab of jealousy. Ani looked quite happy sitting next to Forbes and they started to chat about painting and art courses. They both bent over her drawings, excluding me. A more unpleasant thought came to me – did Forbes fancy her? But he was so old, he couldn't, surely.

I ignored him and looked round at Fiona. She smiled.

Ibiza

"Are you enjoying your holiday?"

"Yes, thanks. How long have you been here?" I asked.

"Two months," she said, picking up a piece of cheese and nibbling at it. "I came out here to paint. I'm broke, but my friend Digby came to the rescue and lent me this flat, which is very lucky. I would still be sleeping on the beach over at Cala Gració if he hadn't offered me this."

"How exciting – I'd love to do that!"

"Well, it can be a bit grotty – you know, not being able to wash anywhere, but yes, it's fun for a while," said Fiona.

"That sounds disgusting," interrupted my mother. "I've heard about these hippies on the beaches, and the police trying to break them up."

Fiona just laughed and changed the subject.

Meanwhile, Forbes was getting friendlier with Ani. "You would be lovely to paint," he said in an insinuating voice, lifting up a strand of her golden hair. I wondered if it was such a good idea to go off with him.

"I'm going to the toilet, are you coming?" I butted in, giving her a stern look.

"Upstairs on the left, darling," said Forbes. But Ani stayed put.

I found the toilet and inspected my face in the mirror. I thought I looked quite pretty and adult. In fact I looked as good as Ani any day. I fiddled with my white top and pushed my hand through my hair.

Yes, not bad at all. Ani and I should try and get off with some Spanish boys at the hotel. Some of them are really good-looking. Better than fat old uncles.

I heard footsteps on the stairs outside and then Ani's voice.

"What are you up to, Pony? Why are you taking so long?"

"Hey," I said, "come in here a minute."

"What is it?" Ani pushed the door open and came in. I grabbed her arm.

"Ow!"

"What are you *doing* with him?" I demanded.

She giggled. "Oh, it's OK. He's a bit of a dirty old man, but I'm used to artists," she said airily. She went on. "Your dad said we can go on a boat trip tomorrow to some amazing caves. The boat has a glass bottom and you can see all the fish!"

"Yeah, all right. But listen – what about Forbes?"

"What about him?"

"D'you want him to take us to Barcelona with him? Is that it?"

"Well, we could escape that way. You're always going on about it." Ani twisted a long piece of her hair and looked out of the window.

"Yeah, and what d'you think he'd do to us?"

"Oh, it's just talk. He's harmless," she said in a superior voice. "Some men are like that. Come on, let's go down and find out about the boat trip."

I held back. I wasn't sure what I wanted any more, to escape or stay. But I had a funny feeling about Forbes and suddenly knew that we absolutely mustn't go to Barcelona or go around with him.

Downstairs, Forbes was telling a funny story. Fiona and Mum were laughing their heads off, but my father didn't look very amused. He caught my eye.

"There you are! Ready to go, then?" he asked.

"Yes, OK."

But my mother broke in. "Oh, let's stay a bit, Ron. This is such fun."

"Hmm, the girls are tired," he said, and looked tense.

Forbes laughed and said, "Ah! The joys of family life. Never got involved myself. Must get going, though, back to jolly old Barcelona. Need to see a man about a dog. Work thingy."

"That makes a change, working," muttered my father in an aside.

Fi took a puff of her cigarette and said, "Why don't you girls stay with me in San Antonio one night? I can show you round."

"Yess!" chorused Ani and I.

"That sounds fun," said my mother. "If they're not a nuisance."

"No problem at all," said Fiona. "There are two camp beds in my art studio."

"There you are, then, that'll be super for you girls," said Forbes, leaning back in his chair and stretching. His shirt rode up and a bit of dark, fat, hairy stomach showed. I shuddered.

"Bring Ani and Hazel tomorrow afternoon if you like," said Fiona.

"Smashing," I said. "Can we, Dad?"

"I should think so, if you're good," said my father. "Come on, now, back to the hotel."

"Can we go in the pool?" I asked.

"Yes, of course," he said.

Forbes stood up. "Super to see you all," he said. "Keep in touch."

"Yes, I'm sure we will," lied my father. "Thank you, Fiona, for the lunch." He was itching to get away. He herded us women up and we headed back to the ferry.

When we got back, my father reverted to usual strict mode and said, "Now, I want to talk to you about San Antonio. It's a big city and there are some funny people there. You stay with Fiona at all times."

"Why, we're not three-year-olds. What's gonna happen?" I said rudely.

He added, "I want you to have an early night tonight, after all these late nights and discos. And don't say 'gonna'."

"God, so boring!"

I kicked at a table leg. I immediately regretted this and was afraid he would lose his temper, but instead he said, "That's enough, Hazel. I'll see you both at supper," and went.

Ani and I looked at each other and then she giggled. "Your old man's got a severe case of middle-class uptightness."

"I know," I said. "But if we're goody-good tonight I think he'll let us go tomorrow. We might as well pack now."

Ibiza

We went up and flung various items in our shoulder bags – pants, beach hats, shorts and a bumper packet of biscuits.

I bossed Ani about and said, "Have you got your passport? And money? And take lots of clothes."

"Why? We're only going for one night, Pony."

"You never know, something else might happen."

"You twit, you're not still on about escaping! I thought you'd gone off Forbes!"

"There might be another way," I said, and left it at that.

But she packed everything. Then we went to the pool until the evening.

We behaved like two angels at supper, smiling and being polite to everyone. And miraculously, we were given the go-ahead to visit Fiona.

We went to bed early. But I couldn't sleep. It was a hot night and I tossed and turned in bed, pushing the duvet off and then pulling it back on. Gran couldn't hear because of her deafness. But it disturbed Ani.

"Will you shuddup, Pony!" she whispered.

"Shut up yourself."

Ani made an exasperated "Hmmph" sound and mumbled, "Some people have got ants in their pants." She rolled over.

I lay there for a long time while Ani went quiet and began to breathe steadily. My grandmother snored. But I didn't sleep for hours; I was busy planning.

CHAPTER 24

BREAKOUT

When I woke the next morning, I stretched out in my soft, white bed. I had slept eventually, despite the events of yesterday. I looked over at Ani's bed. Just a white hump. I looked beyond. My grandmother was asleep and snoring softly. I picked up my watch – six twenty. I got up and tiptoed on to our little balcony.

The weather looked perfect. The swimming pool was shining in the morning light. A few empty cans of Coke and bottles were lying on the ground from the night before, but no people were there yet. I loved this time of day, when the world was silent and fresh.

A voice behind me said, "You're up early."

Ani stood there in her mini nightdress.

"Hi, Hippy. Want to go down to the pool for a bit? Not for a swim, just to sit."

"Yeah, let's."

We dressed swiftly and crept downstairs. Reception was already staffed – with our flirty young boy.

"*Hola, guapas,*" he said, giving a low whistle.

"*Hola, burro,*" said Ani. He laughed and blew her a kiss.

We sat by the pool and dabbled our brown feet in the warm water.

"Only five more days here," remarked Ani, swishing her feet about.

"I know. I don't want to think about it – school again and all. It's so lovely here, with you. I'll never forget it."

"Yeah. The thought of Sherwell High makes me sick, though. To be honest, Pony, I wish I could go to Dartmoor Manor sooner."

"What?" I was horrified. "You're not going yet, are you? I thought you said in a few years. You can't leave me!"

"Don't get your knickers in a twist, dear," she said, patting my arm. "I can't go yet, anyway. There aren't any places."

I linked my little finger in hers. "We'll always be friends, Hippy."

We returned to our room and slept a little more.

* * *

My mother called on us and we went to breakfast. She announced that she would be taking us alone to San Antonio, as Gran was overcome with the heat, and Dad wanted to relax and read the English newspapers. I was pleased – Mum alone was usually more laid back and interesting.

We crammed into the little passenger ferry to San Antonio, along with boys and girls with guitars, some old ladies in black and a priest.

My mother squeezed my arm. "I hope you two enjoy yourselves with Fiona. It'll be a change for you."

"Thanks, Mum." I thought back to the afternoon at Fiona's. "Mum…do you think Forbes is a bit odd?"

"Yes – he's eccentric. And he's a restless soul. Is that what you mean?"

"Well, he was *very* interested in Ani. I mean, a bit too much. He was sitting right next to her, touching her and going on about how pretty she was."

"Was he? I must admit, I was distracted by Fiona and her stories about Ibiza. Oh my goodness, that's not on. Ani – was Forbes being too pushy?"

Ani shrugged. "Yeah, he was a bit. But I wasn't too bothered. I know some old men are like that."

I also suspected she thought I was a bit jealous.

I frowned. "Well, I don't like him very much any more. I'm glad he's gone back to Barcelona."

My mother nodded. "Yes, he's out of the way now. I don't think we'll see him again. You two stay with Fiona, and you'll be all right."

I remembered the way to her flat exactly. The others had to follow me.

She was in the courtyard, smoking a cigarette and drinking a tiny cup of coffee.

"Hi, guys," she called. "Your room is upstairs on the right – with the two beds. Go on up."

"Are you sure this is all right, Fiona?" asked my mother. "Can I have your phone number, just in case?"

"Absolutely, Fenella," she replied. She smelt of patchouli oil.

We spent the day going round the shops with Fiona. She was quite pleasant to us, somewhat vague and dreamy, but that suited us. Ani and I bought floppy hats and big shirts with flowers all over them and Fiona went round a market, buying fresh food and more wine.

That evening, Fi cooked some strange fish for us, with potatoes. She gave us some red wine and water to drink, and we got tipsy. She switched on the TV and we all watched some Spanish film about a war, but we couldn't understand much. I was just getting bored when the phone rang. Fiona said, "Oh, shit, what now?" and got up slowly.

"Oh, hi, Digby," she said. "What? Oh God, right. Well, I guess I could." She glanced at us and listened while Digby told her more. She didn't mention us. "No, no I know. Yeah…OK… yeah." Yeah sounded more like '*Yah*'.

She hung up and started getting her bag and cigarettes.

"Umm, sorry but I need to go out for a while. Can you two stay here? Just do what you fancy – have more wine or hang out or go to bed when you want. I should be back by midnight." She hurried out of the flat and disappeared without waiting for an answer.

We looked at each other and chewed our lips and then started giggling.

"Hey, what shall we do?" said Ani. "Get drunk? Eat all the food?"

"No, something better – we're gonna run away."

"Uh? Really?" Ani looked shocked.

"Yep, let's head for the beaches and sleep out!"

What I really meant was, *Let's start a new life.* Our moment had come.

"You are definitely nuts," she answered. "I didn't think you were like that."

"Well, you're wrong for once, Ani Rydle."

I had never felt so sure of things. This was it – our chance. The big escape and no more Plymouth, no more parents, no more Dartmoor Manor for Ani, either. I would have Ani to myself.

"Get all your stuff," I ordered her. "I'm going to write Fiona a note."

I found a sketchpad flung on a dirty chair. I sat down and thought quickly.

"OK, this is what we do. We'll say my gran is ill and that we had to go back. We'll say my mum rang here."

Ani looked doubtful, but then grinned. "I can't believe you're doing this, Pony."

I chewed the end of the Biro and then wrote a short message. Ani took a swig of wine and picked up the note. She laughed.

"Genius," she said. "Where are we going, then?"

"You remember Fiona was talking about her friends sleeping on the beach? It was called 'Cala Grassy' or something. Let's go there now."

"What about food?"

I grabbed some off the table. "Here, take this. Now, let's get our bags and go – just in case Fi comes back early."

We asked a promising-looking hippy boy where Cala Grassy was and he said, "Oh, Cala Gració. Yeah, it's that over there." And he told us the way. We started walking out of San Antonio, northwards.

It was a hot night, and we sweated as we walked along. Other people were on the streets, flower-people, locals doing late-night shopping, little children in pushchairs in their pretty clothes. No one bothered about us. We looked older than thirteen.

I held my head up and strode ahead. I had never felt so sure, so strong. At last I was free – free from parents, from Plymouth, from my stupid little life. There was no past and no future.

Ani was quiet, following me. We were coming to the outskirts of San Antonio. Some houses looked quite poor. People were sitting outside on plastic chairs, smoking, talking together or holding babies on their laps. Ibizans never seemed to sleep.

We were coming to a small beach. The sign said 'Cala Gració'.

"This is it, come on," I announced. Ani followed silently.

We could see small groups of young tourists on the beach. Someone had lit a fire and a little group sat round it. Others just lay there and one or two were smoking large cigarettes. All of them were scruffy, in jeans or long skirts. I led our way to the end of the beach, near people but not with them.

"This'll do," I said. "We'll sleep here." I took out a big shirt and spread it out on the soft cream sand.

Ani made a little bed for herself with her clothes and bag. We both sat and looked out at the black sea. The lights of San Antonio shone in the distance. I handed out some food and we chewed it in silence.

"What'll we do tomorrow?" Ani asked, sounding a little anxious.

"No idea," I answered. "Tomorrow's a long way away."

I lay back and listened to the waves and the soft sounds of the other beach-people.

So our beach-life began. No one did anything terrible to us, and we survived. I woke early every morning and watched the sunrise. After having biscuits for breakfast, we ran into the sea to wash; we swam in our shorts and bras. The toilet was a problem, but we went behind some pampas grass and decided to go to a café later for the more difficult business. We had enough money for now. I loved it all.

Ani didn't love it as much as me. But she went along with it.

I didn't care; I felt I had found my true self. I was a girl of nature, who enjoyed the salty taste of the sea, the smell of cooking fires and cigarettes, the strumming of the hippies' guitars.

* * *

Breakout

We camped out through the Ibizan summer, getting friendly with the other beach nomads. They didn't judge us because we were young; they accepted us. They called us 'the fairy children'. We learnt how to live outside and survive.

Finally, I was like a girl in the Sunday colour supplements. My hair got bleached blonde by the sun and it grew thick and wild. I slowly forgot my old life in Plymouth. I learnt Spanish and some of the Catalan language, and in the end I met a local boy who was a musician and stayed with him. Ani became an artist.

* * *

Except we didn't really. I'm sorry but this is all a lie. We spent one night on the beach, and in the morning the Spanish police picked us up. One of the more responsible hippies had noticed us and told the patrolling police officers. They were kind and took us back to Fiona's. She had been up all night, searching in the area with Digby, not daring to tell my parents.

After the initial shock, she soon calmed down and laughed at our escapade. We agreed we wouldn't say a thing to my parents. It would only stir things up. We showered the beach salt and grit off ourselves while Fiona washed our clothes. They dried in minutes in the fierce heat. Fi took us back to the hotel, and that was that.

I didn't mind. I knew I really would escape one day, when I was old enough to know the ropes. It was just a question of time.

CHAPTER 25

THE END OF THE RYDLE YEAR

We got home in late August, two sunburnt teenagers trailing after middle-aged parents and a weary grandmother, clutching souvenirs and duty-free drinks.

We dropped Ani home first. Mel came out to the door with the little ones to meet us and she kissed Ani. She looked happier now.

"Hi there! All OK, then? Thank you, Fen and Ron. I'll ring you tomorrow, Fen, about the am-dram."

"Thank you so much," said Ani, blowing a kiss to me. "It was a fab holiday."

"When will I see you?" I asked. An inexplicable wave of sadness hit me.

"Oh, soon, I'll ring you soon," she said, picking up Josh and playing with Tal's hair. The Rydle family. They might fight and complain, but they belonged to each other. I didn't belong. I turned and walked back to our car.

"All right?" said Dad.

"Yeah," I said, biting my lip.

"Home then," he said, and we drove off.

The End of the Rydle Year

The grass in the back garden had grown long and yellow, and the flowers were dying. My father hurried out to cut it and tidy up, while my mother started learning her lines for the next am-dram show and ironed her office clothes, ready to return to her job at the theatre. She didn't seem to mind; she liked her new life. I felt as if I'd been away for months. The air was getting cooler in England. I slipped on my new daisy flip-flops and went round the house, checking up on everything and chasing Hedley about. He was hysterically happy to be home and to see me.

"I'm so glad to be home! They can keep their Ibiza!" announced Granny Lil, struggling upstairs and sitting down heavily on her bed. I wasn't sure. I viewed everything in a more cold and critical light.

I wondered if Rick was in. We still weren't really boyfriend and girlfriend, but I liked him. I hadn't given him a thought in Ibiza, except on the last day.

"Going to see Rick," I shouted to anyone who was listening.

I rang the Atkinsons' doorbell and Custard barked somewhere in the background. Chas answered.

"Oh, it's you, been anywhere hot?" he said, lounging against the doorpost and looking me up and down. Custard rushed out and I bent to stroke him.

"Yeah. Is Rick in?" I stared back at him.

"I'll just check – *Ricky*!" he yelled. "One of your women here."

Women? I hoped Rick didn't have another girlfriend. I was unreasonably possessive about him.

Rick appeared, his mouth full of food. He half smiled when he saw me.

"Oh, hi – just back?"

"Yep, and I've brought you something." I held out some chocolates from Ibiza airport. Chas made a grab at them, and Rick shoved him off, then Chas laughed and went bounding upstairs.

Rick said, "Come in the kitchen if you want."

"Did you go camping?"

"Yeah, it was all right," Rick said.

Boys were never great talkers. I sat at the table.

"Ibiza was OK. Sort of interesting. Did you know it's a dictatorship?"

"Yeah, I did actually. Franco and all that." He opened the chocolates and pushed the box towards me. "Want to go for a walk with the dogs?"

We heard the front door opening and Judy came in from work.

"Oh, hello, Hazel. Lovely to see you. Ricky's missed you."

He blushed scarlet and I felt my cheeks warm up too.

"No, I haven't," he mumbled. Considering Judy was a psychiatrist, she was pretty tactless.

I took Rick down to the fields in Compton, my favourite secret place. They had started building ugly new houses there, but there was still some land left wild. We sat on a log and I confessed about escaping to the beach, for one whole night. Rick whistled.

"Wow! I feel like escaping sometimes."

He looked at me and I thought, *He's going to kiss me.* But he didn't.

"Got A levels to work on now," he said.

I wondered if he was hinting that he didn't want to see me. You never knew with boys. I didn't mind too much, and then a fresh thought came to me: there was a youth club starting at the church. My mother had found that out recently at am-dram. Maybe I would meet other boys there. It wasn't as if I was really in love with Rick; he was more like a friend. Perhaps it didn't matter.

* * *

There were still two weeks of holiday left and Ani hadn't rung me. But I was strangely happy alone for a little while. I went into Plymouth on the bus and wandered around. Some new boutiques were opening and there were more new cafés now. It wasn't too bad there, really.

One day I got all my horse drawings out and looked at them. Mel had said they were "quite good" and I was upset. However, she was right. I would never be *very* good. Ani was much better than me.

But maybe I could do other things.

I looked at myself in the bathroom mirror. A thin, tanned face looked back at me. My hair was growing long and reached my shoulders now.

"You look good," I said to my reflection.

I went to my bedroom cupboard and got out The List, read through it, and nodded. I had done all of it – Levi's, bra, haircut. Meeting boys. A best friend. And an escape, of sorts! Anyway, escaping was a stupid, childish idea. I now knew that it was completely impractical for me, a thirteen-year-old. I would have to bide my time and get away in a few years. But The List was finished. *Until I write the next list.* There would always be more lists. I was about to tear it up, when I stopped and looked at '*Make Ani my best friend*'. How could I tear that up? Ani wasn't something I could just tick off, like a task to be done. I drew a little heart next to it. Then I carefully tore out that bit and placed it back in my secret box. The rest I took out to the garden and burnt in my father's incinerator.

* * *

At the very end of August, Ani finally rang me.

"Hello, stranger," I said, not entirely friendly.

"I know – sorry. We've been busy here doing family stuff. Art shows and things. Sarah wants to say goodbye to you before she goes to Paris. And I want to tell you about something. Will you come round for a coffee?"

I didn't say yes right away, because I was annoyed with Ani. She'd had a brilliant holiday with us, then neglected me. But I couldn't resist seeing the Rydles and wondered what she wanted to tell me.

"OK," I said, "when?"

"Oh, just come now," she said. The Rydles were too unconventional to be organised.

I got the bus to their house and Tallulah answered the door. She was growing. Today she was wearing a little pair of jeans and plimsolls, like a miniature teenager. Someone had curled her hair. She even had some rather crooked lipstick on.

"Hi, Pony," she said. "We're having cake in the kitchen."

She grabbed my hand and led me up the stairs. We went into the orange and brown kitchen, where Mel, Josh, Sarah and Ani were sitting round the pine table. I could smell coffee and warm cake.

"Hi, Hazel," they all said. Sarah got up to hug me. And Ani came over and had a hug too.

Mel got up and said, "Now, darling. Do you want some coffee? Or tea?"

"Coffee, please," I said. It was a year since I'd first come to their house and been amazed by their kitchen. Now, it seemed normal to have chunky mugs and a yellow dishwasher and brown-and-orange walls.

I sat down between Ani and Sarah and helped myself to a slice of gooey chocolate cake.

"When do you go, Sarah?" I asked.

"Today," said Sarah. She looked radiant. "I'm driving to London right after this and my flight's this evening."

It was so sad. But Sarah had said we could visit her. So it wasn't a real goodbye.

"Hazel," said Ani. "I've got some news – well, the thing is..."

"What?" I was instantly on red alert.

"Well, the thing is…Dad knows how much I hate Sherwell High, so he rang Dartmoor Manor and they have one place spare. Someone dropped out."

I stared at her, aghast. I said, "When do you go?"

"Next week." She wouldn't look at me but fussed over her cake.

"Nest week," echoed Josh. "Ani going." He didn't have a highchair any more; he was sitting in a normal chair on a cushion.

"Yes, well we decided it was better for me to go early, get settled in. But Nadia's there, actually, so I'll know someone."

Of course, her half-sister. One of the Manchester Rydles. It was such a big family. I drank some coffee.

"You look great, Hazel," Sarah broke in, looking embarrassed. "I love your jeans and baggy T-shirt."

"Thanks. The shirt's from Ibiza," I said, staring at my plate.

"Josh! Stop it!" shouted Mel, making us jump. Josh was throwing icing at Tallulah. Tal tried to smack him and Josh screamed, slid down from the chair, and ran out of the kitchen with Tal in pursuit.

"Oh, God, this family!" said Sarah, but she smiled.

Mel ignored the little ones and lit a roll-up. "Have more coffee, Hazel? No? Anyway, we'll have to see you at half term, or Christmas at least."

"Will you write to me?" I asked Ani.

She laughed. "You know I'm rubbish at writing letters, Pony, but I'll try."

"Yes, try," I said. My heart turned to ice.

"Let's find Josh and cheer him up," said Ani, and we went down to his brightly coloured bedroom, and played crocodiles with him and Tal until Sarah was due to leave. I said very little.

"Pony," said Ani, "what's the matter?"

"You *know* what's the matter! How can you do this to me?" I started sobbing.

Ani put her arms round me, but I pulled away. I felt like hitting her and instead lashed out a pile of picture books, which crashed onto the floor. Josh and Tallulah stared at me wide-eyed, unused to seeing me crying and behaving badly like them.

"You *knew* I wanted to go to Dartmoor Manor. I'm like a fish out of water at Sherwell. I never kept it secret. But you're still my friend and we'll see each other." Ani stood, hands on hips, but slightly guilty nonetheless.

"It's all right, Pony," said Tal. "You can play with *me* sometimes."

This made me cry even more.

"What's going on here?" Sarah had appeared in the doorway.

"Hazel's sad," said Tallulah.

I wiped my eyes roughly and tried to stop. "I'm OK, it's nothing."

Sarah looked from Ani to me. She knew what was going on.

"Come on, come and freshen up in the bathroom, Hazel," she said and I followed her.

The bathroom looked as messy as ever. Sarah handed me some tissues and patted the bath's edge for me to sit with her.

"Ani can be a selfish so-and-so sometimes," she said.

"I didn't think she was going yet, that's all." I bathed my sore eyes and sat, drooping with misery.

"Life can be tough, but I know Ani thinks a lot of you."

I didn't know if I believed that.

Ani appeared in the doorway. "All right? What's going on?"

"Nothing, it's OK. Let's go and have some lunch," said Sarah. Part of me wanted to scream at them, run out, head for home. But I couldn't resist the lure of the Rydles, even now.

We had a snack lunch, the three of us. Not much was said, just mundane conversation about the food, Sarah's flight, the Austrian au pair, who had started at the Rydles'. But time was passing and the clock was running down.

The moment had come.

"I'm off, everyone," Sarah called.

Her red sports car was stuffed full of luggage. She got in and started up the engine with a roar. We all waved her off and then went back in and hung around in Ani's bedroom, while she thought about her boarding school packing. It was torture for me, but I couldn't tear myself away.

"I'm just taking lots of jeans and long skirts, 'cause we don't have a uniform at Dartmoor Manor, thank God. We can wear anything."

"I know, lucky you," I said. "Think of me at bloody Sherwell High."

I started to cry again and Ani hugged me. "Sorry, Pony. We'll stay best friends, I promise. It's just…I don't fit in at Sherwell High. You know that."

The Austrian au pair, Hannelore, arrived back from her English language lessons and came in to chat with us.

"I'm starting German next term," I told her.

"Very good, Hazel, you can practise with me if you come round."

If. If I ever come back here.

"Austria is a beautiful country, you know. Shall I show you some photos?"

So Hannelore fetched her photos of huge mountains, villages and green fields. It was gorgeous. I decided immediately that I would visit Austria one day. Strange how ideas form in our minds and affect our life course.

It was time to go, although I didn't want to. We went down the stairs in the upside-down house, to the front door.

"Remember when I first met you outside school," I reminded Ani. "You had white shoes on."

"And you called me Anita and were so shy! It's ages since then."

"We were just stupid little kids," I said.

"And now we're stupid teenagers," Ani said and we couldn't help laughing. It's the strangest feeling, laughing when you want to cry.

I looked at my watch. "I'd better go," I said.

"You don't have to," said Ani.

"No, I need to help Mum with the supper. She hasn't got much time nowadays, with her new secretary job and am-dram."

"OK, well – see you in a few weeks, Pony." Ani hugged me.

"Yeah."

As I left, Tal and Josh appeared at the door and called out, "Bye, Pony, bye."

I looked back and saw them all standing there together, the three Rydle children in their fashionable clothes.

"Bye," I said and turned away.

* * *

On 14th September I went back to Sherwell High School, in the third year. Things were just the same, except for Ani not being there. I began German classes and was put in the top stream for maths. My old friend Pat sat next to me and it was oddly comforting to make plans and arrange to go riding on her ponies. Other friends were about, too, and invited me to do things.

Two weeks later, I had a letter from Ani.

I pulled it out of the envelope and took it into the TV room, where I was watching a programme about the Concert for Bangladesh and wishing I could have gone to London to see it. It was written on purple paper, with a garland of leaves drawn around the edge. The writing was untidy, as if she had been in a hurry. It said:

Dartmoor Manor
CHUDLEIGH
Devon
15th September 1971

Dear Pony

Well here I am at Dartmoor Manor at last and it's so fantastic I don't know why I stayed at Sherwell so long. It's so free here! We can wear what we want, old jeans or no shoes or anything. I've made a few friends, who are OK. I share a bedroom with Beth from London. We can see the moors from our window.

There are stables here and Dad says he'll buy me a pony next year and I can keep it here.

I'm not sure if I'll be back till Christmas cos Beth has asked me to see her in London.

So what you doing? Have you seen Rick?

Love

Hippy xx

I read it through twice, said "Huh!" and dropped it on the floor. Then I picked it up and put it on the coffee table. Ani didn't seem real. She was a long way away. I would write back sometime, but not yet.

It was Saturday and I should have been doing homework but was lazing about instead. My gran put her head round the door.

"Did you get a letter from that Ani, then?" she asked.

"Yes, she's gone to boarding school now," I shrieked.

"Do you mind?"

"Sort of," I said. "I'd rather be at home here, though."

I knew one day I might leave but the time wasn't ripe.

"There's no place like home," said Gran. "What are you doing today?"

"I think I'll go out with Hedley, and I'm seeing Pat and Wendy later, in town," I replied, getting up and pulling on a baggy blue jumper. My parents were both out buying antiques and the house was quiet.

I went and found Hedley curled up on a chair in the best living room.

"Come on," I said. "Walks."

He jumped off the chair and I clipped on his lead. We walked all the way to Central Park and climbed a hill. We sat together on the grass, on my jumper, gazing at the panoramic view – we could see Plymouth Hoe and the sea, Dartmoor to the north, and the city's sprawling suburbs on the other sides. I thought about the past year, about Ani and the Rydles, Forbes, René, Rick's party, my parents and grandmother and my jeans, the *right* jeans. It was quite a mix. At that moment, I felt good. I was Hazel James, teenager. The years stretched out ahead of me. Anything could happen.

CHAPTER 26
THE RYDLE YEAR REVISITED

Plymouth 2013

Matti's living with me in Plymouth now. I've done up my mother's house and am based here, doing my translating work and writing fiction. Life is good. I might stay here or I might move on again. Plymouth has changed so much, from a sleepy town at one end of England to an international city. Plymothians haven't changed so much, though: they still say 'proper job' and are as straight-talking as ever. I like that. Tobi and I have parted and it's for the best. Matti is going to study marine biology in Plymouth, which is great. He'll probably move out in a few months to a shared student house.

* * *

London 2013

I hoped she wouldn't be late. It was a quick day visit to London and I had other things to do. I was curious. Would I even recognise her, after forty-two years?

I sat in a Costa café near the Embankment, sipping a decaf tea. I checked my mobile phone – one message from a translation agency, chasing some work. A text from my Matti, asking which train I was getting back. They could wait. I put the phone down and checked the time – one fifty-five. Not long now.

A few people came into the café and I inspected them quickly. There was a blonde woman – could it be…? But, no, she was too tall and scruffy. I couldn't imagine her being scruffy.

I looked at my phone again and clicked on the BBC icon to glance at the news. Awful habit. I put the phone down.

Then I heard a voice.

"Pony? It must be you!"

I looked up and there she was. Tallulah.

Would I have recognised her? Possibly. The same smile, the unruly hair, although silvery-blonde now and cut in a wavy bob. Her face looked lined. But she was stylish – in a white tailored shirt and smart denims. Minimal silver jewellery.

Tallulah came up to me and hugged me, then stood back.

"I'd have recognised you anywhere, Pony," she said. "You've hardly changed."

I winced slightly at that – was I still like the Hazel of long ago? Or it could be just a throwaway remark.

But anyway, I was looking pretty good that day, in my black velvet jeans and leather jacket and my dangly green glass earrings. I still loved clothes.

"Short hair, though – and a nice colour – red!" she went on. "You look great."

"You too. Let me get you a drink."

"A flat white please."

We settled ourselves down and tried to catch up on forty-plus years.

"I guess you became an artist, like the others," I said.

"No way! There are enough artists in our family – I became a GP." Tallulah laughed at me. "Your face!"

"When I googled you, it said '*Dr Rydle*' but I thought you had done a PhD or something."

She went on. "And I went to Devonport High. I just loved the uniform and all the structure. Mum was appalled. You can have too much free expression and art, you know."

I remembered her tantrums and the adults talking about 'self-expression'.

"I always envied your family, compared with my strict parents. It was so exciting at your place."

Tallulah shook her head and said, "Yes, well it's not always a good thing, being allowed to fall asleep when you want, or having meals anytime, or swearing at adults. I liked your mother and gran, actually. They were always so kind to me but didn't stand any nonsense. Your house was peaceful and organised. Your dad was a bit scary, though."

"We were such horrible girls in some ways, really sulky spoilt teenagers. But I guess that's normal." I drank some tea. "Anyway, how's Ani? I couldn't find her online."

"Oh, you wouldn't. Ani's mostly off-grid. Well, she does deign to use the phone – I ring her most weeks. She went off to live in Canada, with a wealthy art dealer. Toronto."

That sounded like Ani.

"Is she happy?"

"As far as I can tell. She runs her own vintage shop and paints. How about you, Pony? What have you been up to?"

"Well, I studied German and Swedish and ended up in Vienna as a translator. And I married an Austrian, Tobi. But that's over, which is OK. I've got a lovely son, Matti. He's living with me in Plymouth for now. Have you got kids?"

She laughed. "Yes, two. Both grown up. And I was strict with them. Ani hasn't got any – probably put off by me and Josh. We were little horrors."

"You were sweet, too. I was so fond of you as I was an only child."

"You and Ani seemed so grown up and sophisticated to me. I was probably a pain, following you around all the time."

"No, it's OK."

"You meant a lot to Ani, I know that. She was pretty insecure, really, having no mother and all. She looked up to you."

"Really? I was in awe of her, well at first. That was a very special year."

I paused and braced myself.

"But why did she go off to Dartmoor Manor and leave me? I've always agonised over that."

Tallulah stirred her coffee and looked thoughtful. "Well, I was only little when she went, but it seems to me that she had to get away. I know she hated Sherwell High and didn't fit in there. And she and Mum didn't always see eye to eye, although Mum tried. The kids at Dartmoor Manor were really her tribe. But she missed you, that I do know. She felt guilty, torn two ways."

I nodded. It was comforting, hearing this. Strange to think that Ani had, in fact, escaped. What I always wanted to do as a child.

"So it wasn't something I did?"

"God, no. It's just – well kids are sometimes thoughtless."

We carried on talking all afternoon, reconnecting and exchanging news. Josh was a photographer now in the west country, doing well. He *had* gone to Dartmoor Manor and thrived. Sister Sarah was well, but Tallulah didn't keep in touch with her much. I had lost touch with her after a year or two but always remembered her with affection, the sister I'd never had. Jim had died recently and Mel had gone to live in Spain. I thought of her and her 'herbal cigarettes', which I now realised were weed. I wondered whether to mention that to Tallulah, but she was a GP and might disapprove. Occasionally I had indulged in it myself. I said nothing.

"My mother left my dad for a while," I told her. "She took me to France for six months. That was such fun. But we went back. He softened a bit in the end. She really stood up to him, thanks to all that Women's Lib – God, it seems so dated now. Some women are even against it now, aren't they?"

Tallulah's phone pinged and she picked it up. "Oh shit! My evening surgery starts soon. I'll have to go."

She scowled and I caught a glimpse of the old child-Tallulah, rebellious and temperamental. But she stood up, looking professional.

"Let's keep in touch. Shall I tell Ani about you when I call her? She might get in touch."

Did I want to talk to her again? Would it somehow spoil things, the old memories and magic of those far-off days? Ani might not want to reconnect with me, either. I paused, then said, "Yes, send her my love and give her my number. I'll leave it up to her."

"OK, Pony. Will do." She blew a kiss at me and was gone.

I looked at my phone. If I hurried, I could catch the 5.15 train from Paddington. But I wasn't in a hurry. I decided to have a stroll by the Thames and mull things over. It had been an intriguing and emotional afternoon. I liked the adult Tallulah very much; she had turned out well. And Ani? Did she ever think of me forty years on, busy with her Canadian life and wealthy partner? Impossible to know. All I knew was, I would never forget her.

Thank you for everything you gave me that year, dear sweet amazing Ani. You'll never know what you meant to me.

I set off along the Embankment, humming a seventies rock song.

THE END

ACKNOWLEDGEMENTS

I would like to thank all my writing teachers for setting me on the right road.

Thanks to Chelsey Flood for her great mentoring.

Also thanks to my friends, especially Diana Turner, for cheering me on.

Last but not least, thanks and much love to Stuart and Ciaran for putting up with me writing, cursing and keeping going.

ABOUT THE AUTHOR

Angela Joyce was born in Plymouth in 1959 and spent her childhood there. At eighteen she left to travel and study languages. She now lives in Cumbria and began writing seriously at the age of sixty.

The Rydle Year is her first novel.

Printed in Great Britain
by Amazon